OF A PENSIONER

A gripping British crime mystery full of twists

P.F. FORD

A Slater & Norman Mystery Book 9

Originally published as ***What's in a Name?***

JOFFE BOOKS

Revised edition 2024
Joffe Books, London
www.joffebooks.com

First published as *What's in a Name?*
in Great Britain in 2017

This paperback edition was first published
in Great Britain in 2024

Cover art by Dee Dee Book Covers

ISBN: 978-1-83526-598-7

To my amazing wife, Mary — sometimes we need someone else to believe in us before we really believe in ourselves. None of this would have happened without her unfailing belief and support.

PROLOGUE

Wednesday 24 August, 2016. 7.19 a.m.

Joe Dalgetty was sixty-two years old, but he looked like a man in his eighties. This was partly due to the arthritis that was slowly destroying his mobility, but if anyone had asked — and been given an honest reply — he would have told them the biggest cause of his early ageing was worry — and loneliness. Not that anyone ever *did* bother to ask. Joe kept himself to himself, and apart from his neighbour and friend Rosie Hewitt, he rarely spoke to anyone. Becoming a loner had been an unforeseen — and unavoidable — price he had had to pay. It wasn't the only thing he had come to regret, and it was these burdens from his past, added to his enforced loneliness, that had aged him so.

Joe was in the habit of doing his shopping very early in the morning to avoid meeting too many people. There was a supermarket about half a mile away from his house, and he made a point of being there at seven o'clock in the morning, as soon as the doors opened. He had it down to a fine art now, and he could be in and out in less than fifteen minutes. He had worked out the quietest days to go, and by avoiding eye contact with any member of staff who tried to engage him in conversation, and going to a different cashier each time, he was quite confident he was more or less unmemorable, which was exactly what he wanted.

That morning, the doors had opened a few minutes early, and as he had been in there barely ten minutes, he was back at his own front door just before seven twenty.

* * *

It would be fair to say Kerry Jones had lost his way. Just two years ago he had been a kid with a bright future, but now, at just eighteen years old, he seemed to have no future at all. His parents were in despair. They had no idea why their son had suddenly gone from hard worker to non-worker. He hadn't just dropped out of school; he seemed to have dropped out of everything. They didn't know where he got his money from, but they were quite sure it wasn't in exchange for an honest day's work. There had been a spate of burglaries locally targeting older people, and although they had no proof, they feared the worst.

That morning, Kerry was breaking into the house of an old guy he had identified as an easy target. The old man went shopping early in the morning at the same time, on the same days, every week, and he moved pretty slowly, like he couldn't walk properly. Today was the day Kerry had selected to rob this particular victim, and he knew this was going to be really easy. He looked at his watch as he reached the old man's back door. It was almost seven twenty. He should have at least ten minutes. That would be plenty of time.

He tried the handle of the back door to the old man's house and gently leaned against it. *The silly old fool hadn't even locked it.* This was good. The old guy was inviting someone to come in and rob him, and Kerry was only too happy to oblige. It wasn't his fault if people didn't lock their doors, was it?

He eased the door open and slipped inside.

* * *

Joe Dalgetty pushed the key into his front door and twisted. The key turned with almost no effort on his part. The old lock had become so stiff he could hardly turn it, but this new lock he'd paid to have fitted was as smooth as silk. It had been worth every penny. He pushed the door open and stepped painfully inside. His knees were bad this morning, but in a minute or so he would be able to sit down and take the weight off them. Silently, he closed the door behind him and turned to walk down the short, narrow hallway into the kitchen. An unexpected movement caught his eye, and he realised there was someone standing in his kitchen staring at him.

The shock seemed to turn him to stone. He had always worried this might happen one day, and now it seemed his worst nightmare had come true. Somehow they had tracked him down, and now they'd come for him. It was a case of flight or fright, but flight was never going to be an option for Joe. It was fright that won through. In the same moment he realised he'd been found out, he felt a stabbing pain in his chest. He clutched at his heart as he fell, gasped once from the pain, and was dead before he hit the ground.

* * *

Kerry Jones stood, mouth agape, staring at the fallen man. He couldn't quite believe his eyes, and a jumble of thoughts rushed into his head. *What was going on? This wasn't supposed to happen. What was the stupid old fool doing back early? He shouldn't have been back for at least another ten minutes. And what was he doing on the floor, clutching his chest? Shit. He'd had a heart attack or something, hadn't he? They'll think I did that. But I don't hurt people, I don't even take their possessions, I only ever steal cash they leave lying around.*

Knowing he was close to panic, Kerry focused on regaining control of himself. This was a serious and unexpected situation to have to deal with, but that just made it all the more important to keep calm. He wasn't going to allow himself to lose it now. He closed his eyes for a few seconds and concentrated on his breathing, making sure to take long, deep breaths. Then, as he began to calm down, he opened his eyes and took in the scene again. Now he could assess the situation with a much more detached eye, it was easy to decide what he should do.

The old man hadn't moved, and he didn't appear to be breathing. A small part of Kerry suggested he should do something to help, but a much bigger part realised there would be a lot of explaining to do if he hung around. Almost reluctantly, he turned and quietly tiptoed back across the kitchen and out through the back door. It was a shame he hadn't had time to find any cash, but at least he hadn't left any evidence. With any luck, no one would even realise he had been there, and the obvious assumption would be that the old guy had suffered a heart attack.

As he slunk away from the unfortunate Joe Dalgetty's house, Kerry sought to rationalise what had just happened. *People have heart attacks all the time, and he couldn't be held responsible for someone having a weak heart, could he? If the old bloke* did *have a weak heart, it would have packed up sooner or later anyway. So, really, when you think about it, there was no real harm done. In fact, he'd probably done the old bloke a favour, because it looked as if he was living a pretty miserable, lonely existence anyway.*

But despite his attempts to justify his behaviour, Kerry experienced a strange, alien feeling. Most people would have instantly recognised it as guilt, but for Kerry this was a new experience, and its meaning was lost on him. He knew it made him feel uncomfortable, but he had no idea why. He was going to have to think about that.

CHAPTER ONE

It was a typically busy Monday lunchtime in the Brewer's Arms, just a short walk from the centre of the small town of Tinton. The air was filled with the smell of good food and the voices of noisy punters trying to make the most of their all-too-short lunch breaks.

Unnoticed, a small, tidy, fair-haired lady pushed the door open and stepped inside. She looked around, taking in as many faces as she could, but as she didn't really know who she was looking for, it wasn't much help. Her resolve began to waver momentarily, but then she remembered exactly why she had come here and, drawing herself up to her full height of five feet three-and-a-half inches, she marched determinedly up to the bar.

'Excuse me,' she said to the barman, who looked up and smiled at her.

'Yes, love, what can I do for you?'

'I wonder if you can help me?'

She explained who she was looking for, and the barman looked around the busy bar. Finally, he pointed to two figures sitting at a table by a window on the far side of the bar. The lady looked uncertainly over her shoulder, following the direction indicated by the pointed finger. Then she thanked the barman, bought a glass of orange juice, and made her way towards the two figures. She had thought the barman must have been mistaken when he pointed out the two overall-clad figures, but as she approached, she could see one was clearly much larger than the other, which was what she had been told to expect.

'Are you the two detectives?' she asked as she reached the table.

The larger, rather roly-poly, man was the first to turn towards her, his curly hair making a valiant attempt to conform to some sort of style, but failing miserably and falling across his face as he turned.

'That's us,' he said, sweeping the curls out of his eyes.

'If you don't mind me saying, you look more like decorators,' she said.

'Good disguise, huh?' said the curly-headed man with a conspiratorial wink. 'We're undercover.'

The second man had turned towards her now, and he gave her a warm smile.

'Don't take any notice of him,' he said. 'We're not undercover at all, we're decorating our new offices. My name's Dave Slater, and this is my colleague, Norman Norman. Here, come and sit down.'

* * *

Slater moved his own chair to one side and placed one for her between himself and Norman.

'My name's Rosie Hewitt,' the woman said, sitting down. 'I was told you were the best people to talk to.'

'Oh really?' said Norman. 'Who told you that?'

'A detective. I forget what he said his name was.'

'DS Biddeford?' suggested Slater.

She looked horrified. 'It certainly wasn't that ignorant so-and-so!' she said, adamantly. 'He didn't even want to talk to me. No, this was a much nicer man. Smarter dressed, he was, too. He had a very smart suit. Pinstripes, you know? And he had nice manners.'

Slater looked at Norman, but it was obvious he didn't recognise the description either.

'We both used to work at Tinton,' said Norman, 'but we don't recognise anyone like that. Then again, things are changing there, so maybe it's someone new. Anyway, why would he suggest you came to us?'

'All he said was the police couldn't help me, but you two were retired police officers and maybe you could.'

Slater and Norman exchanged another glance.

'Why don't you tell us what's bothering you?' suggested Norman, before adding, 'Don't worry, we won't charge you for talking to us.'

The look on her face told him she hadn't even thought about that, but it soon passed.

'Seven weeks ago,' she began, 'my friend and neighbour Mr Dalgetty was found lying dead in his hallway. He'd had a heart attack.'

'I'm sorry to hear that,' said Norman. 'How old was he?'

'Sixty-two. At least that's what he said he was.'

'He's the right sort of age,' said Slater. 'These things can happen without warning. Did he have a problem with his heart?'

She thought about this for a moment. 'I know he had arthritis in his knees, but as far as I knew, he had no heart problems. He certainly never mentioned it, and I'm sure he would have. I mean, he was always going on about his knees. Anyway, the police were called and there was a post-mortem. They concluded it was a case of accidental death.'

'You don't sound convinced,' observed Norman.

'Well, I might have been,' she said, 'but since he died, some funny things have happened. I told the police, but they seem to think I'm round the bend. The only one who seemed to take me even slightly seriously was a young slip of a girl, although she didn't seem to be able to help me, and then there was this other one who told me about you two.'

Slater knew the 'young slip of a girl' would be DC Naomi Darling who, despite being in her twenties, still managed to look about sixteen, but he still couldn't put a face to the mysterious male detective. He was sure he couldn't possibly have forgotten someone who wore a pinstriped suit to work.

'So what are these funny things?' asked Norman.

'Well, first of all, there was his will. He had no relatives so he left everything to me.'

'Was that a surprise?'

'I'll say it was. I'd known him for over five years, and in all that time he'd given me the impression he struggled to make ends meet, yet he left me twenty-five thousand pounds! Where would he get that sort of money from? And if he had it, why live like a pauper?'

'Maybe he just didn't like to spend his money,' suggested Slater. 'Perhaps he preferred to keep it in the bank.'

'But he didn't trust banks. He thought they were just there to bleed us all dry. He said he only kept an account open so he could have his pension paid in to it.'

'Perhaps that's how he saved all that money.' Norman rubbed his chin. 'Maybe he didn't need to touch the pension and it just grew over a few years.'

'But he told me his pension was all he had. That's why he lived so frugally.'

'I understand it must have been a surprise,' said Slater, 'but he wouldn't be the first person to live like that and have a small fortune stashed away somewhere.'

'No.' Rosie shook her head firmly. 'I can't see it. He couldn't even afford to put the heating on half the time. No one would choose to live like that if they had money, especially when there's no family to pass it on to.'

'You must have meant a lot to him,' said Norman.

'I think I was his only friend,' she said. 'I used to do little jobs for him, and if his arthritis was really bad I'd get some bits for him when I was doing my own shopping, you know? The solicitor told me Joe had left it to me for my kindness, but I would have done it for any friend, I didn't expect a reward for it.'

'People have been left a lot more for doing a lot less,' said Slater.

'Yes, but the solicitor told me Joe had only made his will a couple of weeks before he died. It's as if he knew he was going to die, and he'd set it up ready.'

Slater glanced at Norman. He could see his partner's interest was growing, just like his own.

'You said some funny *things* had happened, as in more than one, Rosie,' said Norman. 'Tell us what else.'

'A couple of weeks after he was buried, someone was in his house.'

'What, you mean you saw someone?' asked Slater.

'No, I didn't see anyone, but I know someone had been in there.'

'Did you call the police?' asked Norman.

She sighed. 'Yes, and a fat lot of good that was. They said the house hadn't been broken into and as far as they could see, nothing was missing. The thing is, there's someone going round breaking into old people's houses and stealing cash. According to them, if anyone had been in his house, that's who it was. They said as I couldn't say for sure if anything was missing, and it didn't look as if anyone had broken in, they couldn't really do much about it.'

'If there was no damage and no sign of a break-in,' said Slater, 'why are you so sure someone had been inside?'

'Because everything had been gone through!' Rosie fixed Slater with a piercing stare. 'I've heard about this person who breaks into old people's houses. He's only looking for cash. He never takes anything else, and he only seems to check kitchens and bedrooms. Now, I know someone was in that house and they went everywhere.'

'How can you be sure?' asked Slater.

Rosie drew herself up and flashed him a look that immediately made him regret opening his mouth.

'When he died, I went around there and cleaned the place and made sure it was all neat and tidy. I didn't actually take an inventory, but I know damned well someone has been in there and gone through everything!'

'I'm sorry,' said Slater. 'I'm not trying to suggest you don't know what you're talking abou—'

'I had enough of this with the police,' she said. 'I was hoping you might be prepared to hear me out.'

'We are prepared to listen, Rosie,' said Norman, soothingly, 'but you have to understand — we need to ask questions too. We just want to make sure we don't miss anything. I'm sorry if that means we sound a little like the police, but that *is* where we did our training. I promise you, we're not trying to question what you say. We just like to be thorough, and that's why we're pretty good at what we do. That's why you came to us, right?'

This seemed to placate her, and she visibly relaxed.

'Has anything else happened we should know about?' continued Norman.

'Yes,' she said. 'My own house was broken into just last week.'

'Jeez,' said Norman. 'Did they do much damage?'

'Well. . .' Rosie's cheeks went slightly pink. 'When I say someone broke in, what I really mean is — someone let themselves in.'

'Ah!' said Slater. 'You leave a key outside?'

She nodded her head and sighed. 'Under a flowerpot by the back door,' she admitted. 'And I know what you're going to say, so spare me the lecture.'

'Did you call the police?'

'I did, and they told me the same thing about this man who steals from pensioners again. I said I thought it was too much of a coincidence, but they just reminded me what they had told me before. When I pointed out there was cash in the kitchen drawer that hadn't been touched, they insisted I must have disturbed the burglar before he got that far. That seemed a bit funny to me because whoever had been in there had been inside long enough to go through all my drawers and cupboards upstairs. But then I'm just a stupid old woman. What do I know?'

'Is that when this other officer told you to contact us?' asked Slater.

Rosie nodded. 'Yes, that's right. That ignorant detective sergeant . . . Biddeford, is it? He seemed to think I was just wasting his precious time. I think it was beneath his dignity to use his breath on the likes of a silly old fool like me, and it was obvious he thought they should be doing something much more important. The nice man came next day and told me they couldn't do anything because their hands were tied, whatever that meant, but then he said I should come and see you two.'

'Did you get his name?'

'I'm afraid not. I'm not sure he ever actually mentioned it.'

'Okay,' said Norman. 'Not to worry. I'm sure we'll be able to find him. If he made a special journey to see you, he must think there's something worth looking into.'

'What about you, Mr Norman, and you, Mr Slater?' Rosie looked at each in turn. 'Do you think there's something worth looking into? I can pay, you know. I've got a spare twenty-five thousand pounds, and I want to know what's going on.'

Slater looked at Norman. Like everything else to do with how their business was going to work, what they were going to charge was something they hadn't actually discussed yet.

'Err, well, look, let's not worry about costs just yet,' said Norman, hastily. He looked at Slater, who nodded his approval. 'If this other police officer thinks there's more to this than meets the eye, I think we're both inclined to think we should take a look. But first we need to understand this other officer's suspicions.'

'It'll be useful if he can give us some insight into this guy who's stealing cash from old folks too,' said Slater. 'If what he can tell us backs up what you've told us about the person who broke into your house and your friend's house, then I think we've got somewhere to start.'

For the first time since she had come into the pub, Rosie smiled. 'Thank you both for listening to me and not making me feel like a silly old fool who's just wasting your time,' she said. 'What happens now?'

'We'll try to arrange a meeting with this officer as soon as we can,' said Norman. 'If you can let us have your address and phone number, we'll get in touch as soon as we've spoken to him.'

She stood, ready to leave, and they stood with her.

'There is one more thing I'd like to ask,' said Slater. 'Did Joe ever ask you to look after anything for him?'

'I don't think so,' she said, thoughtfully. 'No, I'm sure he didn't.'

He gave her a reassuring smile. 'Okay. Not to worry.'

'We'll be in touch in a day or two,' said Norman, as he ushered her back out through the pub and onto the street.

* * *

'Are we actually ready to take on a job?' asked Slater, once Rosie was gone and Norman was back in his seat. 'I mean the paint's barely dry, and we've got no computers or anything—'

'And basically we have no idea how anything's going to work because we haven't actually discussed it yet,' finished Norman, pointedly.

'Well, yeah, and that too,' agreed Slater, sheepishly.

When the idea of setting up in business together had first been suggested, it had seemed like a great idea, but Slater's initial enthusiasm had quickly faded, and now he'd had time to think about it, he wasn't so sure it really was what he wanted to commit to. As a result, he was feeling extremely guilty. If he didn't join Norm, he felt he would be letting him down, but if he did join him and then found he didn't like it, he'd be letting him down again. Which was worse? It was a real dilemma.

'Having said all that,' said Norman, 'I think it would be wrong to turn a job down. We can still ask questions, and we have your laptop. We'll be fine, you'll see.'

Slater wasn't convinced, but before he had a chance to voice his concerns, Norman spoke again.

'Have you any idea who this detective in the pinstriped suit is?'

'Not a clue,' said Slater. 'The only thing I can think is that they've drafted someone in from Merryton while they're closing Tinton down, but even then, I thought I knew everyone from over there, and I'm sure no one wears a pinstriped suit.'

'Let me see if I can get hold of Naomi.' Norman reached for his mobile phone. 'Maybe she can tell us who this guy is.'

DC Naomi Darling, the 'slip of a girl' Rosie had mentioned earlier, was a former colleague of Slater and Norman and seemed to be the only person at their old station who didn't resent the two of them. She was usually happy to offer them help if she could.

While Norman called Darling, Slater went across to the bar and bought two more pints. As he walked back to their table, he could see a frown creasing Norman's face as he spoke into his phone.

'Naomi asks if we're sure Rosie's not senile,' said Norman, as he ended the call and placed his phone back on the table.

Slater's only response was to raise a single eyebrow.

'She says she's never seen anyone over there dressed in anything that could even vaguely be described as smart, or a suit, and certainly not in pinstripes. And, no, they haven't had anyone drafted in from anywhere else.'

'Rosie seemed to have a full set of marbles to me,' said Slater.

'Yeah,' said Norman. 'I thought so too, so I wonder who this guy is?'

'It's going to be a bit difficult to find out what he knows if we don't even know who he is.'

'Yeah,' agreed Norman. 'The pinstripe guy does seem to be a bit of a mystery, but Naomi assures me there's only been her and Biddeford involved so she doesn't see how anyone else could have known what to say to Rosie.'

'Are we starting off in the dark then?' asked Slater.

Norman smiled. 'I thought of that, and I've got it covered. Naomi's going to come over later and fill us in with what she knows.'

'You'd better go and find your wallet then, because Naomi drinks like a fish and I've just paid for lunch, so you'll be buying later.'

CHAPTER TWO

'And you're sure you and Biddeford are the only ones who know about Rosie and Joe?'

Slater watched as Naomi Darling took a mouthful of beer and placed her pint glass down on the table. He had never quite got used to the idea of such a tiny girl drinking pints, and he couldn't help but smile to himself.

'Of course I'm sure,' she said. 'The only other person who would know anything is the Wicked Witch of the North, and no one could mistake that evil cow for a nice-mannered man in a pinstripe suit, could they?'

The evil cow she was referring to was her boss, DCI Marion Goodnews, who had initially been heralded as some sort of living legend, but then, bit by bit, the gloss had begun to chip away until she was finally revealed to be an evil-tempered, manipulative control freak, as far as Slater was concerned.

The mention of Goodnews had reminded them all of someone they'd rather forget for varying reasons. In Darling's case, she had been more or less hung out to dry by her boss when she had been falsely accused of assault. In Norman's case, it had been DCI Goodnews who had ensured he was forced to retire on the grounds of ill health. In Slater's case, an ill-advised relationship he should have known better than to get involved in had been the final straw that had led to his decision to leave the force. Neither man could come up with a reason to disagree with Darling's assessment of their former boss, so instead, they settled for taking a drink.

'So, what can you tell us about the person who's robbing pensioners?' asked Norman.

Darling considered the question for a moment. 'I can't tell you much for definite,' she said, 'because whoever this person is, he's clever, and he's obviously put some thought into what he's doing. For instance, he knows not to take anything that might be easily traceable. He only ever takes cash, and he doesn't hang around. We think he's figured out his victims tend to keep cash in a kitchen drawer, or the bedroom, so that's all he bothers to check. He never enters a house when there's someone inside, which on the one hand is good, because he's never hurt anyone, but then it's also not so good, because no one's ever seen him. We think he's also in and out in less than five minutes, and if he doesn't find what he's looking for in that time, he just leaves empty-handed.'

'Wow!' said Norman. 'It must take a lot of discipline to resist turning a house upside down once you've got inside and you know there's no one in there.'

'Yeah,' agreed Slater. 'To me, it sounds like someone who's been round the block a few times and learnt some lessons. It sounds like you're convinced it's a man, so I take it you're looking for someone middle-aged?'

Darling chuckled quietly and gave him a sympathetic look. 'Now that's exactly what Goodnews and Biddeford think. They've put together what they rather grandly call—' she made quote marks in the air with her fingers — '"*a profile*". In reality, of course, it's just a guess based on a hunch.'

Slater didn't much appreciate Darling's condescending attitude towards him, and he bridled at her considering him on par with those two, but he swallowed back his thoughts and kept them to himself.

'So, what do you think, Naomi?' asked Norman. 'Who would fit your profile?'

'Mine's a guess too, if I'm honest, and I don't know if it's any better than theirs, but at least I haven't just plucked an idea out of thin air. Based on a couple of witness statements, even if they are rather vague and uncorroborated, my best guess is it's a young male, late teens to early twenties.'

She stopped to take a sip from her drink. Slater was verging on apoplectic by now. *Cheeky cow. Who did she think she was? He hadn't just 'plucked an idea out of thin air', he'd based it on what she had just told them.*

'And you're sure about this, are you?' he asked. 'Only in my experience, kids that age tend to be tearaways, trashing houses without a thought for any damage they might do, or any distress they might cause.'

She gave him a sweet smile but didn't say anything. He thought she seemed amused that she'd managed to push his buttons quite so easily. But then perhaps it was just that he still felt guilty about what had happened to her and how he hadn't got off his arse and helped her when he could have. Maybe she wasn't deliberately winding him up, but even if she was, could he really blame her? He decided to let it go; after all, he was supposed to be a big boy now, and she had come here to offer them help.

'Is there anything else you can tell us?' asked Norman.

'That's about it,' she said. 'After twelve confirmed robberies, and another three where we think he broke in and took nothing, we believe it might be a middle-aged guy, but then again it could be a young man. Then again, we have no definite sightings, so he could even be a she!'

She took in the combined expressions of both men. 'I know, it's bugger all, but really, that's all we've got. Like I said he — or she — leaves no clues.'

They all took another sip from their drinks as they considered what little they had to go on. It was Norman who spoke first.

'Rosie Hewitt says the police think your middle-aged teenager was the guy who broke into her house, but she says whoever it was went through the house from top to bottom.

That doesn't seem to fit with what you've just told us about the other robberies.'

She nodded her head vigorously. 'I agree with you, but what do I know? According to my bosses, I've still got a lot to learn. The way they see it, it's the same guy, he's just getting bolder.'

'But there was cash in a kitchen drawer and he didn't take it!' said Norman.

'Apparently, he was disturbed and didn't have time to take it,' she said. 'The fact that he's never missed it before, and never searched a whole house before, doesn't seem to bother those above me.'

'What about the break-in at Joe Dalgetty's house?' asked Slater. 'How do they explain that?'

'They don't even accept anyone was ever in his house. There was no sign of a break-in and nothing was missing.'

'So, what? Rosie made it up?' asked Slater.

Darling shrugged. 'It doesn't help that there was no damage, and she insists she locked the door last time she was over there. Maybe Biddeford would have taken her more seriously if she hadn't kept on about coincidences and suggesting there was some sort of conspiracy going on. You know how patient he is when people try to offer their own ideas.'

'It sounds like Tinton Police has gone to pot,' said Norman.

'You're not far off the mark there,' said Darling, 'and I'll tell you why. First off, DS Dickhead Biddeford is sulking, big time, because *she* won't let him have any responsibility. He thought promotion meant he was going to enjoy the freedom you had and that he would be top dog, but the reality is he's just the tail of the dog, and she's the one who decides when it wags. And then there's Goodnews herself.' Darling cast a glance at Slater. 'She's still pissed off because you had the audacity to dump her, and on top of that, she's sulking because she's losing her precious police station. The result is neither of them can see past the end of their own noses. They wouldn't see anything even if it smacked them in the face.'

Slater felt his face redden at the mention of his brief dalliance with Goodnews and decided he should make his position clear.

'Look, people start relationships, realise it's not for them, and then split up,' he said. 'It happens all the time. I made a mistake getting involved with her, and I regret it, but it's not as if we had a wedding planned or anything! We just spent a couple of nights together, that's all.'

'Hey, look, you don't have to explain yourself to me,' said Darling. 'What you do in your private life is none of my business, but I'd watch your back if I were you, because she's definitely got something brewing in her cauldron, and sooner or later she's going to be hurling thunderbolts in your direction.'

Slater felt the beginnings of a shiver run down his spine. Darling might be making a joke of it, but he knew his ex had all the makings of a classic bunny boiler, and he didn't doubt she would make his life hell if she found the opportunity. But he wasn't going to dwell on that right now.

'So you're convinced the guy Rosie has reported isn't the same guy who's pinching pensioners' cash, right?' he asked Darling.

'I'm sure of it,' she said. 'The MO is so different it can't be the same guy.'

'D'you think you're going to catch your young, middle-aged guy?' asked Norman.

Darling took another draught of beer. 'He's become a one-man crime wave and he's either very clever, or very lucky, and I'm beginning to think the only way we might stop him is if *we* suddenly get lucky, or he suddenly grows a conscience and stops of his own accord.'

'If he had a conscience, he wouldn't be doing it in the first place,' said Slater, taking a swig of his own beer. 'You'd better hope you get lucky soon.'

'I'm not so sure he's even still around,' Darling said. 'There hasn't been a robbery reported for a few weeks now.'

'Maybe he's taken enough for what he wanted,' Norman said thoughtfully. 'Or perhaps he's on holiday.'

'Whatever.' Darling put her glass down emphatically. 'As long as he stops, I don't really care. I'll be happy if we never hear of him again. The only good thing is he never hurt anyone.'

Slater drained his glass and set it carefully down on the table, then he bought the other two another drink, made his excuses, and headed for home. He could feel Darling's curious stare on his retreating back, but he didn't have the energy to explain why he had to get back. Norman would probably explain it anyway.

CHAPTER THREE

It was 6.45 a.m. In the half-light of the early morning, two figures, a man and a woman, could be seen jogging side by side along the canal path.

'You don't have to get up and come with me every morning,' said the woman. 'I could do this on my own. It's something I need to do for myself, after all.'

'Yeah, I know you could, Jenny,' said Slater, puffing slightly, 'but until I'm convinced you're not in any danger, I prefer to keep an eye on you. Besides, I would never have started running again on my own, and it's doing me good, so you're doing me a favour.'

'I think it's you who's done me the favour,' she said, flicking a glance out the corner of her eye at him. 'Taking poor old homeless Jenny in when you'd only met me once ages ago.'

Slater had first met Jenny Radstock when she had been involved in a case he had been asked to investigate a couple of years ago. By coincidence it was actually the first case he had worked with his friend, former DS Norman Norman. Slater and Jenny had got on reasonably well at the time, but then lost contact until a few weeks ago when she had turned up in Tinton, penniless and homeless. It soon became clear she had managed to make some powerful enemies, and she had actually taken to living on the streets as a means of hiding.

Slater wasn't the sort of guy who could stand by and let a friend carry on living like that, so he had offered her his spare room and fully intended to help her sort her life out once she was ready to start fighting back. In the meantime he felt it was his duty to protect her while she recuperated and built her strength up.

Slater shrugged and tried to catch his breath. 'You made an impression on me, Ms Radstock,' he said, holding up his hands. 'What can I say? I'm just hoping one day you'll trust me enough to tell me who you're hiding from.'

She looked at him for a long moment and then smiled sadly. 'So, when are you going to make your mind up about working with Norm?' she asked as they crossed the footbridge and began to run back down the other side of the canal.

'Ha! Yes,' said Slater. 'That's a good question.'

'So, what are you going to do?'

'I dunno, to be honest. I can't even explain why I'm reluctant to work with him.'

'Oh, that's easy,' Jenny said. 'You like the order and structure working for the police gave you, whereas he's happy to fly by the seat of his pants. It may work fine for him, but you're not sure it works for you.'

'Yeah,' Slater said, nodding slowly, 'that's probably not far from the truth.'

'Have you actually told him about your doubts?'

'Err, no, not yet.'

'Oh come on, Dave. That's not fair, is it? He's going to be really upset when he finds out you've been keeping him in the dark.'

'Yeah, but if I decide to work with him, he won't need to know I had any doubts, will he?'

'And you think that's okay, do you? What happens if you decide not to work with him?'

'Jesus, Jenny, don't keep on. It'll be fine.' He tried to increase his pace as if he could outrun the uncomfortable conversation.

'I hear you telling me that,' she said, 'but you don't exactly sound convinced, and you're certainly not convincing me.'

'Yeah, well, my head's still in a bit of a whirl from everything that's happened recently.'

'I've never thought of you as being indecisive,' Jenny said, peering at him.

'It's a big decision,' Slater said, defensively, 'and I want to get it right, so I think being extra cautious is the way to go.'

'Is this extra caution why you won't let me have a front door key?'

'We've been through this before,' said Slater. 'There *should* be a spare key in the kitchen drawer—'

'Yes, but it's not there, is it? You told me you must have lost it and you were going to get a new one cut.'

Slater sighed, and his face flushed guiltily. 'You're right. I *did* promise I'd get one cut, it's just that what with trying to get my head together, I haven't got around to it. Why d'you need one so desperately anyway?'

She snorted derisively. 'How about because I'm beginning to feel like a prisoner?'

'That's unfair,' said Slater, feeling a touch aggrieved. 'I'm just trying to keep you safe.'

'Yes, I know that, but I can't even go out and do a bit of food shopping! You must be getting fed up with me giving you a shopping list every couple of days. It would be much easier if I could just go and do it myself.'

'Well, yeah, but—'

'Look I really do appreciate what you're doing, but you can't protect me forever. Anyway, I can look after myself, you know.'

Slater fixed her with a stare. 'No offence, Jenny, but weren't you looking after yourself when you got into this mess?'

This prompted the stony silence he had expected but, even so, he felt it had needed to be said. They ran on in silence for a hundred yards or so before she spoke again.

'You don't have to keep rubbing it in.'

'I'm not trying to rub it in, and I *do* understand why you think it's your fight, but you also need to realise there's no shame in accepting help when the odds are stacked against you.'

She didn't say anything — and her face told him nothing — so he made a peace offering.

'I'll get you a key cut, but you have to promise me you won't do anything rash, and you'll let me know when you're going out and where you're going, otherwise I'm going to be worried sick if I come home and you're not there.'

They ran another hundred yards while she considered his suggestion. For a moment, Slater wondered if he was being over-protective, but she was in danger, there was no getting around that.

'All right,' Jenny conceded at last. 'It's a deal.'

Slater couldn't stop a small smile from flashing across his face. He understood her desire to come and go as she pleased, but until he was convinced she was no longer in danger, he was reluctant to allow it. This was a compromise he could live with and getting her to agree to it was a small victory.

They turned away from the canal so they were now running alongside the road; Slater moved over so Jenny was on the inside, furthest from the road. At this point, they were only a steady twenty-minute jog from Slater's house.

'Anyway, I don't think you should be in any rush,' he said. 'I don't think you're ready to take on the world just yet.'

She opened her mouth to argue, but he beat her to it.

'Yes, I know you seem to have got your head together, but you're going to need to be physically fit as well, and right now you've got plenty of room for improvement.'

He grinned at the sharp glance she gave him in response. She was definitely getting to be much more like the feisty Jenny Radstock he'd known before. He didn't have long to wait before she rose to his challenge.

'Okay, Mr Superfit, why don't we race home from here and see who's breathing hardest when we get back?' she suggested. 'Then we'll see who's fit.'

'I'm not really the yardstick you want to be measuring yourself against.'

She snorted. 'Ha! You're just saying that because you know I'll beat you!'

'Is that right? Okay, let's get across this road, and then we'll race from there.'

The route they followed every morning took them diagonally across the road, just ahead.

'As soon as we get to the other side?' she asked.

'Once we're safely across the road,' Slater said.

There was no traffic to worry about, so they jogged safely across to the other side. Now they were on the opposite side of the road, Slater was on the inside, where a bushy hedge bordered the path.

'Okay,' said Jenny, 'I'll call out ready, set, and then we can start on go.'

'Whatever.' Slater shrugged nonchalantly. 'I'll beat you anyway.'

She grinned wickedly. 'Ha! In your dreams, Buster. Ready, set, oops, sorry!'

'What the—'

Before Slater knew what was happening, she had given him a good hard shove into the hedge, where he frantically flapped around trying to find something to grab hold of to keep him upright. But all his flapping was in vain because the hedge was so deep and overgrown, there was nothing substantial to hold on to. He was gradually swallowed up as he sank slowly into it and then to the ground. As he fell, he could hear her fading footsteps as she raced away.

It was only a few seconds before he extricated himself from the hedge, covered in bits of twig and assorted detritus, but by then her slim figure was a good forty or fifty yards ahead — and she wasn't hanging around. A broad grin filled his face as he quickly brushed himself down.

'Right then, Miss Radstock,' he muttered as he set off after her. 'Let's see just how fit you *really* are.'

CHAPTER FOUR

It was nearly 9.30 a.m. by the time Slater eventually made it to what Norman referred to as their 'office', which was actually a pair of converted stables at the back of what had formerly been the town's brewery. Norman's landlord owned the site and was redeveloping the old buildings into small business units. He had offered Norman the stables rent-free for two months in exchange for them decorating and adding the finishing touches. It was a good deal, and Norm had jumped at the chance, even though his handyman skills weren't exactly top drawer.

As Slater walked in, he was greeted by the sight of a rather generous overall-clad backside pointing his way. The owner of the backside was on his knees, trying to figure out which screws went where as he attempted to put together one of the workstations he had bought. He looked round as Slater pushed the door open.

'I'd be stopping an hour's pay if you were working for me!'

'Err, yeah, sorry about that,' said Slater, sheepishly. 'I got a bit carried away. I didn't realise how late it was.'

Norman looked at Slater's guilty face. 'I think I can guess what you were carried away doing, but it's none of my business, and I'm not going to ask you to confirm or deny it,' he said. 'Anyway, we're working for nothing, I don't think we have actually agreed a start time, and it's not as if we're rushed off our feet, is it?'

'Well, yeah, I suppose when you put it like that . . .'

Slater looked at Norman and his attempt at building a workstation. 'D'you need a hand with that?'

'That would be good.' Norman pointed at the instruction sheet spread out on the floor in front of him. 'The pictures look all right, but the instructions might as well be written in Chinese, and the screws all seem to be the wrong sizes.'

Slater grinned wickedly. 'Are you sure it's not the holes that are the wrong sizes?' he asked innocently.

'Really? I hadn't thought of that,' said Norman, completely missing the point at first, but then slowly catching on. 'Oh right, I get it. Joke, huh?'

'Here,' said Slater, sinking to his knees beside Norman. 'Let me have a look.'

'Oh, thanks.' Norman heaved his bulk up from the floor. 'I'll leave you to it then!'

Slater frowned at him. 'That wasn't exactly what I meant.'

Norman gave him a winning smile. 'Yeah, I know, but you're good at this handyman stuff,' he said. 'There's other stuff I'm better at.'

'Yeah, like eating,' muttered Slater as he reached for the instruction sheet. He stared at the instructions. 'Have you actually tried following these?'

'Err, not exactly, no.' Norman looked sheepish. 'I looked at the pictures, but me and instructions, well, we sort of don't get on too well.'

'I didn't think so,' said Slater. 'Because if you *had*, you would have noticed that they actually are in Chinese.'

'Jeez, how is anyone supposed to make sense of that? It's no wonder people have problems building these things.'

Slater sighed and turned over the sheet of paper in his hands. 'If you had looked at the other side, with the instructions in English, I think you might have found it a tad more useful.' He started to sort through the small heap of assorted screws Norman had poured onto the floor. 'It also helps if you don't mix up all the screws. And I'm sure you'll find the screws are all the right size as long as you try to fit them in the right holes.'

'Oh. Right,' said Norman. 'Well, that sort of proves my point about you being better at this stuff, and you're definitely better at pointing out mistakes. Is there anything I can do that might actually help?'

Slater knew the small kitchen hadn't been plumbed in yet. 'Yes, there is,' he said. 'How about you go and make me a cup of coffee?'

'Ha!' said Norman. 'You mean you want me out of the way, right?'

Slater looked up, shame-faced.

'It's okay,' said Norman. 'I understand what you mean. I'm a pain in the arse when you're trying to do something fiddly like that. I know. I'd want me out of the way too. How long do you want?'

'Twenty minutes?'

'You got it. I'll bring cakes, too.'

Slater watched fondly as Norman retreated through the door. It was true Norm seemed to be in a permanent state of near-chaos, whereas he preferred order, but then he was good company, and it was their differences that made them such a good team, wasn't it?

* * *

'I'm afraid Joe's solicitor might not be very helpful,' said Norman later that morning as they settled into Rosie's comfy chairs, ready to try to get some background on Joe Dalgetty.

'Why's that?' asked Rosie.

'He can't see us until tomorrow afternoon, but already he's talking about client confidentiality and how he might not be able to help us much.'

'But Joe's dead! Does the solicitor think he's going to rise from the dead and sue him if he talks to you? What a load of nonsense! Why don't people use common sense any more? It's ridiculous!'

As soon as they had entered Rosie's house, Slater had been outmanoeuvred by Norman's claim of: 'I don't seem to have a pen, or a notebook . . .' and so had scowlingly become the official note-taker. He looked up from his notepad now.

'We can't quite see how it applies when the man's dead,' he said, 'but unfortunately we can't make him talk to us if he doesn't want to. We're going to try to make a start by looking into Joe's background, and we were just wondering if he ever told you anything about where he lived before he came here, or maybe something about where he grew up. It might give us somewhere to begin.'

Rosie stared off into the distance and screwed her face up in concentration. 'Well, I can tell you for sure he never told me anything about his recent past, but he was a lot more forthcoming about his childhood. We had quite a few chats about what we remembered from when we were kids, although he often seemed to get confused about when things happened. I'm sure he told me he went to school in Windsor until he was about seven, and then he moved to Germany. His father was in the army, you see, and he got posted out there for a few years.'

'Did he say where he was posted?' asked Slater as he scribbled away.

'If he did, I'm afraid I don't remember. I know he must have been out there for six or seven years because he told me he came back when he was thirteen. Or was it fourteen?' She looked at Slater for inspiration. 'Well, it was when he was at the younger end of his teenage years, anyway.'

'Do you know where he came back to?'

'Oh yes,' she said, looking pleased with herself. 'It was Windsor again. And he must have been a bit brainy because he went to the grammar school. I remember that bit because I was surprised.' She leaned towards them, conspiratorially. 'He didn't seem all that bright to me.'

'So when would this have been?' asked Norman.

'Well, if he really *was* sixty-two, that would have meant he was born in 1954. So he would have gone to Germany in about 1961.'

'You say if he really *was* sixty-two, as if you didn't quite believe him,' said Norman. 'Why is that?'

'If he was sixty-two, he looked a lot older,' she said. 'All right, maybe he had a hard life, but I know men ten years older who don't look anything like as old as he looked. And when we talked about old times, he sometimes had different memories to me. It was like he thought things happened later than they really did. I'm sixty-three, see, and I know The Beatles became really big around 1963, when I was ten, yet he seemed to think they didn't happen until he was in his twenties. He would accept he was wrong if I pointed it out, but I always thought it was bit strange. He said his memory was going, but I was never convinced.'

She stopped talking and almost seemed to be looking back into another time. They kept a respectful silence for a few moments, but they didn't want to be there all day.

'This is all good stuff, Rosie,' said Norman encouragingly. 'It'll be a great help. What about when he was older, after he left school? Did he tell you anything about that?'

For a few seconds, she looked at him as if she had just woken up and had no idea who he was, but then she seemed to snap out of it.

'I'm sorry,' she said. 'I was miles away there for a minute. What was that you asked?'

'What did he do after he left school?'

'He never really spoke much about what he did after he left school. It was all a bit vague. He was some sort of builder I think. He did tell me some stories about when he was working in Germany. In the eighties, it was. There was a slump in the building trade and it was hard to get work, so he went to Germany. He'd grown up there, you see, so it made sense. He ended up with a bunch of men from Newcastle. They sure did get up to some stuff! From what he told me, it's a wonder they ever got any work done. He must have enjoyed it out there because he seemed to have such clear memories of it. He could even remember all their names.'

'I don't suppose you can recall any of them?' asked Slater.

'Oh, I'll never remember them all. I'm sure there was a Neville, or was it Dennis? I'm not sure now.'

'Any idea where in Germany this was?'

'I'm not good on place names. Would it have been Doosel-something?'

Düsseldorf?' suggested Slater, looking up from his note-taking.

'That's right!' she said.

'And these others were all Geordies?'

'I don't know about all of them, but certainly most of them. I'm sure that's what he told me.'

Slater looked thoughtful, nodded, grunted, and went back to his notebook.

'We can check all this out when we get back,' said Norman. 'You've been really helpful, Rosie.'

'I'm sorry it's not more. It's only now, when you've asked me to sit down and try to remember what he told me, it's occurred to me he actually didn't tell me much at all.'

* * *

'You have a strange look about you,' said Norman as they climbed back into the car. 'Are you hacked off about the note-taking? I promise I wasn't pulling a fast one. I genuinely did forget to bring anything with me.'

Slater smiled. 'No, I'm not hacked off about the note-taking. I'm worried about what Rosie has just told us.'

'Why? What was wrong with it? I thought she was quite helpful.'

'Well, it might be helpful if any of it's true, but if this stuff really *is* what he's told her, I think old Joe might not have been quite as dim as Rosie thinks.'

'You think it's not true? But why would she ask for our help and then feed us a load of crap?'

'Oh, don't get me wrong. I'm sure she's recalling things Joe told her, I'm just beginning to think he's fed her a load of bullshit.'

'But why would you think that? We haven't even started checking yet.'

'I might be wrong,' said Slater, 'but that stuff about a group of Geordies in Düsseldorf, with guys called Neville and Dennis. Doesn't it ring any bells with you?'

'Should it?' asked Norman.

'Back about twelve or fifteen years ago, there was a revival of a TV series about a group of guys who had worked together in Germany in the eighties. The original series, way back in the eighties, was called *Auf Wiedersehen, Pet*. It was about the exploits of seven Geordie builders who can't find work in England and end up in Düsseldorf.'

Norman swore quietly. 'So you're telling me all that stuff about him working in Germany was just him retelling the story of a TV series?'

'Well, we don't know all the details about what he told her,' admitted Slater, 'but it's a bit of a coincidence, don't you think?'

'How come you know so much about it?' asked Norman. 'You would have been a little boy back in the eighties.'

'Yeah,' said Slater. 'But I enjoyed the revival so much I found the original series and watched it. It was a bit dated, but it still made me laugh.'

'Crap!' said Norman, unhappily. 'So where are we with this case? Are we wasting our time?'

Slater beamed at him. 'Well, I don't know about you, but as far as I'm concerned this case has just moved up from the "maybe worth a look" category to "definitely worth checking out further"! I don't think old Joe would have fed Rosie all that bullshit unless he had a good reason, and I'd like to know what it was.'

Norman smiled happily. 'Yeah, you're right. Count me in.' He thought for a few seconds and then spoke again. 'Do you think all that stuff about being at school in Windsor is bullshit too?'

'It has crossed my mind,' confessed Slater. 'But we won't know for sure until we start checking it out. I just hope my laptop can cope.'

'Shit, yeah, I'd forgotten about that,' said Norman, glumly. 'I should have had some sort of computer system sorted out by now.'

'Actually, I think I'm as guilty as you,' said Slater. 'Although, to be fair, I don't think either of us expected to have any work to do just yet. Let me get my laptop on the way back and I'll see if I can start doing some research.'

CHAPTER FIVE

The 12.50 train from Waterloo pulled slowly into Tinton Station and squealed to a halt. A man disembarked from the train, placed his briefcase carefully on the ground, and looked at the clock on the wall. It was two o'clock and, to his great surprise, the train was on time. The quiet inactivity of a small town like Tinton came as a shock to the newcomer, who had got used to the hustle and bustle of central London. He had guessed his journey was going to deposit him into something of a backwater, and judging from the shabby look of the platform and its surroundings, he had made an astute assessment. After the noise and vibrancy of his normal surroundings, the first thing that came to mind here was a dull greyness. And where were all the people?

Involuntarily, he brushed himself down, as if the grubby surroundings had somehow got into his clothes. Or maybe it was simply that he had exchanged his normal suit for jeans and a casual jacket, and he genuinely felt untidy. Finally, satisfied with the state of his attire, he picked up the briefcase and set off towards the exit. He had a somewhat strange imagination, and as he walked, he amused himself with the thought that maybe he'd managed to slip through some sort of time warp and had somehow arrived in a moment of time when no one else existed. It certainly felt that way.

The doors of the train let out a heavy sigh as they squeezed themselves closed, and then the train let out a series of small screeches as it began to trundle onwards down the line towards the next station. As the rumbling train gathered speed behind him, the man made his way along the deserted platform, through the small station building, and out onto the street beyond.

He had made good use of online maps the previous evening, so he knew the place he was looking for was less than a mile away. He had even drawn himself a rough sketch so he knew exactly which way to go. The sun was doing its best to add to the warmth he now felt towards this little town, so he decided to walk. It shouldn't take more than fifteen minutes.

The Old Brewery was formerly Tinton's own brewery which, in days past, had supplied the Brewer's Arms and other pubs in the area with the finest real ales. Sadly, those days were long gone, and the huge old building had recently been redeveloped and now housed several small businesses. To one side, separated from the main building, stood the old stables where the brewery horses had once lived. Now, gutted and refurbished, it was in the process of being made ready for business by its new occupiers.

The Old Brewery car park had vehicular access from a road that ran parallel to the High Street, but there was a pathway that ran from the High Street, allowing pedestrian access. The man turned down that path. He followed it into the car park at the back of the new offices and across to the old stables. There was no sign to tell him he was at the right place, but he confidently pushed open the door and stepped inside.

A man was sitting on a fold-up chair, hunched over a workstation, studying the screen of a laptop. He looked up in surprise as the door swung open.

* * *

Slater took in the newcomer as he walked into the room. He reckoned the man was around fifty years old, must be a couple of inches over six feet tall, and looked reasonably fit. He was wearing jeans, a shirt and a jacket, but it didn't look quite right, somehow, and Slater got the impression he had felt the need to dress down to come here. The briefcase clearly didn't go with the outfit, and he got the impression the man would normally wear a suit. He had the air of someone privately educated and was probably used to the old-school-tie way of doing things. That could be a bit awkward; he and Norman were anything but.

'Mr Slater?' the man asked, extending his hand. 'My name's Robin Bradshaw.'

Slater closed his laptop, jumped to his feet, and shook Bradshaw's hand. The confident handshake matched his manner perfectly.

'Err, we're not exactly open for business,' Slater said, indicating another folding chair set up by a second workstation. 'But now you're here, you'd better have a seat.'

Bradshaw looked distrustfully at the chair. 'It won't collapse, will it?' he asked.

'The guy who usually sits on it weighs at least half as much again as you,' said Slater, 'and he hasn't managed to break it yet.'

'That must be Mr Norman,' said Bradshaw as he lowered himself carefully onto the proffered seat and placed his briefcase on the floor next to him.

'So, what can we do for you?' asked Slater, warily.

'How's business?' asked Bradshaw.

Of all the questions he could have asked, this was one Slater hadn't anticipated. 'I'm sorry?'

'You're a new business, aren't you? I just wondered how things were going.'

'It's not actually *my* business,' said Slater.

'Oh! I understood you were going into business together.'

'That's a possibility,' admitted Slater. 'But nothing's set in concrete. Right now, I'm just here to help a friend get started.'

'And that friend is Mr Norman, isn't it?'

Slater frowned suspiciously. 'Is there something I can do for you, Mr Bradshaw?'

'It's not really working out though, is it?' said Bradshaw, ignoring the question. 'You don't have any work. Is that why you're no longer part of the business plan?'

'There is no business plan,' said Slater, testily, 'and officially we're not open for business yet, so we're hardly going to have people fighting for our attention.'

'*We*?' asked Bradshaw. 'I thought you just said it was your friend's business?'

'All right,' said Slater. 'So *he's* not open for business yet.'

Bradshaw looked a little puzzled. 'And you say you're not part of the business?'

'That's correct.'

Now Bradshaw looked thoughtful. 'Hmm, that makes it a whole new ball game,' he said. 'Maybe I didn't need to rush down here after all.'

'Look, do you have a problem we can help you with?' asked Slater, 'or are you doing some sort of survey into new business start-ups?'

Bradshaw gave him a ghost of a smile. 'I see you've still got the feisty attitude, Mr Slater.'

Slater sighed. 'What exactly is it you want?'

'It's about you and the police force.'

'I'm not in the police force. I resigned a few weeks ago.'

Bradshaw gave him a condescending smile and gave a barely perceptible shake of his head. 'Ah, but did you?' he asked.

Slater folded his arms. 'Yes, I, bloody well did.'

'Ah, but you didn't, did you?' said Bradshaw. 'We both know you were persuaded to change your resignation to a request for a short sabbatical instead.'

Slater frowned at him.

'A leave of absence,' said Bradshaw.

'Yes, I know what a sabbatical is, thank you,' snapped Slater. 'I just don't understand how *you* know about that!'

'Ah! Yes, I should have made that clear from the start,' said Bradshaw. He fished in his pocket and produced a warrant card, which he handed to Slater before continuing. 'You see, we don't think you really want to resign at all. That's why you were persuaded to take a sabbatical — so you would have time to reconsider.'

'Chief Superintendent Bradshaw,' read Slater from the warrant card. 'You're from the police? But I've still got a few weeks to go before I'm supposed to confirm my decision to leave.'

'Yes, we heard you were thinking of making the sabbatical a permanent break. I'm here to make you an offer so that doesn't happen.'

'*We heard*? What do you mean *we heard*? Who told you that?'

Bradshaw said nothing.

'Yeah, well, you're wasting your time,' said Slater. 'This sabbatical was a stupid idea. You should have just let me go in the first place.'

'But we didn't think you really wanted to leave. The assessor you spoke to felt you were acting in haste for personal reasons rather than work reasons.'

'What's that supposed to mean? What else could I have possibly meant when I wrote a letter of resignation?'

Bradshaw inclined his head as if to acknowledge Slater's point. 'Well, of course, I can't say for sure what you meant,' he said, 'but it was felt your unfortunate relationship with DCI Goodnews might have had rather more to do with your decision than anything work-related. You're not the first officer to resign in this way.'

Slater felt his face redden. If Bradshaw had intended to get under his skin, he had done an excellent job. 'Who the hell do you think you are?' he asked, angrily. 'How do you know all this stuff? And what's it got to do with you anyway?'

'Oh, don't get me wrong, I'm not here to pass judgement,' said Bradshaw, hastily.

'I think we're probably done here,' said Slater. 'Unless you've actually got some sort of problem that needs investigating, I don't feel inclined to listen to anything else you have to say.'

Bradshaw said nothing for a moment and then smiled at him. 'I just want you to understand that it's possible for you to come back in a completely new capacity — well away from DCI Goodnews.' He paused for a moment. 'How does Detective Inspector Slater sound?'

Slater almost fell off his chair. 'What? I think I must have misheard.'

'I said it's not too late to come back,' said Bradshaw, patiently. 'You've had the break you needed, so why not come back and work for me in a completely new position?'

'Why would I want to do that?'

'Because I believe you're much better suited to the working environment I can offer than working for yourself alongside Mr Norman.'

Slater studied Bradshaw but said nothing. This had come as something of a shock, and he needed time to think about it.

'How's Miss Radstock?' asked Bradshaw.

The question caught Slater completely off guard, and his mouth flapped open in silent surprise.

'Oh, sorry,' said Bradshaw. 'Is she supposed to be a secret?'

'I don't know who you're talking about,' said Slater hastily, trying desperately to regain his composure.

Bradshaw spread his hands in appeal. 'Oh, please!' he said. 'How stupid do I look? I do hope you never have to lie your way out of trouble, because if there was a prize for the world's most transparent liar, you'd win it hands down.' He watched Slater struggling to contain his anger. 'Oh, I see. You want me to play silly games. Perhaps I should ask how is the former Miss Radstock, who sometimes calls herself Ginger, and up until a few weeks ago, was living on the street?'

Now Slater was getting worried. 'What do you know about that?' he asked, nervously.

'I know she had a rough deal, was unfairly dismissed from her position, and then driven to the brink of bankruptcy. She felt she had to go on the street to hide, did you know that?'

'Yeah, she told me,' said Slater.

'And now she's living with you.

'How d'you know all this?' demanded Slater. 'Are you spying on us?'

Bradshaw said nothing, which Slater took as an admission of guilt. 'If you think you've come here to try and get your hands on her—'

'Your chivalry is very honourable, but you needn't waste it on me,' said Bradshaw. 'You should calm down and start thinking, Mr Slater. As far as I'm aware, she hasn't been accused of committing any crimes, so I'm not here to arrest her. And, would I really come in here and tell you, if I intended to do her any harm?'

Now Slater felt slightly foolish.

'I'm on your side, and on hers too, come to that,' said Bradshaw. He looked at the puzzled face before him. 'Ah. I see you don't understand.'

'Don't understand?' asked Slater. 'That's a bloody understatement! You turn up, unannounced, insisting I want to come and work for you. And then, as if that's not enough, you start dissecting my private life, and now you want to bring Jenny into it. Yeah, you're right. I don't understand!'

'Whatever Miss Radstock did, she came to you for help,' said Bradshaw.

'I don't think she sought me out deliberately,' said Slater. 'It was more of a chance meeting.'

'Whatever. The point is she ended up with you, and she's *still* with you, which tells me you've chosen to look out for her.'

'She's a friend,' said Slater. 'Of course I'm going to look out for her.'

Bradshaw raised his eyebrow for a moment and then smiled slightly. 'Now, if I'm any judge of character,' he said,

'I think you would like an opportunity to find out who did this to her and to set the record straight.'

'The thought has crossed my mind.'

'But how are you going to do it?'

'I'll find a way.'

'It would be a lot easier to do it if you were inside an organisation like the police force.'

Slater folded his arms in front of him. 'I've had enough of the police force.'

'Which is exactly why I'm here,' said Bradshaw. 'I can make sure that when you finish your sabbatical, you're recruited into a new team, and a quite different environment to the one you were in before.'

'For the last time — I might have been persuaded to go on a sabbatical to think things over, but I never withdrew my resignation, and I still intend to stick to my decision and leave the police force.'

Bradshaw leaned down and opened his briefcase. He removed a folder, placed it on his knee, opened it, and removed a couple of sheets of paper.

'According to this, you simply requested a sabbatical,' he said, offering the sheets of paper to Slater.

Slater's face creased in confusion as he took the pages and studied them. 'I didn't write this,' he said, angrily, brandishing the pages.

'I think you'll find a handwriting expert would confirm it was your hand.'

'But that's bullshit! Where's my resignation letter?'

'Yes, it's a puzzle isn't it, old chap? You keep talking about this letter, but there's no sign of one in your file, just a letter requesting a sabbatical, which you'll see I myself graciously granted.'

'Don't "old chap" me, you condescending arsehole,' snarled Slater, jumping to his feet. 'This is—'

'Look, I understand this is all very confusing,' said Bradshaw, genially.

'Confusing? It's not bloody confusing, it's blackmail!'

'Oh, come now, don't you think that's rather dramatic? I didn't say you had to re-join, just that you *could* if you wanted to. I certainly don't remember making any threats about what might happen if you didn't come back. But, let's face it, some people aren't cut out for working for themselves. You like organisation and proper structure and procedures to follow, whereas Norman has always been more than happy to muddle along in a mess and fly by the seat of his pants.'

Slater's mind was in turmoil.

'I'm not saying either of you is right or wrong,' added Bradshaw, hurriedly. 'People are different, that's just how it is. But how long would it be before you got fed up clearing up behind him, and he got fed up with you complaining about the mess he makes? You could end up getting sick of the sight of each other. Is that what you want?' He gave Slater a couple of seconds before he continued. 'And there's another thing to consider. We both know Mr Norman has no problem with crossing lines. While you were in the force, he could only stray a little way off the path. Do you think working for himself is going to offer more or less control?'

'He's good at what he does,' said Slater, feeling he ought to stick up for his friend.

'I'm not denying that,' said Bradshaw. 'I'm just telling you what you already know. You need to be a part of a bigger organisation. He doesn't.'

Slater had a feeling of déjà vu. Hadn't Jenny said much the same thing? He shook the thought from his head. 'I'm not sure I want to come back. I really was sick and tired of the police force and trying to work with my hands tied behind my back. There are so many rules favouring criminals these days, it gets harder and harder to convict them, even when there's no doubt they're guilty.'

'I understand your frustration,' said Bradshaw. 'That's why we lose so many good people. But you need to understand — what I'm putting together isn't the police force as you know it. This is police work unshackled by so many rules.'

Slater couldn't deny there was something appealing about this idea. 'I need to think about this,' he said.

'Of course you need time to think,' said Bradshaw. 'I'm not looking for a decision right now. But let me ask you a question: didn't you ever wonder what happened to those officers from the Serious Crime Unit you crossed paths with when you worked with Miss Radstock? An old case, wasn't it? Ruth someone or other.'

'Ruth Thornhill,' said Slater.

'That's the one.'

'It wasn't our brief to follow up with those guys,' said Slater. 'Our job was to find Ruth's killer.'

'Well, yes, I understand that,' said Bradshaw, 'but didn't you ever think about it?'

Slater didn't want to admit that he had often wondered what had happened. 'So what did happen to them?' he asked casually.

'Well, that's just my point,' said Bradshaw. 'Nothing happened.'

'But they were as bent as corkscrews!' Slater exclaimed.

'Which just goes to show it's not what you do, but who you know that counts,' said Bradshaw. 'Don't you think it's high time that all changed?'

'Is that what you want me to do? Chase bent coppers?'

'Not specifically, but it will happen sometimes. You've never had any qualms about doing that in the past.'

'I wouldn't have any qualms about doing it now,' said Slater. 'But I need to understand how it's going to be any different from before.'

'I want you to come back as a DI and work for me, leading part of a much bigger team spread across the country. We won't be as visible as the main force, and we won't have to follow quite so many rules. We will be more interested in results rather than following procedure. If we can fill the barrel with enough good apples, it'll be a lot easier to find the bad apples and weed them out.'

Slater couldn't help but let out a cynical snort of laughter. 'Ha! Isn't that how it's supposed to work *now*?'

Bradshaw inclined his head to acknowledge Slater's point. 'So, you think we should just give in to the bad apples, do you?'

Slater conceded the point. 'But I don't know you from Adam,' he said. 'I don't recall ever hearing your name before, and yet here you are expecting me to hop into bed with you just because you've forged a letter. If I'm honest, there's a big part of me that thinks I should tell you to piss off and let me get on with my life.'

'Come now, Mr Slater. It's not like you to be so fussy about who you hop into bed with, is it? Perhaps we should ask DCI Goodnews, or maybe Miss Radstock? I'm sure they could both give an interesting answer.'

Slater's mouth flapped open.

'The bed-hopping analogy was yours,' Bradshaw said simply.

'You're barking up the wrong tree with Jenny Radstock,' said Slater, guiltily. 'I already told you — I'm just doing a friend a favour. She has her own room, and there's no more to it than that.'

Bradshaw smiled indulgently. 'Yes, I'm sure that must be the case,' he said, 'but I'm not actually here to discuss your sex life. I'm sure it would be a fascinating subject, but it's getting off the point. Don't you think Miss Radstock deserves to have her life back?'

'I already told you, I'll help her when she's good and ready,' said Slater, 'but not because some clown wanders in off the street and says so.'

'Well, I suggest you don't take too long about it,' said Bradshaw, 'because if I could find her, it stands to reason *they* could too. For all you know, they could be biding their time right now, just waiting for the right moment.'

Slater shook his head fiercely. 'That's a load of old bollocks.'

'Is it?' Bradshaw leaned back in his seat. 'I found her quite easily.'

'She's quite safe where she is.'

'And you know this for certain, do you?' Bradshaw fixed him with an intent stare. 'Hasn't your house been broken into before? Wasn't there an incident with some Russian chappie with a gun?'

Now Slater wasn't so sure of himself. Bradshaw really *did* seem to know a lot about all of them. What if he wasn't quite so full of shit after all?

He peered at Bradshaw suspiciously. 'How do I know you're not just feeding me a load of crap?'

'Have I got any of my facts wrong so far?' Bradshaw stared at Slater, as if challenging him to prove him wrong. Slater shifted awkwardly in his seat but said nothing.

'By the way,' said Bradshaw, 'how's Mrs Jolly getting on? It's a shame about her husband turning on your friend Norman like that, but then again, every cloud has a silver lining, doesn't it? I wonder . . . do you realise just *how* close she and Norman have become?'

Slater said nothing. He wasn't sure exactly what Bradshaw was suggesting, but whatever Norm and Jane were up to was none of his business, and he certainly wasn't going to judge them.

'My, my, isn't this a cosy setup?' said Bradshaw. 'Two happy couples! I almost feel like a gooseberry.'

'Well, I did think you were a bit of a prick,' muttered Slater. Then he said, more loudly, 'This is all very well, but I still don't know if I can trust you.'

'Ah! But how do you know you can't?'

'How about because you just walked in off the street and showed me a forged letter? That warrant card could be another forgery for all I know. Any one of a hundred people could walk in here with one of those and make accusations to try and persuade me to work for them.'

Bradshaw stared at Slater for a few seconds, then picked up his briefcase and stood up. 'I'm sorry you feel that way, Mr Slater. I was hoping you would be interested in joining me. But before I go, here's something to consider — how many of those hundred people who might have walked in off the street would know how you've come to arrive where you are right now, and exactly which accusations would push your buttons? And would they know about Miss Radstock and her situation?'

Slater considered this as he stood up.

'I thought you would be interested in the job I'm offering,' said Bradshaw, 'but obviously I must have got it all wrong.'

'I've already got a job, right here,' said Slater.

'Yes. Joe Dalgetty, isn't it? How are you getting on with that?'

Slater was beginning to feel decidedly concerned about just how much Bradshaw knew. 'How the hell do you know about that?' he asked.

Bradshaw stared impassively back at him, and Slater felt the hair on the back of his neck prickle.

'Wait. Are you the guy in the pinstriped suit?'

Bradshaw smiled another condescending smile, but still said nothing.

'You're beginning to make me feel uncomfortable,' said Slater. 'Is there anything about us you *don't* know?'

'I won't claim to know everything,' said Bradshaw, 'but when we decide to research someone, we are quite thorough. Trust me, there isn't much I don't know.'

'Is that even legal?'

'That's a moot point, especially if you speak to the civil liberties lot, but we live in a digital, technological age. It's just about the only way to keep up with people these days, and even then, the major criminals are still managing to keep ahead. I did tell you we're a bit different from the police force you know.'

Slater was really struggling to know what to make of Robin Bradshaw, and he was becoming increasingly intrigued by this job offer.

'So, how are you getting on with your case?' asked Bradshaw, pointing at Slater's laptop. 'I expect you're finding it a bit difficult to find out what you need to know, especially now you don't have the resources you used to have at your fingertips. Google will only get you so far, won't it?'

Slater couldn't argue with that. 'It takes a bit of getting used to,' he admitted. 'But we've only just got the case. We've barely started to scratch the surface. We'll work it out.'

Bradshaw gave him an indulgent smile. 'But even if the information you need was so easily available, it will take so much longer,' he said.

'You still haven't told me why you sent Rosie to us.'

'Perhaps it's a test,' said Bradshaw, mysteriously.

'What are you? Some sort of cold-case handler, is that it?'

Bradshaw said nothing.

'But then, this case can't be cold, can it?' continued Slater, thinking aloud. 'Old Joe only died a few weeks ago.'

He turned his attention back to Bradshaw, who stared back impassively. 'It would all be so much easier if you had access to those old resources again, wouldn't it?' he said.

Slater pulled a face. 'Somehow, I don't think there's much chance of us being allowed to link up with the police databases,' he said.

Bradshaw's eyes widened; he was obviously trying to look innocent. 'But, if you *were* to come and join me . . .'

'What are you? MI5?'

Bradshaw gave a small snort of laughter. 'I think you watch too many spy films.'

'All right, so let's assume you *are* something to do with the police,' said Slater, 'and let's assume I *did* come back. What then?'

'You'd be promoted to DI, and you'd get to run your own team.'

'Based where?'

'I don't know that yet,' said Bradshaw.

'What sort of cases?'

'You would be working on cases that I think need further investigation. You would also be in a position where you can look at people of interest when the need arises.'

'Who would I be looking at?'

'You don't need to know that right now.'

'So, this is going to be a bit like a cold-case squad, but it's not necessarily cold cases we'd be investigating, right?'

'As I understand it, they normally use retired officers for that,' said Bradshaw.

'How do I check you out?' asked Slater. 'There has to be some way of proving you're for real. Where can I find you online?'

'Now that would hardly be discreet for someone in my position, would it?' said Bradshaw.

'Oh, bloody terrific!' said Slater. 'So, I can't check you out at all? You're not some nutter who gets his kicks playing out some elaborate cloak and dagger game and pretending to be James Bond, are you?'

Bradshaw guffawed. 'Good grief, he's far too active for me. I'm not the action man sort. I prefer using my brain to using my fists.'

'I'm glad you think this is funny,' said Slater, sarcastically. 'But I'll tell you this: so far, you're doing a good job of convincing me I don't want to get involved.'

Bradshaw shrugged. 'I think you probably need time to think about what I've told you,' he said. 'I completely understand your reticence. To be honest, it's a good thing, and it's no more than I expected. I would have been concerned if you had rushed in without thinking. Perhaps if I was to make a gesture of good faith, it would help to ease your concerns.'

'Yeah, right,' said Slater, getting to his feet as Bradshaw reached for his hand. 'Good luck with that.'

'Oh, I'm sure I can come up with something to convince you,' said Bradshaw as he shook Slater's hand.

He turned and headed for the door, but stopped as he reached it and turned to Slater. 'Goodbye, Mr Slater, or should I say DI Slater. It's been a pleasure. Until the next time.'

CHAPTER SIX

'Did I see some guy leaving?' asked Norman, as he set down the promised coffee and cakes on one of the recently finished workstations.

Slater was busy trying to clear the assorted decorating rubbish that was strewn all around. Norman wondered how they had managed to generate quite so much rubbish, but didn't feel inclined to deal with the matter himself.

'Yeah,' said Slater, noncommittally.

'Was it another job?'

'Err, not exactly,' said Slater. 'He was looking for me.'

'Oh, right,' said Norman, uncertainly. It wasn't like Slater to be quite so unforthcoming.

Norman watched Slater as he headed for the door, carrying a huge box filled with empty paint tins and yet more assorted rubbish. He was definitely looking uncomfortable about something.

'Can I ask a question?'

'Jeez, Norm,' said Slater, peering over the top of the box. 'When have you ever needed permission to talk?'

'I'm serious,' said Norman. 'We can't keep on avoiding the elephant in the room. It needs sorting out, and it needs sorting out now!'

Slater lowered the box carefully to the floor, looking taken aback by Norman's sudden outburst and slightly shame-faced.

'What elephant in the room?' he asked innocently.

'The one we've been tiptoeing around for the past week while we've been decorating this place,' said Norman. 'The very same one we've actually been tiptoeing around ever since we agreed to start working together!'

'Ah, right,' said Slater. 'You mean *that* elephant.'

'I hope there's not another one,' said Norman, 'because if there is, I'm not aware of it.'

Slater shifted from one foot to the other. 'No, there isn't another one,' he said, slowly. 'What do you want to ask?'

Norman grabbed the two rickety folding chairs and arranged them opposite each other. He parked himself on one and pointed to the other. 'Come and sit for a minute.'

Slater shuffled obediently across and settled into the chair.

'A few weeks ago, I thought we were both pretty keen to set up in business together,' began Norman, 'so I want to ask, why is it every time I suggest we sit down and talk about it you come up with an excuse not to?'

'That's a bit harsh, Norm,' said Slater. 'You know I've got Jenny staying back home and I worry about her.'

'Don't use her as an excuse. I seem to recall you suggested her story would be our first investigation.'

'Yeah, but she's still not saying much,' said Slater, 'and until she comes up with some names, we've got nowhere to start.'

Norman fixed him with an intense stare. 'Does that mean we were only ever going to take on that one case?'

Slater was beginning to look distinctly uncomfortable. 'No, of course it's not that, it's just . . .' His voice trailed away into silence.

'Can I make an observation?' asked Norman.

Slater gave an unhappy nod of his head.

'It seems to me your heart might have been set on working with me a few weeks ago, but now your head's had a chance to get involved, it no longer seems quite such a good idea. Am I right?'

Slater's face was a picture of misery. 'It's not that I don't want to work with you, Norm. We've always made a great team, and we have a lot of fun—'

'Wait a minute,' said Norman. 'I didn't think there was a problem with you and me. I think I can tell when someone doesn't like me, and my radar isn't detecting any anti-Norm vibes coming from you. I'm not trying to pick a fight here, and I'm not judging. I'm just trying to get you to tell me what you really think.'

Slater looked puzzled. 'I'm not following,' he said.

'Well, forgive me if I'm wrong,' said Norman, 'but it seems to me you're not convinced you really want to start a business and work for yourself, with me. Am I right?'

Something that could have been relief passed across Slater's face.

'I'll go even further,' Norman continued. 'I think that you think you're going to be letting me down if you don't join me in this business.' He sat back and watched Slater's face.

'I feel really bad about this,' said Slater. 'It's just that the more I think about it, the less sure I am about what I really want to do.'

Norman spread his arms. 'I get it. Working for yourself isn't for everyone, but it's not something you should be feeling bad about. Jeez, you'd be an idiot to join me if you weren't sure, and imagine if you did join me, and then a few months down the line you hated it? Then I'd be the one feeling bad!'

Slater looked uncertain. 'You don't mind?'

'Aw, come on, Dave, of course I don't mind. I was going to set up on my own before you quit, remember? If you really wanted to join me that would be great, but if you don't, well, that's okay too.'

At last, a glimmer of a smile crept onto Slater's face. 'I really wanted to tell you, but I've been feeling so bad about letting you down,' he said.

'But that's just the point, you're not letting me down,' insisted Norman. 'You could do it just to keep me happy, but then you'd be letting yourself down, and trust me, you don't wanna start doing that. I do understand where you're coming from, honestly. I mean take a look around you.' He waved his arms around the room. 'I'm a bit haphazard, right?'

Slater nodded enthusiastically.

'That's just how I am,' continued Norman, 'and am I going to change now? It's not gonna happen. I'm too old to change now. In the same way, you like things orderly and tidy, and there's no way you're changing any time soon, is there?'

Slater nodded again and smiled. 'No chance,' he agreed.

'Exactly,' said Norman. 'I think you would feel compelled to keep cleaning up behind me, and in the end, we'd get on each other's nerves. I don't think either of us would want that to happen, do you?'

This time Slater shook his head. 'Definitely not,' he said. 'No way.'

'I bet, if you're really honest, you miss the order and structure of the police force, don't you?'

Slater sighed. 'I dunno if that's what it is, to be honest,' he said. 'So much has happened in such a short space of time, what with finding my dad, and then him passing almost straight away. And then there's Jenny. I never thought I'd see her again, and suddenly here she is, sharing my house.'

'You forgot to mention getting tangled up with the Black Witch,' said Norman. 'That woman is enough to mess anyone up. I think Naomi's hit the nail right on the head with that name for her.'

This was the second reminder Slater had been given of his ill-fated fling with Marion Goodnews, aka the Black Witch, in the last twenty-four hours and judging by the look on his face, he didn't need any reminder of just how much he regretted it.

'Yeah, I admit I was a bloody fool getting involved with her,' he said, gloomily. 'I suppose I've buggered everything up and created my own mess. Jenny seems to be the only good thing that's happened to me recently.'

'You could always go back to the force,' suggested Norman. 'They're losing good people all the time, so I should think they'd welcome an experienced guy who actually wanted to come back. Personally, I think maybe you just needed to take some time away from it, not leave altogether.'

Slater sighed and took a deep breath.

'Actually,' he said, 'there's something I've been meaning to tell you about that.'

But before he could say any more, Norman's mobile phone began to ring.

'That'll be Jane!' cried Norman, and he rushed across the room to answer it.

It was a full ten minutes before Norman ended his call. From what Slater had been able to glean, he was taking Jane out on a date this evening, and he was obviously excited about it.

'I gotta go,' said Norman, reaching for his jacket. 'What was it you wanted to say?'

'Oh, it's okay, it'll keep until the morning,' said Slater.

CHAPTER SEVEN

It was Wednesday morning. Their appointment with Joe Dalgetty's solicitor wasn't until the afternoon, and Slater's laptop had decided it wasn't going to work, so they had decided to call Rosie and see if she still had a key to Joe's house. To their delight, she not only had a key, she was actually about to head over there to make sure everything was okay and to make sure there was no post lying around. She told Norman she had been to the post office and asked them to stop delivering Joe's post, but she wanted to be sure they had listened. She would be happy to wait for them and they could all go over together.

It was barely sixty yards from her house to Joe's, but as they neared the house, Rosie seemed to slow down.

'Here,' she said, thrusting the front door key at Norman. 'I hate going in there now it's empty. It's so quiet it gives me the creeps, and I'm always worried whoever was in there before might have come back.'

'I doubt he'll come back here again,' Norman said. 'If he was as thorough as you said, he either found what he wanted, or he's certain it's not here.'

'D'you think it was the same man who broke into my house?' A sudden look of worried realisation spread across her face, and she turned to Slater. 'Is that why you asked me if Joe had left anything with me?'

'If we assume he was looking for something, and he knew you and Joe were friends, it's possible,' Slater admitted, wishing she hadn't asked the question, 'but it's more likely the police were right and it was the guy who's been targeting pensioners.'

She gave him a hard stare. 'Don't patronise me, Mr Slater,' she said. 'I might be getting on a bit, but I can assure you I still have a full picnic basket. We all know it wasn't someone after my money because it was there in the kitchen drawer, and he didn't touch it.'

Slater blushed guiltily. 'I'm sorry. I didn't mean it to sound quite like that.'

'Am I going to be safe?' she asked.

'Honestly? I don't know for sure, but this person has been pretty careful to avoid attracting too much attention. So far, he's managed to convince the police he doesn't exist, but that would soon change if someone got hurt.'

'I think Dave's right,' said Norman. 'He wouldn't go to all the trouble of doing this invisible man thing and then hurt someone. In my opinion, he knows whatever he wants isn't here, and now he knows *you* haven't got it either.'

'I'd love to know what he's looking for,' said Rosie.

Norman placed the key in the lock, and it slipped smoothly into place and turned easily. 'Yeah, that's our starter for ten,' he said. 'Maybe we'll get lucky and there'll be something inside that gives us a clue.'

'Right now, I'd settle for a simple clue about Joe's past,' said Slater. 'At least it would be a start.'

The door swung quietly open and Norman stepped inside, closely followed by Slater. Rosie hung back for a moment and then followed.

The first thing Slater noticed was the eerie quietness that Rosie had remarked upon, then the coldness of the empty house seemed to embrace him like an unwanted caress and he gave an involuntary shiver.

'It's because there's no one living here,' said Rosie from behind him. 'Empty houses always feel cold and damp.'

Feeling slightly embarrassed that Rosie had seen him shiver, Slater said nothing and followed Norman along the hall. As Norman turned left into the kitchen, Slater turned right into the lounge. As they disappeared from view, Rosie turned to push the door closed, then bent down to gather a couple of letters that had been swept aside as the door opened.

'Lazy buggers,' she mumbled to herself. 'I went all the way down there to tell them to stop Joe's post and send it to the solicitor. Waste of my time that was.' She squinted at the letters, but without her glasses it was a futile exercise, so she stuffed them into her coat pocket and followed Norman into the kitchen.

'What is it you're looking for?' she asked.

'Something that might give us a clue to his past,' said Norman, rummaging through one of the kitchen drawers. 'An address book perhaps, or a letter from a relative, anything like that would help.'

'I don't recall seeing anything like that,' she said. 'Now I think about it, I'm not sure he *had* any friends or relatives. He never used to get cards at Christmas time, or for his birthday.'

'So, how come all his stuff is still in this house?' asked Norman. 'I would have thought the landlord would have wanted the house cleared so he could put a new tenant in place.'

Rosie looked surprised. 'D'you know, I hadn't even thought about that! I suppose I ought to let him know Joe's dead.'

'Surely the solicitor would have done that. How long's he been dead now?'

'Getting on for eight weeks,' she said.

'How did he pay his rent? Was it monthly?'

'I'm not sure, but I think he was probably monthly direct debit, in advance, the same as me.'

As Norman considered this, he spotted Slater passing the kitchen door. 'Hey Dave,' he called.

Slater stopped in the doorway and leaned into the kitchen.

'Joe's solicitor would have control of his bank account now, right?' asked Norman.

Slater nodded. 'Yeah, he should have.'

'So, he would have notified the landlord and cancelled the direct debit, right?'

'I would have thought so.'

'Me too,' agreed Norman. 'Yet nothing's been done about getting Joe's stuff out of here and getting ready for a new tenant.'

'Maybe these things take time.'

'My landlord's a great guy,' said Norman, 'but letting property is a business. If I passed away tomorrow, I don't reckon he'd leave my room empty for eight weeks. Sure, he might give my family a week or two to clear my stuff out, but eight weeks? That's not good business, is it?'

'Right. I see what you mean,' said Slater.

'Then again, I'm not sure it matters much,' said Norman.

'Wouldn't hurt to check it out. That's another question we can ask Joe's solicitor this afternoon, but first we need to get finished here.'

'Yeah, you're right,' said Norman. 'I'll have a quick shufty through the rest of the cupboards and drawers in here, and then I'll join you upstairs.'

'I don't think you'll find much,' said Rosie to Norman as Slater made his way upstairs. 'I can't remember seeing anything like you're looking for.'

Norman methodically went through the handful of cupboards and drawers in the kitchen, but apart from a couple of old recipes that had been torn from magazines, there was nothing of interest. In the last drawer he opened, he found a cheap flyer for a locksmith. It was the sort of thing someone might have knocked up themselves on a PC.

'Is this the guy who fitted the new lock?' asked Norman, showing the flyer to Rosie.

She squinted at the flyer. 'What's it say?'

'It's a flyer for a locksmith.'

'He never said, but I suppose it could be.'

'I'll give this guy a ring,' said Norman, folding the flyer and slipping it into his pocket.

'I'm sure whoever got in here must have had a key,' insisted Rosie.

'Well, if this is the guy who fitted the new lock, he'll know how many keys there were. If we can't account for them all we'll know someone has a key who shouldn't.'

By the time Norman was ready to make his way upstairs, Slater was on his way back down.

'That was quick!'

'It doesn't take long to look through two drawers and find nothing,' said Slater.

'Crap!' said Norman. 'I was hoping we'd at least find something.'

CHAPTER EIGHT

Jeremy Pearson had made it quite clear from his frosty attitude that Slater and Norman were anything but welcome, and he launched into them as soon as the formality of the introductions was over.

'According to the police, Mr Dalgetty died of a heart attack with no suspicious circumstances,' he said. 'In my book, that's natural causes, so why are you investigating his death?'

'His neighbour, Rosie Hewitt, thinks there's more to his death than meets the eye,' said Norman.

'And she knows more than the police? Who does she think she is? Miss Marple?'

'Since he died, his house has been broken into and so has hers,' said Slater. 'Don't you think that's a bit of a coincidence?'

'They're both pensioners, aren't they?' said Pearson dismissively. 'Half the pensioners in town have had their houses broken into in the last few weeks. That's the only coincidence I can see.'

'Is there any particular reason you're being so obstructive?' asked Norman.

'You're not even police officers, are you? No, of course you're not, so I don't have to tell you anything, do I? It's not about being obstructive, it's about confidentiality.'

'We thought you might like to help us clear up one or two issues that are worrying us,' said Slater.

'Have you never heard of client confidentiality?' insisted Pearson.

'Mr Dalgetty is dead. Surely that must give you some leeway.'

'I was engaged by Mr Dalgetty to look after his affairs after his death, and that's what I intend to do.'

'So how about if we were to ask some questions that you could answer without divulging anything?' said Norman. 'What if we tell you some stuff and you just tell us if we're right or wrong.'

Pearson sighed. 'It's still the same thing. I can't tell you anything.'

'Are we right to think Joe has no family?' asked Norman.

'I can't tell you—'

'The police say we're right,' said Slater.

'Do they?' asked Pearson, curiously.

'Are you saying they're wrong?' asked Norman.

'Well, no, of course not,' said Pearson, exasperated.

Norman smiled at him. 'There, that wasn't so hard, was it? And you didn't tell us anything we didn't already know.'

'Yes, but—'

'Why are you still paying his rent?'

'I'm sorry?' said Pearson, not quite able to keep up with the quick-fire questions and change of subject.

'The rent on his house. It's still being paid. Shouldn't you have stopped the direct debit payment by now?'

'I can assure you, I have notified everyone he was paying and stopped all the payments,' Pearson said haughtily. 'It's a matter of preserving his estate, so it's not something I take lightly.'

'Are you sure?' asked Slater.

Pearson gave him a dirty look. 'Do I look incompetent, Mr Slater?'

'Well, no, I wasn't trying to imply you were incompetent. It's just that we believe his rent is still being paid because the landlord hasn't tried to repossess the house.'

Pearson angrily opened a folder on his desk and thumbed through it until he found the page he wanted. He ran his finger down a short list. 'There's nothing here that looks like a regular rent payment. What's the landlord's name?'

'Bennet, Swift,' said Norman.

'There's no payee by that name,' said Pearson.

'There must be,' said Slater.

Pearson glared at him. 'There most certainly is not!'

'So how was he paying his rent?' asked Slater.

'I have no idea,' said Pearson, 'but I can assure you it wasn't through his bank account.'

'What about council tax?' asked Norman.

'You're starting to try my patience,' said Pearson, tapping his fingers on the desk.

'Utilities, then,' insisted Norman. 'Electricity, heating, stuff like that. Everyone pays those by direct debit, don't they?'

Pearson glanced down at the list in front of him again. 'It appears Mr Dalgetty liked to be different,' he said.

'What, none of them?' asked Slater, in surprise.

'People *do* still pay these things by cash,' said Pearson. 'You can do it at post offices and banks.'

'Yeah, but my guess is he had his pension paid into that bank account, and if I'm correct that means he would have to withdraw the money to make those payments from his account first. Am I right?'

Pearson looked down at his list again and then back up at them again. He was looking a little uncomfortable now.

'How much is in that account?' asked Norman, then he held his hand up before Pearson could reply. 'I know, you can't tell me, right? So, let me make a guess. My guess is he's never drawn a single penny out of that account.'

Pearson gulped loudly. Norman smiled a big wide smile.

'We'll take that as a yes, then, shall we?' he said. 'Let me try another one. My next guess is that he gave you twenty-five grand, in cash, a while ago so you could transfer it to Mrs Hewitt when he died. How am I doing so far?'

Pearson had turned pale.

'Didn't you think it was strange? I mean, twenty-five grand in cash? And you know it didn't come from his bank account. Didn't you wonder where he got it from?'

'I think you should leave now,' mumbled Pearson. 'I don't think I have anything more to say. As I've already told you—'

'Yeah, we know,' said Slater, 'it's that client confidentiality thing again, right?'

'You know what's worrying me now?' asked Norman. Pearson gave an almost imperceptible shake of his head. 'I have to wonder if you're serious about this client confidentiality bullshit, or if you're just hiding behind it. You've probably noticed I have a pretty big gut.' He patted his stomach affectionately. 'The thing is, my gut's telling me there's something not right here, and being as it's so big, I have to listen to it.'

'And, in my experience, he's usually right,' said Slater. 'You should think yourself lucky we're not the police, or you'd be sitting in an interview room and possibly spending the night in a cell. As it is, we're not going to stop investigating this, and you need to understand that you're on our radar. We're going to leave now, but when we're gone you might want to have a think about that confidentiality bollocks and whether you're really doing the right thing hiding behind it.'

As they got to their feet, Norman smiled at Pearson. 'Don't get up,' he said, 'we'll see ourselves out.'

Pearson's lips curled, but he said nothing. As soon as he was sure Slater and Norman had gone, he reached for his phone.

* * *

It was approaching four p.m. as they drove back to their office, so they had decided to call it a day and knock off early. Norman had been invited around to Jane Jolly's for dinner. This was a significant step forward in their relationship, and he wanted to make sure he wasn't late. Slater was going to take his laptop home and see if he could make any progress in his attempt to find some information about Joe Dalgetty.

CHAPTER NINE

On Thursday morning, Slater made an extra special effort to get to the office early, just to prove to himself he could still do it when he really wanted to. To his surprise, Norman was already there, out in the small kitchen at the back of the main office. Although there was no water plumbed in yet, they had both got fed up with having to go out every time they wanted tea or coffee, so they now had an electric kettle, a five-gallon water holder, six mugs, a small refrigerator for the milk, and a supply of tea and coffee.

When Slater poked his head around the kitchen door, Norman was pottering around making coffees, but it was a far more subdued Norman than Slater had left the previous afternoon. He was almost afraid to ask the question, but decided he needed to know.

'So, how did the big dinner date go?'

'It was okay,' said Norman, glumly.

'What do you mean it was *okay*? You couldn't wait to get there yesterday. What happened?'

'Well, I guess maybe I got the wrong end of the stick,' said Norman, sadly. 'I mean we had such a great time the night before, I thought we were moving up a gear, you know? I mean we've been friends for quite a while now, and I thought . . .'

'Ah! I see,' said Slater, sympathetically. 'So, she doesn't see it quite the way you do?'

'Oh no, that's not the problem. She feels the same as me. The thing is, this was never going to be a normal relationship, was it? I mean with our past, there's always going to be that complication, right?'

The complication in question was Jane's husband, who was currently staying at Her Majesty's Pleasure after allowing himself to be convinced, incorrectly, that Norman was having an affair with his wife. It was his subsequent kidnapping of Norman that had led to his incarceration and Jane's breakdown. She was in the process of divorcing him, but even so, he was still the father of her three children.

'So, what's happened?' asked Slater.

'He's about to come out on parole, and he wants to see his kids. Jane's frightened one of the kids is going to mention me and he's going to kick off about it. Then again, the guy has every right to want to see his kids, and I completely understand that.'

'Yeah, I can understand how that's a complication,' said Slater. 'What are you going to do?'

Norman heaved a big sigh. 'I don't know,' he said. 'Part of me says I should stay away so I don't inflame the situation, but another part of me says I should be there just in case.'

'What does Jane say?'

'She says he won't do anything to upset the kids. He thinks the world of them, and he's really missed them while he's been away. I mean, he has to be allowed to see them, doesn't he?'

'I'm sorry, Norm, but I don't know what to suggest.'

'I didn't think you would,' said Norman. 'I doubt if anyone really knows how to handle these situations. I can only do what I think is right and hope for the best, so I'm going to step back and let Jane make the call. She knows I'm there if she needs me.'

A knock on the outside door interrupted their conversation.

Slater looked over his shoulder. The top half of the door was glass, and through it he could see a young woman with dark hair, tied in a ponytail, leaning against the door frame and peering in at him.

'Are you expecting company?' he asked Norman.

'Not that I'm aware of,' said Norman, coming to look over Slater's shoulder. 'Maybe she's looking for someone.'

She was looking straight at Slater, and now she began to wave.

'Yeah, and it looks like it's one of us,' Slater said.

'But there isn't a sign up or anything,' said Norman. 'How does she know it's us?'

'The same way Rosie knew, I guess, but there's only one way to find out for sure.'

He walked across the office towards the young woman, Norman following in his wake. As he opened the door, she levered herself away from the wall and, using the walking stick in her left hand, stood up as straight as she could. Slater couldn't be sure, and he couldn't have said why, but he got the distinct impression the stick was a prop rather than a necessity.

'Can I help you?' asked Slater.

'Are you Mr Slater?'

'Yes, that's right.'

She grabbed his hand and shook it firmly. 'Jolly pleased to meet you, sir!' Then she stepped forward and grabbed Norman's hand. 'And you must be Mr Norman!'

'Well, you seem to know who we are,' said Slater, somewhat taken aback by the whirlwind greeting. 'Perhaps you could introduce yourself?'

'DS Samantha Brearley, but you can call me Watson, everyone else does. Mr Bradshaw sent me,' she said, turning to Slater. 'He said to tell you I'm the goodwill gesture.'

Slater's mouth dropped open.

'Goodwill gesture?' asked Norman, looking accusingly at Slater. 'Does Jenny know about this?'

'Oh gosh, no!' said Watson, blushing furiously. 'I'm not that sort of goodwill gesture. I'm sure I'd be hopeless at that! I've been sent to help out with your case.'

'Case? What case?' asked Slater, dumbly.

'Mr Dalgetty, deceased in uncertain circumstances,' she said.

Norman turned to Slater in surprise. 'Help out with the case?'

'Jesus!' said Slater, his eyes glued on the girl. 'He was serious?'

'Oh, yes, very much so,' she said. 'He meant every word.'

'I hate to interrupt,' said Norman, 'but would someone mind telling me what the hell is going on, and why a young woman has been sent down here to help us?'

'You mean you don't know?' Watson asked.

'Do I look like I know?'

'Now you come to mention it . . .' She turned her attention to Slater. 'Didn't you tell him?'

'Well, no. I didn't actually think anything was going to come of it, and I certainly wasn't expecting him to send a young woman down here.'

'Hello?' called Norman, indignantly. 'Like I said, I hate to interrupt your conversation, but I think, as this is actually *my* case you're talking about, I deserve some sort of explanation.'

He stepped back to allow the young woman to enter, waving his hands to usher her in the right direction.

'Right, young lady. Step inside. I wanna know what's going on.'

The young woman bent down to grab the enormous suitcase she had brought with her.

'Here, let me help you,' said Slater.

'It's fine. I can manage,' she insisted. It was something of a struggle for her, despite the fact the case had wheels, but she was obviously determined to show she could manage, so the two men stood respectfully aside and tried not to stare as she dragged the bag inside. Slater thought it would have been a lot easier if she had let go of the walking stick, but kept his thoughts to himself.

She might have been independent enough to insist on carrying her own bag, but when Slater dragged a chair across for her to sit on, she sank gratefully onto it, her left leg stretched out before her.

Norman arranged two more chairs so they were all facing each other and then he sat down. Slater took the remaining vacant seat.

'Right. Let's hear it,' said Norman, looking pointedly at Slater.

'Err, well, it's a bit difficult to know where to start,' he explained, awkwardly.

'Try from the beginning,' said Norman. 'I find that tends to work best.'

Slater was squirming inwardly and cursing himself for not telling his friend about this from the beginning.

'Yes, of course. From the beginning. Right. Well, it's a bit difficult, and you're probably not going to like this. What I mean is, I should have told you about this weeks ago, and I feel really bad that I haven't been able to tell you, but—'

'If you're about to tell me you're on a sabbatical,' said Norman, 'then yes, you should have told me, and yes, you deserve to be feeling bad for not telling me about it from the start.'

Slater stared at Norman, agog. 'You knew?'

Norman spread his arms. 'I'm a detective, right?'

'Yeah, but how?'

'I'm not gonna reveal my sources.'

'It was Jenny, wasn't it? But when did she tell you? And why?'

'Well, she did tell me you were regretting not telling me from the start, and that now you didn't feel you *could* tell me because you didn't want to disappoint me over the business. But I already knew before that. In her defence, she felt she had to tell me because it was tearing you apart and because she cares about you, and she was worried we might fall out over it. Why do you think I keep asking you all those pointed questions about the business? I've been creating opportunities for you to come clean all over the shop, and you've missed every one!'

Watson was sitting perfectly still watching the two of them, absolutely enthralled.

'You've known about it all along, and you let me suffer all that guilt?' asked Slater, taking his turn to be the indignant one.

Norman beamed a megawatt smile at him. 'I think you'll find that was your choice. You could have told me right from day one, but you chose to keep it to yourself—'

'And the longer it went on, the harder it got,' finished Slater.

Norman turned to their guest. 'What would you have done, Watson?' he asked.

'Oh, I'm with you, Mr Norman, sir,' she said. 'If he did that to me, I'd make him suffer — every time.'

'Hey, wait a minute,' said Slater. 'You're supposed to be *my* goodwill gesture, not his!'

'Yes, sir. Sorry, sir,' she said, contritely. 'I got a bit carried away in the moment, but Mr Norman *did* ask.'

'You don't have to call either of us "sir". We're just two ordinary guys,' said Norman. 'I much prefer it if you call me Norm, and he's Dave.'

'I might find that bit difficult,' she said.

'Why's that?' asked Slater.

'I'm not sure I can say, sir. Not if you haven't told Mr Norman about Mr Bradshaw's visit. It's not my place, is it?'

'Bradshaw was the guy who came to visit when I was out yesterday, was he?' asked Norman.

'Yeah,' said Slater.

'And he came here to offer you a job, right?'

Slater's face reddened. 'Well, yeah, but I told him I'd think about it. That's when he offered what he called a "goodwill gesture", but I wasn't even sure he was for real, so I thought it would come to nothing.' He looked at Watson. 'I certainly didn't expect him to send an assistant down here. I'm not sure what he thinks you can do that we can't.'

'I'm not some sort of secretary,' said Watson, indignantly. 'I'm a DS with specialist skills. I've even got a warrant card here somewhere.' She made to start searching through her bag, but Norman stopped her.

'That won't be necessary,' said Norman. 'I know who you are.'

'You do?' asked Slater, confused.

'When Robin left here, I ran into him outside. He told me he was going to send someone down to try and persuade you he was for real.'

'Robin?' echoed Slater. 'You mean you *know* Bradshaw?' He was becoming more incredulous by the minute.

'We worked together for a few months up in the City years ago,' said Norman. 'He was a high-flyer back then, destined for great things. Looks like he's done well.'

'So all that "what's going on here?" indignation bollocks was just you winding me up, was it?' asked Slater. 'When, in actual fact, you've been conspiring behind my back.'

'Yeah, I suppose you could put it like that,' said Norman thoughtfully, 'but whereas you see it as conspiring, I see it as getting you back where you belong. And before you start complaining, it's no worse than you keeping your sabbatical secret, is it?'

Slater couldn't really argue with that. 'So, if you knew about this before Jenny told you, exactly how long have you known?' he asked.

'Robin got in touch with me when you were in Thailand. He knew we had been working together and he wanted to know what I thought of you, why you really wanted to leave, and if I thought you could be persuaded to go back and work for him. That's when he told me you'd been talked into taking a sabbatical.'

'And I suppose you've been in touch with him ever since I got back.'

'I couldn't possibly say,' said Norman with a wink.

'You crafty old sod,' said Slater, affectionately.

Norman turned to Watson. 'You'll have to excuse the future DI Slater's language. He's not always like this. Usually he's much worse.'

'I don't suppose for one minute he's as bad as you say,' she said with a smile. 'And anyway, I went to a private girls' school, so I'm sure he doesn't know any words I haven't heard before.'

'So, are you going to be my DS if I take this job?' asked Slater.

'That's my wish,' she said, flexing her knee, and sitting up straighter. 'At the moment, I'm afraid I'm just your back-room support staff. I've not been able to get around so well since I stopped a bullet with my left knee. I wouldn't recommend it, unless you really want your knee smashed to pieces. They've done a good job of replacing it — I'm a bit like the bionic woman now, or at least my knee is — but we won't know if it's working properly for a few more weeks.'

'So you do need the stick, then?' asked Slater, guiltily.

She looked scornfully at the stick which lay on the floor next to her chair. 'The medical people insist I have to use it,' she said, 'but I'm quite sure I don't really need it anymore. I think the knee's perfect just now, but they insist everything has to be done to their timetable, and I daren't step out of line.

'I was actually invalided out because of it, but the boss thought it was a waste of a good brain, so when he got the go-ahead for this new squad he brought me back in and even gave me my rank back. He said, at the time, that I might not be any good out on the street, but I'm bloody good with paperwork, which I'm sure you probably hate, and I'm pretty hot with computers. And then I got the chance to have the bionic replacement, so I'm ever hopeful.'

'Is that why Bradshaw calls you Watson?' asked Norman.

Slater had been puzzling over this as well, but the penny had yet to drop.

'Oh, come on, Dave!' Norman started chuckling. 'It's obvious.'

'Not to me,' said Slater.

Watson was grinning at both of them. 'It's because I'm very good at working with HOLMES,' she explained.

It took a couple of seconds, and then Slater's face broke into a smile. 'Ah! Right. Yeah, of course,' he said. 'I get it.'

HOLMES — or Home Office Large Major Enquiry System — was an IT system police forces used to co-ordinate major crime investigations.

'I'm quite useful with other systems too,' she explained. 'I've had plenty of time to learn how to use them all while I've been deskbound.'

'So now we're all on the same page, how exactly are you going to help us?' asked Norman.

'I understand you've been trying to use a laptop and the internet to access information,' she said.

'Trying is the word,' said Slater. 'It's a bloody nightmare.'

'Yes, I know. I've tried it myself. But you don't need to worry about that now.' Watson patted the enormous suitcase she had kept close by. 'I have in my possession a force laptop with access to all the usual databases, and one or two you wouldn't normally have access to. It's not lightning fast, but it'll do for now. I've been sent here to do all your background research so you can focus on what you do best.'

'But why would he send you here to do that?' asked Slater.

'To remind you what you're missing, technology-wise,' said Norman. 'And so you can get to know young Watson here.'

Watson nodded enthusiastically. 'And as well as being here to show you what I can do, and remind you what the equipment can do, I'm also here to answer any questions you might have about the job you've been offered and how we operate.'

'Bradshaw's got a lot of trust in you, hasn't he?' asked Slater.

'Chief Superintendent Bradshaw is a brilliant boss,' she said. 'He trusts me, and I trust him. Granted, he can come across as a bit of a twit sometimes, but he's the best I've ever worked for.'

'Well, I suppose now you're here it would be churlish to turn you away,' said Slater. 'So, what do you need to get set up? We're a bit short on furniture at the moment, but we've got a couple of workstations. You can use one of those if you like.'

She took one look at the workstations Slater indicated and wrinkled her nose.

'I'm afraid I need a bit more room than that,' she said, looking around. 'Don't you have any desks?'

'Err, not yet,' admitted Norman. 'It's on my "to do" list.'

'Do you need that door through to the kitchen?' she asked.

'Sorry?' Slater followed her gaze to the kitchen door.

'If you take it off, we could lay it between the two workstations. It'll be just about big enough for what I need.'

'And where do *we* work?'

'Well,' replied Watson, 'if you're really that desperate for a desk, you could always go out and buy one, but surely you can manage without, can't you? I was working on the assumption you wouldn't actually be doing a lot of paperwork, and with me doing the donkey work here, I assumed you two would be out conducting interviews and things.'

'I was just starting to get used to the idea of me and Norm having to do everything,' said Slater.

'But you won't have to if you come back t—'

'Yes, thank you, Watson,' said Slater. 'I think you can rest assured I've got the idea now.'

'Righto. Sorry, sir. Message understood.'

Slater could hear Norman chuckling in the background.

It didn't take him long to remove the kitchen door, take the handle off, and set it between the two workstations to create what was effectively a desk about six and a half feet long.

'It'll do for now,' Watson had assured them. 'I've worked with a lot worse, I can assure you. Now, why don't you two go and find something useful to do while I get set up? Just leave your case file for me so I can get started.'

'Case file?' said Norman.

'You must have *something*,' she said. 'What about some interview notes?'

'Notes?' repeated Norman.

'What? Nothing at all?' She looked appalled. 'This is even worse than I expected!'

'I've got the notes I took at Rosie's the other day,' said Slater. 'I just haven't got round to writing them up yet.'

She sighed and gave him the sort of look a nursery teacher might give a naughty boy.

'I should make you both stand in the corner,' she said, 'but I suspect it's probably a bit late to try and change your ways now. Are your notes legible?'

'I think so,' said Slater. 'I'll get them for you.'

'I can do all the paperwork you want back in the office, but I can't follow you around taking notes so, in future, you'll have to make any notes legible if you want me to turn them into anything useful for an investigation.'

'Right,' said Slater, handing his notes to her. 'I'll bear that in mind. Could you just remind me which one of us is going to be the DI?'

She opened her mouth to speak, but then saw the smile on his face and grinned back at him instead.

* * *

Having no particular activity in mind, the boys had decided to walk to the nearest coffee shop to get some decent coffee and cakes to try to make Watson feel a little more welcome.

'So, what do you think?' asked Norman, as they walked.

'What? You mean Watson? She's a bit jolly hockey sticks,' said Slater.

'Don't tell me you're going to let your inner inverted snob speak for you?'

'I'm not a snob, inverted or otherwise,' said Slater, indignantly. 'I'm just saying she speaks a bit posh, that's all. But I suppose it makes her a good match for Bradshaw. He's definitely an old-school-tie guy.'

'There you go again, judging people just because of the way they speak. I promise you Robin's a good guy. You can tell that from the way Watson talks about him. You don't get that sort of praise if you're an arsehole, right?'

'Fair comment,' said Slater.

'Don't hold it against him because he comes from a family with money,' said Norman. 'It's not his fault, any more than it's my fault I grew up in a terraced street in a shabby part of London.'

'Actually, I think Watson's all right,' said Slater, 'although her efficiency's a bit scary!'

Norman laughed. 'Yeah, she'll soon knock you into shape. I can just see you standing in the corner with that dunce's cap on your head.'

Slater smiled. 'Don't joke about it. She's probably serious!'

They walked on in silence for a few more yards before Slater spoke again. 'I wonder how she came to get her knee blown apart?'

'Yeah, that's a shame,' said Norman. 'I suspect she was a pretty good detective before that. Mind you, I reckon she's gotta be shit-hot on the computers. Robin wouldn't have her in his team just because he felt sorry for her. He doesn't believe in carrying passengers. Anyway, when I asked what do you think, I wasn't asking about Watson. I was referring to the job you've been offered.'

'Yeah, that's what I thought you meant,' said Slater.

Norman waited patiently for Slater to expand on his answer, but that appeared to be it.

'Jesus, it's like pulling teeth, talking to you sometimes.'

'What?'

Norman sighed. 'This job offer. Are you going to take it or not?'

'Are you trying to tell me something? Don't you want me around?' asked Slater.

'Aw, come on, Dave, don't be an arse. You know I like having you around. You're the best friend I've ever had, but that won't change if you're working somewhere different, will it? I'd rather have a happy friend I don't see very often, than have to put up with an unhappy friend under my feet all the time.'

Slater looked at Norman and smiled. 'You have such a way with words, you know that? So, what you're saying is, I'm miserable and I'm under your feet, is that it?'

'Now you're just being deliberately obtuse. You know damned well that's not what I mean. I just think working with me would make you unhappy. It worked in the police because there were always other people to do all the stuff I didn't want to do and to clear up behind me. You won't want to do that, and I don't want you to have to do it.'

'I hear what you're saying,' said Slater, 'but, I'll have you know I'm feeling pretty happy and content right now, and there's not a police force in sight.'

'Yeah, I've noticed, but that's because you have Jenny in your life. It has nothing to do with working with me.'

Slater thought about this as they entered the coffee shop. Perhaps Norman was right about the effect Jenny was having on his life.

* * *

'What exactly do you know about this Joe Dalgetty character?' asked Watson when they got back to the office.

'How do you mean?' asked Norman. 'All we really know is he died, the police thought there was nothing suspicious about it, but his neighbour thinks there's a lot suspicious about it.'

'And so does your boss,' added Slater, pointedly. 'He sent Rosie to us, so he must know something. Perhaps you already know more than we do?'

Watson looked him straight in the eye. 'Well, that's all news to me. I can assure you — if he does know anything, he hasn't told me about it.'

They held eye contact for a few seconds, then Slater spoke again.

'It's like Norm said, except we also know his rent is still being paid, which is a bit of a surprise as he's never taken any money from his bank account. Oh, and he managed to give his solicitor twenty-five grand, in cash, for him to give to Rosie when he died.'

'The plot thickens, then,' she said, 'because, according to the records I've managed to find, there's no such person as Joe Dalgetty.'

Norman stared at her. 'But that can't be right! He's lived in that house for five or six years. He had a passport.'

'He might well have had a passport that said who he was, but did anyone check to see if it was genuine?' she asked.

'That we can't tell you,' said Slater. 'When he died, the police were called and they ID'd him. Surely they would have checked?'

'But why would they?' asked Norman. 'As far as they were concerned, there were no suspicious circumstances about his death, and the PM confirmed it, so why would they bother to check if he was who his passport said he was? Plus, they had a neighbour who identified him, and a solicitor, too. You know how it goes. They wouldn't have wasted any more time than they really had to.'

'So who the bloody hell was he then?' asked Slater.

While they were talking, Watson had been typing. Now she leaned forward to study the screen. 'I can't tell you who he is yet,' she said. 'But I might be able to tell you why the rent's still being paid. According to this, the person who's living in that house is called William Harding.'

'Did you say the person who's *living* there?' asked Slater.

'This says he's lived there since 2008, and he pays his rent on the dot every month. He's never missed a payment, or even been late with a payment.'

'William Harding?' said Norman. 'But Rosie said Joe's lived there for the last five years or so. Why would Harding still be paying the bills?'

'Maybe he doesn't know he's paying them,' suggested Slater.

'I think you'd notice if that sort of money was leaving your account every month, wouldn't you?' asked Norman.

'He might not notice if he was loaded,' said Watson.

'We'll need to access his bank accounts to find that out,' said Slater. 'But let's just go back to Joe for a minute. We already know he's not really called Joe, right? And now we know he's living in a house with another person's name as the tenant, and the rent is being paid in that other person's name. Now why would he do that?'

'Because he's hiding,' said Watson almost instantly.

Slater pointed a finger at her. 'Exactly! And why would he be hiding?'

'Because he's done something, or he knows something,' said Norman.

'Right! And that must be why someone broke into his house and searched it.'

'And then they broke into Rosie's house when they couldn't find what they were looking for,' finished Norman.

'It's all starting to add up now,' said Slater.

'Oh, yeah, this is going to be a piece of cake.' Norman rolled his eyes. 'All we have to do is guess what he's done, or what he knows, and we'll be home and dry. Lemme see, there must be about a million possibilities!'

'Don't look so gloomy, sir,' said Watson cheerfully. 'We'll get it sorted, you'll see.'

'Yeah, listen to me,' said Norman, 'and I'm supposed to be the positive one around here! How about I go up and have a chat with Rosie? Let's see if she can tell me anything about this William Harding guy.'

'That sounds like a plan,' said Slater.

'You wanna come?' asked Norman. Then he had a better idea. 'No, on second thoughts, why don't you stay here and ask Watson some searching questions about your new job?'

He grabbed his keys and marched from the room before Slater could think of a retort.

'You don't really want to talk about this job opportunity right now, do you, sir?' asked Watson once Norman had left.

'I've only just met your boss and heard about it,' said Slater. 'And now I find my best mate has known about it for weeks. I'm just a bit confused at the moment.'

'He was only trying to help,' she said. 'And your girlfriend knew too.'

'She's not my girlfriend,' said Slater, hastily.

'Well, whatever, it seems to me they both care a lot about you. You're lucky to have people like that in your life. Don't be too harsh on them.'

'Yeah, I know you're right,' he said. 'I just need to get my head around the whole thing, you know.'

'I understand,' she said. 'And I'm not here to put your back up. Let's just focus on Mr Dalgetty, or whoever he really is, and you can ask anything you want to know when you're ready.'

'Or not,' said Slater. 'Don't take this personally, but I need to get some bits for home, so I'm just going to take a walk to the shops. I won't be long.'

Watson smiled to herself as he left the office and went back to her search.

* * *

Meanwhile, Norman was knocking on Rosie's front door. After a few seconds, it opened a little way and Rosie peered uncertainly at him.

'Ooh! Hello, Mr Norman. I wasn't expecting you.'

'Hi, Rosie. I was just passing and I thought I'd stop by. I have a couple of questions.'

'D'you want to come in?'

'Just for a minute,' said Norman. 'I can't stop long.' He followed her into the kitchen.

'What can I do for you?' she asked.

'What can you tell me about William Harding?'

'Bill?' she asked, surprised. 'Blimey, what do you want to know about Bill for?'

'He was living in that house before Joe, wasn't he?'

'Yes, that's right. He was such a nice man.'

'When did he move in?' asked Norman.

'I can't remember exactly, but he was there at least two years before Joe took over.'

'What happened to him?'

'He just took off,' Rosie said. 'One day he was there, the next he was gone. There was no warning, no goodbye, no nothing. It was so unexpected. He was building a patio in his back garden, and he left that half-finished. It was so out of character. He was such a nice quiet man. I thought him and me were close, you know. I was very upset when he left like that.'

'Do you know where he went?'

'I wish I did,' she said. 'I'd give him a piece of my mind, I can tell you.'

'How long after he moved out did Joe move in? Was it straight away?'

'Ooh, no,' she said. 'It was a good three months or so.'

'Are you sure?'

'Quite sure. I can't forget when Bill left because it was just before my birthday, which is at the end of August. I was so disappointed I won't forget that in a hurry. And I'm sure Joe moved in a couple of weeks before Christmas, and one of the first things he did was finish that patio. It wasn't right, working out in the cold, and with his arthritis too!'

Norman was deep in thought and didn't say anything.

'Actually,' she said, 'now you come to mention him, I've got something. I don't know if it's any use or not.' She walked over to the back door, where a coat hung on a hook. She slipped her hand into one of the pockets and drew out two letters. She walked back and handed them to him.

'These came the other day when we were over at Joe's. I was annoyed because the post was supposed to have been stopped and diverted to Joe's solicitor, so I stuffed them in my pocket. Then, of course, I forgot all about them until you just mentioned his name.'

'That's odd, they *should* go to the solicitor if the post's been diverted,' said Norman.

'No, not these. Look at the name on the envelopes. It's Joe's letters that are being diverted to the solicitor. These are addressed to Bill. You'd think they'd know he didn't live here any more after all this time, wouldn't you?'

Norman looked at the two letters, which were both clearly addressed to Mr William Harding. One was definitely a utility bill, and he thought the other might be from a bank or something similar.

'Well, I'm going to have to get going,' said Norman, glancing at his watch, barely able to contain his excitement. He held up the two letters. 'Can I take these?'

'Are they important?' asked Rosie.

'I doubt it, but they might tell us something. You don't mind?'

'No, you take 'em,' she said, regretfully. 'I don't want the damned things.'

'Thanks for speaking to me.'

'That's all right, dear,' said Rosie. 'It's nice to have someone to talk to.'

Norman made his way out as graciously as he could, trying not to make it too obvious he was suddenly in a great hurry. He climbed into his car, waved goodbye to the watching Rosie, and drove off as slowly as he could. Once he was round the first corner, he pulled over and carefully tore open the first envelope addressed to William Harding. He let out a long, loud whistle. Just as he had thought, it was a statement from one of the utility companies.

'Christ!' he said out loud. 'It's his electricity statement for the last quarter.'

He reached for the other envelope and opened it. This yielded even bigger news. It was William Harding's latest bank statement, and there had obviously been a regular supply of money coming in, more than enough to cover his outgoings. 'Holy crap,' Norman said. 'What the hell is going on here?'

CHAPTER TEN

'While you were out, I called the landlord who owns Joe Dalgetty's house,' said Watson when Slater returned half an hour later. 'I was hoping he might confirm who the tenant was but, surprise, surprise, he started spouting off about data protection and how he couldn't name any names. Even so, I did manage to find something out. He must have thought I was some sort of debt collector because when I told him the address I was interested in, he told me the tenant had never missed a single payment and always paid on the same day every month, just like he had since he first arrived in 2008. He didn't seem to consider that was the data that needed protecting!'

'That's good,' said Slater, not quite sure this information had actually moved them any further forward. 'Well done.'

'Then I went a step further and checked the electoral roll. Lo and behold, I think I now have proof our Mr Dalgetty knew all about William Harding. According to the electoral roll, the person currently registered to vote at that address is one William Harding.'

'Aha!' said Slater. 'Now you're talking. But don't you have to update that thing every year?'

'Well, yes, exactly,' Watson said. 'That's my point. It has been updated every year. The thing is, anyone can fill in a form and send it back, and who's going check if it's the same signature on the form as the year before? And, of course, you can do it online these days so there is no signature to check. But my question is, why would he keep doing that every year?'

'Rosie said Joe had only been living there for about five years,' said Slater. 'But Harding arrived in 2008. What if this Harding guy has a reason for doing a runner? He moves on and leaves everything behind, and then Joe takes over the house. But if we're right about Joe, and he's trying to keep a low profile, it makes sense that he keeps registering Harding on the electoral roll so if anyone does a search for him, they won't find his name.'

'Can I be cheeky and point out a tiny flaw in that theory?' Watson asked.

'Yeah, sure, go ahead.'

'If Harding has fled the scene as you suggested, doesn't that mean someone was looking for *him*?'

'That's one possibility,' said Slater.

'Then wouldn't Joe be taking a risk keeping the electoral roll up to date? He could be inviting Harding's hunter to come and pay him a visit.'

'That's a good point,' said Slater. 'But maybe it proves Joe knew why Harding had gone and knew he wasn't inviting trouble.'

'Gosh, yes! I think you're probably right,' she agreed. 'And keeping the electoral roll updated meant there was no risk of being taken to task for not being registered to vote.'

'Right,' said Slater. 'I still think there's no doubt he was hiding from someone.'

'I found something else I think you'll be interested in—'

She was interrupted by the door crashing open as a jubilant Norman rushed into the office.

'You might wanna give me a standing ovation,' he said as he pushed the door closed behind him.

'Yeah, right,' said Slater, totally unmoved by Norman's antics. 'Let's hear it first.'

'You're going to love what I've just discovered. To quote Alice in Wonderland, this case gets interestinger and interestinger.'

'I think you'll find that's curiouser and curiouser,' corrected Watson.

Norman stared at her, nonplussed, for just a moment, then he seemed to recall who she was and why she was there.

'Yeah, you're probably right,' he said with a smile. 'But who cares? Just wait till you see what I've got!'

With a huge grin, he pulled the two now crumpled letters from his pocket and waved them in the air. 'Tada!' he sang.

'And this is what, exactly?' asked Slater.

'Two letters!'

'Wow! Really? I never would have guessed. But what's so important about them?'

'Note the name on the front,' said Norman. 'The addressee.'

'I'd need binoculars to read that from here.'

'It's William Harding,' said Norman, impatiently.

'Gosh!' said Watson.

'Yeah, that figures,' said Slater, shrugging.

Norman looked suitably unimpressed. 'What do you mean "yeah, that figures"?'

Slater gave him a wicked got-one-over-on-you grin.

'Watson's just been telling me how she called the landlord and checked the electoral roll. To all intents and purposes, William Harding is still living in that house, and he's still paying the rent as he has, every month, for the past eight years.'

Now Norman looked momentarily crestfallen. 'Really? You already know? Crap!' he said. Then he remembered the contents of the letters and his spirits rallied. 'Ah, yeah, but I bet you didn't know he's still paying the electricity bill, and I've got his bank statement!'

Slater beamed at him. 'Now, *that* is something we didn't know,' he said. 'Well done, Norm.'

'Yes, jolly well done,' added Watson.

Norman accepted the plaudits with a little bow and placed the two letters down on Watson's makeshift desk. He spread the bank statement out.

'You can see here—' he pointed at the statement — 'the rent goes out on the first of the month. There's money in the account, but there's only one month here so it's hard to see if it was one big sum to start or if there have been regular payments into it.'

Slater whistled as he looked at the statement. He pointed out one of the payments. 'This looks like a monthly payment for gas, and there's the electricity one. Well, now we know for sure there is definitely something dodgy going on here.'

'It sure smells of something,' agreed Norman.

'It's beginning to look as if Joe knew William Harding,' said Slater. 'That would explain how he managed to move into the house without the landlord knowing.'

'Are you suggesting this Harding guy is some sort of benefactor?' asked Norman. 'Then how come he's vanished?'

'We don't know he has,' said Slater. 'We haven't tried looking for him yet.'

'Noted.' Watson reached for a pen. 'I'll add it to my search list. Actually, I'd quite like to find him. I could do with someone to pay my rent and bills every month.'

'Yeah, me too,' said Norman.

'It's a pity we can't get hold of some more of these statements,' said Slater. 'It would be a real help.'

'Maybe Joe kept them hidden away somewhere,' said Norman. 'I know we had a look around his place, but we didn't exactly turn it upside down, did we? Maybe they're up in the loft.'

'Err, can I make a suggestion?' Watson looked enquiringly at Slater.

'If you're going to work with me,' he said, 'you need to understand I'm not one of those people who thinks he knows everything and everyone else is an idiot. You don't have to ask permission to offer your opinion. If you have an idea, I would love to hear it.'

'I might be able to access those bank statements,' she said.

'You can?'

'If you think it would help. I need to make a phone call to the boss, and it'll probably take twenty-four hours to set up, but I'm sure he can swing it for us if we've got the account number.'

Slater looked at Norman, who smiled back at him and inclined his head. 'He did say it was a bit different from what you're used to, didn't he?'

'I'm beginning to like this idea,' said Slater. 'You make your call, Watson.'

* * *

'Well, now, this is interesting,' said Watson, studying her laptop fifteen minutes later. 'On a hunch, I thought it might be an idea to check the story Rosie said Joe told her about his childhood, so I set up a search for kids in Windsor in the fifties and sixties. It seems there was a little boy called Joseph Dalgetty who went to school there at around the right time.'

'Now there's a coincidence,' said Norman. 'This is beginning to look like some sort of identity theft. Maybe we can follow the trail and see exactly where he fell off the radar.'

'I can tell you *exactly* when that happened,' she said, staring at her screen. 'It was January fifteenth, 1959. He and another little boy, Arthur Bradbury, were knocked down in a car accident. They were both eight years old.'

'Jeez, that must have been bad luck,' said Norman. 'I didn't think there was much traffic around in those days.'

'I don't think bad luck really comes into it when you and your friends are playing chicken by choosing to race across the road in front of oncoming cars. It seems the driver had no chance of stopping.'

'Suicide disguised as selfish fun,' said Slater, shaking his head.

'That's a bit harsh, sir! I don't think they intended to die,' said Watson.

'I don't suppose the driver intended to run them down,' said Slater, 'but he would have had to live the rest of his life knowing he'd killed two small boys.'

'They were only eight years old. They wouldn't have realised the consequences for the driver,' said Watson.

Slater sighed. 'Great,' he said. 'I'm sure knowing that would have been a great consolation to the poor sod who killed them.'

'Was this kid's father in the army?' asked Norman, keen to change the subject.

'As it happens, yes, he was,' Watson said.

'Now that *is* interesting,' said Slater.

'What are you thinking?' asked Norman.

'I'm not sure exactly, but whoever Rosie's friend was, we know Joe Dalgetty wasn't his real name, right? Now I can accept there must be hundreds of ways he could have come up with a new name, but what are the chances of choosing a name at random and then inventing a fact that's actually true?'

'You think maybe he was there when the accident happened?'

'I don't know about that, but it would have been big news in Windsor. If he had been living there, he must have known about it. Maybe he knew the two boys involved, and then when he needed a new ID he remembered the names. He certainly wouldn't be the first person to adopt the identity of a kid who died years ago.'

'And that far back it doesn't have to be exact, does it?' said Norman. 'You know, a year or two in either direction just to blur the edges and make it fit his own appearance. Yeah, it figures, when you think about it.'

'I suppose I might as well cancel this second search,' said Watson. 'Poor little Joe can't have come back from Germany if he was already dead before his father was posted there.'

'No, hang on,' said Slater. 'If Joe told Rosie the truth about going to school in Windsor, maybe he told the truth about going to Germany and then coming back a few years later. Can you do a search for boys coming back around that time?'

'I can search for families with boys,' she said, 'but it would be a lot easier if I had a name to search for. There are two barracks in Windsor, and there were lots of soldiers being posted to Germany and coming back. I could end up with hundreds of possibilities.'

'Can you narrow it down by age of the boys? Rosie said he was a young teenager. Can you try searching for boys aged twelve to fourteen?'

'For the whole of the sixties?' asked a horrified Watson. 'It'll still be like trying to find a needle in a haystack.'

'So let's assume he was the same age as the two boys who died,' said Slater. 'Let's say he was eight in 1959, add on five years, give or take another year or two, try 1962 to 1966, that should narrow it down quite a bit.'

'Hang on,' said Norman, 'don't forget Rosie said she thought he was older than he claimed. You could be ten years out with that search.'

'Crap! I'd forgotten that,' said Slater.

'Why don't I start with this search, and see what we find,' suggested Watson, as she keyed in the search parameters. 'I can always widen the search if we draw a blank.'

Ten minutes later, they reconvened to hear Watson announce the results of the search.

'Well, you won't be surprised to hear there's no one called Joe Dalgetty,' she said. 'But we *have* got six other names.'

Slater smiled a satisfied smile. 'Six? So I did manage to narrow it down for you, right?'

A small smile escaped onto Watson's face. 'No one likes a smart arse, sir,' she said without looking up from her work.

Slater grinned. 'Hey, you're the newbie here. You shouldn't be back-chatting the bosses.'

'Don't include me,' said Norman. 'I agree with the newbie.'

'Creep,' muttered Slater.

'Smart arse.'

'Are any of these names of interest?' asked Watson, reading from the screen. 'Willets, Brown, Major, Roberts, James and Harding.'

'Whoa!' said Norman. 'Did you say Harding?'

'Yes, and the reason they tripped the flag is they had a son, William, who was twelve years old when his family returned in 1965.'

'Now, isn't that a coincidence?' said Norman.

'That's twice they're connected,' said Slater. 'Once by the house, and now by Windsor. That has to be important.'

'It makes you wonder why he was paying the bills for Joe Dalgetty, doesn't it?' said Watson. 'Do you think Joe had something on him?'

'We can ask Harding if we ever find him,' said Norman. 'But, as far as we know, five years ago he seems to have vanished. People will tell you it's impossible to disappear these days, but it's really not that difficult. And it's even easier if you have an accomplice.'

Watson squinted at him. 'I'm not with you.'

'Well, let's say Harding wants to disappear, but he wants to make it look as if he's still around, so he gets an accomplice like our friend Joe to live in his house. The bills are all paid by direct debit so all Joe has to do is keep an eye on the account and maybe pay some money in every now and then. To the big wide world, it looks as if Harding is still where he always was. He would only get caught out if someone comes physically looking for him.'

'I see what you mean,' said Watson. 'But if Joe's dead, who's going to keep up the pretence? Do you think Harding will have to surface now?'

'It's been five years,' said Slater. 'I should think he's been gone long enough not to need to worry. Wherever he's hiding, he's not likely to get found now.'

'So, Joe served his purpose?' asked Watson.

'I suppose you could say that,' said Norman.

'Maybe Harding killed him, then,' she suggested.

Norman looked at Slater in disbelief.

Watson caught the look. 'Sorry,' she said quickly. 'Am I speaking out of turn?'

Slater smiled. 'Not at all,' he said. 'You're just making us look a bit slow and wonder why we hadn't thought of that!'

'D'you think I'm right?'

'It's a logical theory,' he said, 'and we can't dismiss it as a possibility, although I think it's unlikely. If you'd been hiding, undetected, for five years, would you risk everything by coming out into the open to murder someone?'

'Okay,' she said, unconvinced, 'but what if Joe was threatening to reveal where Harding was hiding?'

'But why now?'

Watson gave him a crooked smile. 'Well, I don't know,' she said. 'You're the ace detective, you tell me!' She was clearly quite enjoying this new, relaxed way of working. 'I must say, I didn't realise our job could be such fun!' she added.

'Never a dull moment,' said Norman. 'But it's what you choose to make it. I don't see why you can't have a bit of fun while you're working. I think it makes the job easier, and I know for a fact your new boss thinks the same.'

Slater shot him a look, but Norman just grinned at him.

'So, what do we do now, sir?' Watson asked Slater.

Slater looked at her. 'What do you think we should do next?'

She looked shocked. 'Who? Me?'

'Why not you?' he asked. 'You are a detective sergeant, aren't you? That means you have the power to think. You must have situations where you're in the office and you have to make a decision.'

'Well, yes, but not when there's a DI around.'

'But I'm not a DI. I'm just Dave Slater.'

'He means he's not a DI *yet*,' said Norman. 'But he will be.'

'He *might* be,' argued Slater. 'Don't try to make my mind up for me.'

'I think we definitely need to do background on William Harding,' said Watson, uncertain whether or not Slater and

Norman were about to break into a full-blown argument. 'Maybe we'll get lucky and find a reason he might have wanted to go into hiding.'

'There you go,' said Slater. 'That wasn't hard, was it? But that can wait until tomorrow. I think we've done enough for today.'

CHAPTER ELEVEN

Watson had arrived early and had somehow managed to conjure up a coffee machine from somewhere, much to Norman's delight. Slater noticed his friend had a spring in his step, but he resisted the urge to ask why.

'I've had a message from my boss. He would like to be kept informed regarding the progress of this investigation,' Watson told them.

'Well, that won't take long,' said Slater, with a wry smile. 'We haven't really made any progress yet!'

'Does this mean you're gonna be spying on us?' asked Norman. 'Will you be feeding back every little thing about this case?'

'I wish you wouldn't put it like that,' Watson said unhappily. 'He is my boss, after all. I may be here on secondment, but he's still paying my wages. It's only natural he should want to know what I'm doing while I'm here.'

'I suppose we can't complain. He did send Rosie to us in the first place,' said Slater.

'What makes you think that?' asked Watson.

A sudden silence filled the room.

'A police officer in a pinstriped suit told Rosie to come and speak to us. It was him, wasn't it?' asked Norman.

'I don't think so,' she said. 'As far as I know, the first time he came here was the day he came down to interview Mr Slater. He didn't even know where Tinton was before that. I had to show him on the map and book his train tickets.'

'Yeah, but he could have driven down and then played dumb,' said Slater.

'I would know,' she said. 'I've been his PA ever since he rescued my career. I know where he is, where he's been, and where he's going. And I arrange all his travel, including train tickets. Trust me, if he had come down here I would have known.'

'But you don't know where he is right now, do you?' asked Norman.

'I don't have to as of yesterday, because I'm not his PA any more,' she explained. 'My return was always about getting back to doing real police work. We had a deal that I would do the PA thing until a position came up. This is my first venture back, as it were.'

'So, you have a vested interest in Dave here taking this job, right?' said Norman. 'Because the position won't exist if he says no.'

'Oh, the position will still be there.' Watson looked pointedly at Slater. 'We'll just have to find someone else to lead the team.'

'Well, if *he* didn't send Rosie to us, how did he know what case we were working on?' asked Slater, refusing to be drawn on what he was going to do in the future. 'He knew about Joe, and me, and Norm. He even knew about Jenny and Jane Jolly!'

Watson's face flushed. 'I can't tell you how he knew about the case,' she said, 'but I can tell you how he knew all about you two — and your ladies.'

'So that was you, was it?' asked Slater.

She looked suitably embarrassed. 'He asked me to look into your files so he had plenty of background before he came to speak to you,' she explained.

'What? Both of us?' asked Norman.

'I just do my job. It's not my place to ask what, or why.'

'I guess, if I try really hard, I can just about accept that as an excuse,' said Norman. 'What about you, Dave?'

'I suppose someone has to do the background check,' admitted Slater.

'Anyway, it's not all bad news,' said Watson. 'He's also tracked down someone who might be able to help us with this case.'

'Who?'

'He's a retired DCI called Dennis Stockholm, used to work for the Met.'

Slater looked at Norman.

'The name doesn't ring a bell,' said Norman, 'but that's one huge force. There must be dozens of DCIs I've never heard of.'

'What's this guy's address?' asked Slater. 'If he's willing to talk, we might as well go and see the man.'

'Ah. I'm afraid it's not quite that simple,' said Watson. 'When I say the boss has "tracked down" someone, I mean it. Former DI Stockholm is currently on a three-month holiday visiting family in Australia.'

'Australia!' echoed Norman. 'That's not gonna be much help.'

'Actually, the outlook's not quite as gloomy as you might think,' she said with a knowing smile. 'Thanks to the wonders of modern technology, we can actually speak to him a little later by video link.'

'Isn't it night over there?'

'There's a twelve-hour difference,' she said, 'but that's not going to be a problem. We're linking up at ten thirty this morning.'

* * *

'As you know,' said Dennis Stockholm later, when Watson had hooked them all up and they'd got used to the slight time lag, 'Chief Superintendent Bradshaw suggested I should speak to you.'

'That's right,' said Slater. 'He suggested you could help us, although he hasn't exactly told us how.'

'He's doing me a bit of a favour letting me talk to you, really,' said Stockholm.

'What kind of a favour?' asked Norman, suspiciously.

'I used to deal with robberies,' explained Stockholm. 'The bigger they were, the more I enjoyed them. I had a pretty good record, but there's always one that gets away, you know? Have you ever heard of a gangster called Ronnie Scanlon?'

'I've never crossed paths with him, but I seem to recall the name from years ago,' said Norman. 'Wasn't he from the East End of London?'

'That's him,' said Stockholm. 'He was a nasty piece of work who wasn't averse to a bit of armed robbery whenever he got a bit short of funds. Anyway, back in the eighties, '86, I think it was, he organised this big diamond heist. The gang got away with millions. We never did know the true value of what was stolen because the diamond merchants didn't want to admit how much they'd lost, but my guess is they lost somewhere in the region of twenty million quids' worth.'

Slater whistled. 'Jesus, just a small handful, then?'

'Did you catch 'em?' asked Norman, who was always willing to exchange stories with guys like this.

'Every one of them,' said Stockholm, proudly, 'but we never even got a sniff of the diamonds.' The tone of his voice showed the disappointment still rankled, even now, some thirty years later.

'What? Nothing?' asked Norman. 'Did they smuggle them out?'

'I don't think so. We always thought they'd been stashed away, and if we followed Scanlon when he came out of prison he would lead us to them.'

'What about his family?' asked Norman. 'Someone else could have collected years ago.'

'We thought of that. His wife has been under surveillance for years, and so has their son Stevie, since he grew up. When I retired, Robin Bradshaw took over the surveillance.

He's kept me informed because he knows I'd like to see the case closed, but there's never been even the slightest suggestion the family's fortunes have improved.'

'This is all very well, Mr Stockholm,' said Slater, 'but why are you telling us all this?'

'Because that nice Mr Scanlon's been out of prison for nearly two years now, and the word is someone else has got the diamonds and our old gangster is not very happy about it!'

'But why would that have anything to do with our case?' persisted Slater. 'Are you suggesting our dead man is involved? Only you said you didn't recognise the man in the photo we emailed to you.'

'That's right, I don't recognise him,' agreed Stockholm, 'and before you say it, yes, I know plastic surgery can change appearances. Anyway, if that was all we had, I wouldn't see a link myself.'

'You obviously know something we don't,' said Slater, 'so why don't you get to the point.'

'I understand you got involved because a lady came to you,' said Stockholm.

'That's correct. She was a neighbour, and probably the only friend our dead man had.'

'But why did she come to you?'

'Because some mysterious police detective sent her to us.'

'Well, that's the thing, you see,' said Stockholm. 'That was no detective — and he's no mystery. That was Ronnie Scanlon's son, Stevie.'

'Wow! That kinda raises the stakes a little,' said Norman.

'Does Bradshaw know this?' asked Slater.

'Of course he does, but he wanted *me* to tell you, because it was my old case.'

Slater turned to Watson. 'Did you know about this when Bradshaw sent you down here? Only he obviously knows a lot more about this case than he's letting on, doesn't he?'

'Well, I can't deny it's beginning to look that way, but if he does know a lot more, I promise you he hasn't told me,' she said, awkwardly.

'I don't get it,' said Norman. 'If he knows so much about this case, why doesn't he just share what he knows with us?'

'I'm just a small cog in a big machine,' said Watson, unhappily. 'He only tells me what I need to know.'

'Would he tell me if I ask him?' asked Slater.

'I'm sorry, only he can tell you the answer to that question.'

'What's the best number to get him on? I want to know what's going on here.'

'There's something else you should know, before you forget all about me and charge off to start an argument.' Stockholm's voice filtered through the computer. 'The reason we caught them all was because one of the gang's drivers turned grass in exchange for a very short sentence and a new identity.'

'Well, in that case, I'd put my money on him knowing where the diamonds were,' said Norman. 'He gets everyone else put away for twenty-odd years, while he serves a token sentence. Then he collects the loot when he comes out and he's got a head start of twenty years in which to disappear, sell the goods, and spend all that moolah. It makes sense to me.'

'What are you saying, Mr Stockholm?' asked Slater. 'Do you think Joe Dalgetty was this man? Only he was living like a pauper, not like someone who had twenty million stashed away.'

'Going by that photo you showed me, no he's not the man, but maybe he knew who it was.'

'Who was this driver?' asked Norman.

'His name back then was Kenny Wingate,' said Stockholm, 'but I was never allowed to know what his new identity was. I suppose that's the whole point of the protected witness scheme, but it's bloody frustrating. Like you say, he could have known where the diamonds were, but we weren't allowed to watch him.'

'If you don't know his identity, how can you be so sure it's not Joe Dalgetty after plastic surgery?' asked Slater.

'If your description is correct, your dead man is about six inches shorter than Kenny was. Plastic surgery can change a face, but you can't just chop six inches off a bloke's legs, can you?'

'But if this Kenny Wingate, or whatever his name is now, has made off with the diamonds, that means it could have nothing at all to do with our victim,' said Slater.

'Of course, that's a possibility,' admitted Stockholm, 'but just suppose, for a minute, you were Ronnie Scanlon. You knew you were getting close, and you thought there was a possibility you were being followed. What would be a great way to continue the search without arousing suspicion?'

'Get someone else to do it for you,' said Watson. 'And who better than two private detectives who have just started working together and might be keen to take on a job.'

Slater turned to Norman and exchanged a look of horror, then he turned back to Stockholm on the screen.

'So, you're suggesting Ronnie Scanlon has duped an unsuspecting Rosie Hewitt into asking us to find his missing diamonds. Is that right?' asked Slater.

'Exactly.'

CHAPTER TWELVE

Slater had spent a fruitless fifteen minutes pacing up and down in the car park, trying to get hold of Bradshaw before finally deciding it could wait. When he came back into the office, Watson beckoned him over to her desk.

'There was a flyer for a locksmith in amongst your notes,' she said, 'so I thought I ought to get in touch with him and see what he knows.'

'Good idea,' Slater said. 'Did he say how many keys there were for that front door?'

'I haven't actually spoken to him yet,' she said, 'and I don't expect to any time soon.'

Slater's brow creased. 'Why not?'

'It appears Mr Locksmith doesn't actually exist.'

Slater sighed. 'Not another fake identity. What the bloody hell's going on? Are there actually any real people in this case?'

'It's not so much about a fake ID,' she said. 'This business just doesn't exist, and it never did as far as I can make out. And quite honestly, looking at this flyer, it's the sort of thing anyone could knock up on a PC.'

'So what you're saying is—'

'It's some sort of scam,' Norman said, arriving from the kitchen with three mugs of coffee.

'Exactly,' said Watson. 'I bet this is one of those cases where some enterprising con artist has printed out a batch of these on his home computer, pushed them through all the letterboxes in the street, and waited for someone to call him. It's a good cover when you think about it — someone who fits locks would be perceived to be honest. Once inside, he has a look around and steals what he can, or he decides to come back later if it's going to be worth his while.'

'Bugger,' said Slater, vehemently. 'I was hoping that was going to lead us somewhere.'

'We could still talk to the guy if we can find him,' said Norman.

'How are we going to do that?' asked Watson.

'Maybe another one of the neighbours around there called him in. If we can get a description, I could ask Naomi if they know anything about it.'

'Why not ask her anyway and save some time?' said Slater. 'If someone has reported it, she'll probably know. We might get really lucky and find they know who it is.'

'I'll give her a ring,' said Norman, reaching for his phone. Slater and Watson waited as he had a short, mumbled phone conversation, then he ended the call and looked across at them.

'Naomi agrees it definitely sounds like a scam, but if it is, it's not one they're aware of. No one has reported anything like that, and it's not on their watch list.'

'It must be seriously low key and localised if it's not even on the watch list,' said Watson. 'Maybe it was just a trial run in that area and there weren't enough takers to make it worth the risk of scaling it up.'

Norman thought for a moment. 'Maybe we should get out there and ask some of the neighbours.'

'I'm not so sure you'll turn anything up, but I suppose it wouldn't hurt,' said Slater. 'When do you want to do it?'

'There's no time like the present! I think most of the neighbours around there are retired, so I expect most will be at home.'

Slater started to move but Norman beat him to it. 'It's okay, I'm sure I can manage this one on my own. You've got plenty to do here.'

'What are you up to?' asked Slater, knowing very well there wasn't really a great deal he could do that Watson couldn't do better — and quicker. 'You've been looking particularly pleased with yourself ever since we got here this morning.'

'Who, me? I'm not up to anything. Nothing at all.'

'You can't fool me with that innocent little boy act,' said Slater. 'Come on, what are you up to?'

Norman sighed. 'Okay,' he said, reluctantly. 'I should have known you'd see right through me. You know I've been trying to convince Jane she should come and work for me? You even said as much yourself yesterday. Well, I suggested to her that if we had a little house-to-house to do, she might like to come along and see how she felt.'

'You mean like a trial run?'

'Exactly! I'm sure once she gets back in the saddle, she'll be fine,' said Norman. 'It's just getting over that first hurdle, and this'll be a piece of cake, right? Just knock on a few doors, show a flyer, and ask a simple question. What could be easier? It's the ideal situation.'

'So, what are you waiting for?' said Slater.

'You don't mind?'

Slater was a little miffed Norman would even ask such a question. 'I'm not even going to answer that. You've made it quite clear you think I should be working somewhere else, and if I take your advice, that will make this *your* business. As the boss, it's up to you how you run your business, right?'

Norman looked at him uncertainly.

'Well, go on!' said Slater. 'What are you waiting for?'

'Oh, right, okay. I'll catch you later.' Norman left in such a hurry, he tried to push the door when he should have pulled, but eventually he managed to make his way out and to his car.

'What was all that about?' asked Watson.

'It's a long story,' said Slater. 'Jane used to be part of our team, but there was an unfortunate incident involving her husband and Norm—'

'Oh! Was that when he was kidnapped?' asked Watson.

'Of course, I forgot, you already know about that, right?'

She looked rather embarrassed again. 'Like I said, it was just a bit of background, know who you're going to be working with, that sort of thing.' She was silent for a moment. 'Anyway, I think it's really sweet,' she said brightly. 'Look at him, like a fifty-something teenager in love with the girl of his dreams.'

'Yeah, unfortunately it's not quite that simple,' said Slater.

'Life never is, but I can't see him doing anything inappropriate.'

Slater pulled a face. 'You're probably right about that, but then again, he hadn't done anything last time, and look what happened. The thing is, Jane's husband is due out on parole very soon, and he wants to see his kids. I worry what he's going to make of it all.'

'Gosh, that could be awkward.'

'Quite,' said Slater. 'But they're all adults, and much as I don't want to see anyone get hurt, it's not really our business what they get up to.'

'D'you think there's going to be trouble?'

Slater shook his head. 'I honestly don't know the answer to that, but I sincerely hope not.'

CHAPTER THIRTEEN

'We might as well start with Rosie,' said Norman, as he parked his car outside her house.

'Do you want me to start knocking on some doors while you talk to her?' asked Jane.

Norman looked at her dubiously.

'I'll be fine,' she assured him. 'Like you said, I just need to get back into it, and this should be a gentle reintroduction. That's what you said, wasn't it?'

Norman had thought it would be a breeze, but now they were here, he was beginning to wonder if it really was such a good idea. It was quite ironic she was showing no nerves whatsoever, and here he was full of doubts and second thoughts.

'I'm not sure I'm happy about letting you go door-to-door on your own.'

'Look, you said yourself they're all pensioners along here,' Jolly argued. 'I'm hardly in any sort of danger, am I? On the other hand, what's going to be more intimidating for them — answering the door to find a lone woman on the doorstep or finding a woman with a bodyguard? I'll just show them the copy of the flyer, ask if they've seen it before, and then leave. What can possibly go wrong?'

'Do you know how many times I've heard someone say those words and regret it?' asked Norman. 'I hate it when someone says anything like that. It's almost inviting trouble, and I'd never forgive myself if anything happened to you.'

She patted his knee. 'That's very sweet of you,' she said, opening the car door, 'but I'm nearly forty years old, I'm a mother of three, and I'm old enough to make my own decisions. I promise you, nothing is going to happen to me. I'll be extra careful.'

Armed with a copy of the flyer, she stepped from the car and strode purposefully towards the nearest house.

'Crap!' said Norman quietly to himself as he watched her approach the house. 'Why do women have to be so independent? And how come I feel guilty because I care? How does that work?'

He sighed in resignation and climbed from the car, keeping a watchful eye on her progress the whole time. He closed the car door and stopped to watch. She was showing the flyer to a silver-haired lady at the first house, but the shake of the head made it clear she didn't recognise it. Jane thanked the lady, said goodbye, and turned away from the door. As she walked up the short path, she clocked Norman watching her. She stopped, hands on her hips, and glared at him, making it quite clear she didn't think she needed chaperoning. When that didn't work, she started making little shooing motions with her hands. Eventually, Norman decided he'd better do as she asked.

Reluctantly, he turned away and knocked on Rosie's door, but he couldn't help looking over his shoulder as he waited for the door to open.

'Ooh, hello, Mr Norman,' said Rosie, when she opened the door. 'Come on inside.'

'It's okay, Rosie, I don't need to come inside. This will only take a minute.'

'All right, if you're sure,' she said, disappointed. 'What can I do for you?'

He showed her the flyer before taking another glance over his shoulder. 'Have you ever seen this before?'

She looked at the flyer and then looked up at him as if he were simple. 'Yes,' she said. 'You know I have. I gave it to you the other day.'

'Well, yeah, I know that,' said Norman. 'What I mean is, have you seen it before that? Did you have one of these pushed through your letterbox?'

'The first time I ever saw that was at Joe's,' she said.

'You're sure?' he asked, unable to stop his head automatically swivelling around again.

Rosie stood on her toes and looked over his shoulder. 'What you lookin' at?' she asked, then she spotted Jolly walking up to another door on the other side of the road. 'Who's that, then?'

'She's a colleague,' Norman said, turning back to her, a faint blush on his face.

'Yes,' said Rosie, knowingly. 'Of course she is.'

'I'm just keeping an eye on her.'

'Yes, I can see that. She looks very nice.'

'Yeah, she is,' agreed Norman, his face colouring up even more. 'Anyway, getting back to this flyer — you're quite sure you haven't seen it before?'

'Cross me heart and hope to die,' she said.

'Right. Okay, thanks. That's all I wanted to know. Thank you for your time. I'm sorry to disturb you.'

'That's all right, dear,' she said. 'You get back to your girlfriend. You're obviously worried about her.'

'She's just a colleague,' said Norman as he turned to leave.

'Yes, and I'm the Queen of Sheba,' Rosie said, loud enough for Norman to hear, as she stepped back inside her house and began to close her front door.

Norman thought about a retort, but then he heard the door close, and the chance was gone. He made his way down the road on the opposite side to Jane, calling at each house as he went. She finished her side of the road, crossed to his side, and began working her way back until she met up with him.

'Any luck?' he asked.

She shook her head. 'Not one.'

'Nah, me neither. Come on, let's get back before it starts raining.'

Norman had left his car outside Rosie's, and they were just about to climb in when Rosie's front door opened and she called out to them. For a moment, Norman's heart sank as he envisaged an embarrassing scenario where Rosie interrogated him and Jane about their relationship, but then he realised she was looking a little odd.

'Are you okay, Rosie? Are you feeling unwell?'

'No, no, it's not that,' she said. 'I've just had a bit of a shock. You'd better come on in. There's something I need to show you.'

He looked at Jane, but she was already walking around the car towards Rosie's door, so he followed her up the path.

As Rosie stepped back to let them in, Norman made the introductions.

'Rosie, this is Jane. Jane, this is Rosie. I'm hoping Jane's going to come and work for me.'

'Ooh, that'll be nice and convenient for you both,' she said with a cheeky grin.

'Has something happened?' asked Norman, ignoring the inference. 'You haven't had another break-in have you?'

'Oh, no,' she said, leading them through to her kitchen. 'I've had a letter. Well, more of a small package, really. From Joe!'

'From Joe?' echoed Norman.

'Yes. How can he send me a letter when he's dead?'

'Can I see it?'

'It's there, on the table. The postman only came a couple of minutes before you, but you knocked on the door before I'd had a chance to open it.'

There was a small padded envelope on the table. A brass key lay alongside it, and a small note was scrawled on a scruffy piece of paper.

'Is it okay if I read it?' asked Norman.

'Be my guest,' she said. 'Perhaps you can make some sense of it, because it means nothing to me.'

Norman looked at the note and read it aloud.

Dear Rosie,
You already know I'm gone. This key is for you. You can work out what it opens. Just think of two little ducks.

Norman turned it over to read the other side, but that was it. He passed it across to Jane.

'Is that the key?' he asked, pointing to the key on the table.

'Yes,' said Rosie, 'and I've been wracking my brains, but I haven't got a clue what he's on about. I know two little ducks is twenty-two at the bingo, but I don't understand how that helps. He didn't even play bingo, so I have absolutely no idea what it's for.'

Norman picked up the key, placed it in the palm of his left hand, and studied it, then he turned it over and studied the other side. There were no distinguishing marks of any kind; no clue to its origin or its purpose.

He placed it carefully back on the table and picked up the padded envelope. There was a postmark, but it had been so badly smudged he doubted it would be legible, so no clues there either.

'Can you make out what that postmark is?' he asked Jane, passing the envelope to her.

'How can he send me a letter when he's dead?' Rosie wrung her hands. 'It's quite creepy.'

'I've seen this sort of thing before,' Norman explained. 'How it works is quite simple. You register with an agency. You leave the message, package, or whatever it is you want delivered, and you set up a sort of rolling deadline. For example, you might set up some sort of system whereby you check in regularly, say once a week, or once a fortnight. Then you would set the trigger, which might be the first time you didn't check in, or it might be if you don't check in two times running. Whatever, once the system's triggered, the package gets sent. It's very simple, but very effective.'

'But he's been dead for two months now!'

'But you can make your trigger deadline as long as you like. It could be he set it so it was triggered after one month, but there was a delay of another month built in before it was posted.'

'But why?' she asked, puzzled. 'Who would want to send a message from the dead?'

'You'd be surprised,' said Norman. 'A vengeful wife, maybe, or someone who wanted to frighten someone else, maybe. Or perhaps in this case, Joe just wants you to have whatever it is he's been hiding.'

'What's that supposed to mean?' she asked suspiciously.

'It's a bit complicated,' said Norman, 'but we're beginning to think Joe might have been hiding from someone because he has something they want. Seeing this key might confirm our suspicions.'

'But who's he hiding from?'

'Well, that's just it,' admitted Norman, carefully. 'We have no idea at the moment.'

'If you're suggesting there was something shady about him, I can tell you, he seemed all right to me,' she insisted.

Norman wondered if Rosie thought someone had to wear a striped jumper and carry a bag marked 'swag' to appear suspicious, but he resisted the urge to say so.

'Is it okay if we take all this stuff with us? We may be able to work out what that postmark is.'

'You take it, dear,' she said. 'It's no good to me if I don't know what it's for.'

'If we figure that out I'll let you know,' said Norman.

* * *

'I have to say, I think it's great to see you back out on the street,' said Norman as he drove away from Rosie's house.

Jane laughed out loud. 'Ha! I don't think I'd make much money doing that.'

'What? No! What I mean is, it's—'

She put a hand on his arm. 'It's all right, Norm, I know what you mean, and I must admit, it felt good to be back out there.'

'We always were a pretty good team,' said Norman.

'But I don't think we've set the world alight this time, do you? We haven't even managed to find anyone who's seen one of those flyers, so it was a complete waste of time, wasn't it?'

'I'll think about that and get back to you,' said Norman.

'At least we got the key. That might be useful.'

'Let's hope so,' said Norman. 'But my instinct's telling me we also learnt something useful from the house-to-house. I just haven't figured out what it is yet.'

CHAPTER FOURTEEN

'What? No one?' asked Slater, his disappointment clear. 'Jeez, what a waste of time.'

'Yeah, that's what Jane said, but I think it depends how you look at it,' said Norman. 'Maybe we didn't find anyone who's seen the flyer, but I'm not so sure it was a waste of time. In fact, I would suggest it was quite the opposite.'

'How do you work that one out?' asked Slater, gloomily.

'What if Joe was the only one who actually had that flyer posted through his door?'

'I'm not with you.'

Norman grinned. 'Allow me to elaborate. Here's a theory I've been developing on the way back here. We know Joe's not really Joe, right? Now there could be plenty of reasons for that, but we suspect he's hiding from someone, possibly Ronnie Scanlon, so let's run with that idea for a minute. What if Scanlon, or someone working for him, had tracked Joe down? Now he could just smash his way in, beat the crap out of Joe, and hope to make him talk, but that would probably arouse a lot of suspicion, right? Being cautious, Scanlon would prefer to figure out a way to get into Joe's house when he's not there, so he watches, and observes, and learns when Joe comes and goes. But then, as he's watching, he notices

Joe has bad arthritis in his hands and struggles with the lock on his door.'

Slater nodded his approval. It sounded good so far.

'Go on, Norm,' he said. 'I think I see where you're going with this.'

'Poor old Joe is finding it harder and harder to get his door open,' continued Norman, 'and he knows it's not going to get any easier as his arthritis gets worse, but then, suddenly, lady luck smiles on him and a locksmith pokes a flyer through his letterbox. Joe thinks this is just perfect timing, so he phones the guy, who comes around and fits a new lock. Now Joe's over the moon because he can open his door without struggling, but what he doesn't know is the locksmith is really working for Scanlon, who's also happy because now he's got a key that fits Joe's front door and he can get in any time he wants. What do you think?'

'I think it makes sense,' said Slater. 'The phone number was probably an unregistered mobile, yeah?'

'That's right,' said Watson, 'and the locksmith probably used it to answer the one call from Joe and then ditched it.'

'Yeah, easy peasy,' said Norman.

'I have a question,' said Watson. 'Are we still working on the assumption Joe's death wasn't from natural causes?'

Norman nodded.

'So, are we now saying Scanlon, or one of his cronies, killed him? If he did, what happened to the cautious approach? Why go to all this trouble to get a key if he didn't care whether Joe died? Why not just knock on the door and force his way in?'

Slater and Norman exchanged looks.

'It's a good point,' admitted Slater.

'I never said I had all the answers,' said Norman. 'It was just a theory about where the flyer fits in.'

'There is another scenario,' said Watson. 'What if Joe came home and actually found one of Scanlon's men in his house? Maybe there was a struggle, or perhaps he just died of fright. Perhaps it really was a case of accidental death, but caused by a burglary that went wrong.'

'We still don't know for sure if Scanlon is involved,' said Slater, 'but if you add Watson's accidental death to your theory, it would suggest murder wasn't the motive. I reckon he just wanted to get inside to search for something when Joe wasn't there. If only we knew what that something was.'

Norman flashed them all a beaming smile. 'Well, it just so happens I might be able to help you there,' he announced. 'Cue drumroll . . .' He put his hand in his pocket, and with a suitably theatrical flourish, he pulled out the key he had collected from Rosie's. 'You can applaud now.'

Watson peered at it. 'What is it?'

'It's a key,' said Norman.

'That's a relief,' said Slater, sarcastically. 'For a minute there, I thought I was missing something.'

Norman looked pointedly at him. 'It's a key,' he continued, patiently, 'that Joe had arranged to be sent to Rosie if anything happened to him.'

'Gosh!' said Watson.

'Now, *that's* significant,' said Slater, 'because it suggests he knew someone was looking for him, and he thought there was a good chance he was going to be found.'

'That's exactly what I thought,' said Norman. 'And the recent deposit of twenty-five grand for Rosie suggests he knew he was going to be found soon.'

'Any ideas what the key opens?' asked Slater.

'Not a clue.' Norman fished in his pocket again. 'There's a note here that talks about two little ducks. That's twenty-two in bingo talk. He tells Rosie she's gotta work out what it's for, but she says she doesn't have the faintest idea what he's on about or why twenty-two would mean anything to her. There's also the envelope it was delivered in, but the postcode is so badly smudged I doubt anyone will be able to decipher it, so we don't even know where it was sent from.'

'All right,' said Slater. 'We might not have the details yet, but this key seems to confirm he was definitely hiding something from someone, and now we've spoken to Dennis Stockholm, we know it was probably Ronnie Scanlon he was hiding from.' He looked at Norman. 'I've got to say, Norm, if this is what happens when Jane works with you, I suggest you get her signed up and working as soon as you can.'

'Yeah, I'm working on that,' said Norman. 'But let's not get too carried away. We haven't solved anything yet. There's still the small matter of where the twenty-five grand came from. We know it wasn't taken from William Harding's current account, so where the hell did Joe get that from?'

Slater sighed. 'Yeah, and what about William Harding? Where does he fit into this? It would be quite handy if we could find another bank account, or some sort of savings account, and twenty-five grand had been withdrawn from that, but I have a nasty feeling I'm just being way too optimistic.'

'I can always try searching a little deeper,' said Watson, turning her attention back to her computer. 'You never know what I might find.'

'That can wait until Monday. You're supposed to be catching a train to go home for the weekend, aren't you?'

CHAPTER FIFTEEN

Slater swung his car into the parking space, pulled on the handbrake, and switched off the engine. As he climbed from the car, he idly pondered the merits of having his name, DI Slater, adorning his own space in a new place of work. He still couldn't quite believe he and Norm could well be going in different directions, and he stopped to look at the small, but handsome, red brick building that was now probably going to be Norman's office, but not his.

For the umpteenth time, he wondered if walking away from this was really what he wanted. He had spent hours talking it through with Jenny, who thought the new job would be perfect for him, but even so, he still wasn't sure. However, he had to admit he had been very impressed with Watson, and Friday had certainly felt a bit like the old days.

He pushed open the door and walked inside. Norman had entrusted the interior decor to Jane Jolly, who had chosen colours that managed to achieve just the right balance between formality and friendliness. Slater felt it every time he came through the door. He thought it would be just perfect if Norman could persuade her to bring her beaming smile along so it was always the first thing anyone saw when they walked through that door.

'Morning, Watson,' he said, 'How are you today? Is everything working out with the hotel?'

'I'm very well, and everything is working out just fine, thank you, although I did enjoy being home for the weekend.'

'Has Norm been in yet?'

'He was here before me,' she said. 'He's making coffee, obviously keen to make a good impression.'

Norman appeared in the kitchen doorway. 'I heard that, Watson. I think it was a great idea of mine to have you on secondment for this case, but I could just as easily have you unseconded if you get too cheeky.'

'Is that really a word?' she asked Slater.

Slater shook his head. 'He makes them up as he goes along. It's a lot like the way he works.'

'Careful now, Watson,' said Norman. 'Don't listen to him, and don't push your luck too far.'

She looked at Slater, obviously not quite sure if Norman was joking. He gave her a reassuring wink and nodded his head at Norman.

'Yeah, sure, Norm,' said Slater, 'of course it was a great idea of yours.' Then, to Watson, he said, 'You'll find he always claims credit for all the good ideas. I'm just here to make up the numbers.'

'Listen,' said Norman, looking pointedly at Slater, 'you need an innovative thinker like me — it makes up for the duller members of the management team.'

Slater looked at Watson. 'As temporary office manager, I wouldn't blame you for taking offence at that remark.'

Norman guffawed. 'She knows I didn't mean her.'

'What are you doing here this early anyway,' asked Slater, ignoring the insult. 'Did someone set fire to your bed?'

Norman grinned. 'Was that a joke? If it was, it kinda proves my point about some members of the management here being dull.'

'Did I miss something?' asked Slater, good-naturedly. 'Is it a special get-at-Dave-Slater day?'

'That's never been a special event,' said Norman. 'It's more like second nature. Anyway, let's not discuss your feeble sense of humour. Watson has something you should take a look at.'

Slater walked across to Watson and peered over her shoulder at the screen. 'What have we got, then?'

'I've been looking deeper into William Harding. Apparently, he used to work for a bank, so I wondered if maybe he had something to hide and that's why he disappeared, but there's no suggestion he's ever had his hand in the till. In fact, it would appear he's squeaky clean.

'I've also looked at Joe Dalgetty again, but there's definitely no sign of him anywhere from the time he dies as a little boy until he appears in that house.'

'What if I was wrong about him telling Rosie about that TV series?' said Slater, moving across so he could see the monitor over her shoulder. 'Perhaps he really *was* out in Germany with a bunch of Geordie lads back in the eighties, and maybe he stayed out there. Perhaps it was six years ago when he came back.'

'I don't think so,' said Watson, turning to Slater. 'If he had come back there would be a record somewhere. When I say I've got nothing, I mean I've literally got nothing. He isn't just dead — according to the records, he has never existed!'

'That'll be on account of him being run over when he was eight years old,' called Norman, from the kitchen.

Slater patted Watson on the shoulder. 'Good work. Let me and Norm think about this for a few minutes.'

He headed for the kitchen and joined Norman.

'Right,' said Slater, 'what the hell have we got here? It seems to me we started off with a nice, simple, possibly suspicious, death. Now we've got one guy who's not who he says he is and has no past, except as a dead schoolboy, and somehow he's linked to another guy who seems to have vanished into thin air yet is still paying the rent and utility bills!'

Norman beamed happily. 'And they may well all have been at school in Windsor. Then, of course, there's a possible connection with an old London gangster, who may have sent a phantom locksmith along just to make things even more confusing. I think it's pretty cool, don't you?'

'*Cool*?' said Slater. 'I'm not sure that's what I'd call it, but it's definitely intriguing.'

'So where do we go from here?' asked Norman.

'I'll start by getting Watson to do a search on this Kenny Wingate.'

'I still have a couple of mates in the Met,' said Norman. 'Shall I see what I can dig up about Ronnie Scanlon?'

'That sounds like a plan,' said Slater.

CHAPTER SIXTEEN

'Here we are,' said Watson, reading from her laptop screen, 'Kenny Wingate a.k.a. Kenny the Driver. Born in Hackney in 1952. Sentenced to sixteen years, reduced to six months, in 1988.'

'Well, well,' said Slater, peering over her shoulder. 'What did he do to get his sentenced reduced so drastically? Do you think it was because he shopped all his mates?'

'Well, I hope it was worth his while,' said Watson, 'because most of the people he double-crossed aren't the sort who would forget about it in a hurry. I'm sure there would have been a pretty price on his head.'

'Maybe he thought twenty-million quid's worth of diamonds made it worth the risk,' muttered Slater. 'Is there any way of finding out what happened to him when he was released?'

'There's nothing here to confirm he ever *was* released,' she said. 'He just seems to have been erased from the system after that.'

'That confirms Stockholm's protected witness idea then,' said Slater. 'If only there was some way of finding out who he became after that.'

Watson had been busily poking at keys on her laptop. 'This is interesting.' She leaned closer to the screen. 'It appears Kenny Wingate wasn't kept in solitary confinement.'

'Really?' said Slater. 'That was risky. I thought these guys were always kept in solitary for their own protection. Do we know who he was sharing with?'

'Oh yes,' said Watson, turning to him with a broad grin. 'Does the name Brian Harding seem familiar?'

'Oh, well done, Watson!' exclaimed Slater. 'Now that is a bit of a coincidence, isn't it?'

Watson turned back to her screen, her face slightly pink, and began tapping away at the keys again. It was barely two minutes later when she spoke again.

'Here we are, sir. Brian Harding, born October 1943, and can you believe it, he has the same parents as William. They were brothers, with ten years between them. He's got a record of petty theft, burglary. He's the complete opposite of his younger brother.'

'Sounds like the black sheep of the family,' said Slater. 'I wonder where he is now? Perhaps he knows where William is.'

'Let's see if I can track him down,' said Watson, looking as if she was in her element.

Slater's phone began to ring. It was Norman, who'd gone across to the pub to make his calls in private.

'I just spoke to a guy I know. The word is, Scanlon's officially retired, and his son's in charge these days but, unofficially, it's also a well-known fact he's still looking for his diamonds, and he's the guy who put a price on the head of Kenny the Bigmouth Wingate all those years ago — and it still stands.'

'They've changed Kenny's name,' said Slater.

'Yeah, well, they don't want him to do a driving job any more,' said Norman. 'The name's a reflection of what he's best known for these days.'

'That's good stuff, Norm. It's all helping to build the picture. Watson's just found out Kenny had a buddy sharing his cell when he did his six months.'

'That's unusual. Maybe they were hoping he'd tell them where the diamonds were if he had someone to speak to.'

'Get this,' said Slater. 'The buddy was Brian Harding, William's older brother.'

'Wow! What are the chances of that?'

'Yeah, just a tad coincidental. D'you think you could go and see Rosie and ask her if she knows anything about William's older brother?'

'I'm on my way. I'll speak to you later.'

* * *

Half an hour later, Watson called Slater over. 'Our Mr Brian Harding has been a bit of a nomad,' she said. 'It's as if he's visited almost every town in the country since he came out of prison. For the best part of twenty years, he never stayed anywhere for longer than a couple of months.'

'But he was released in 1991,' said Slater. 'That was twenty-five years ago.'

'Yes, but he's quite elusive. He comes and goes within the system, sometimes disappearing for a year or so and then popping up again. This goes on up until seven years ago, when he disappears once again. Only this time, there's no trace of him ever reappearing.'

'Christ not another one who's disappeared,' muttered Slater. 'I wonder why he moved around so much. And why would he disappear at that particular time?'

'Perhaps he was hiding from someone?' said Watson. 'And maybe they found him, and made him disappear.'

'You mean they bumped him off? It's a possibility, I suppose,' mused Slater, 'but here's another idea. What if he wasn't running away from someone, but was actually *searching* for someone? Remember, he shared a cell with Kenny Wingate. Now, suppose Kenny was one of those people who couldn't help but brag about how clever he was? What if he told Brian Harding he was getting a new ID, and he had a little nest egg waiting when he came out? That might be an incentive to search for someone, don't you think?'

'So, all we need to do is find Kenny Wingate, who has a new identity we know nothing about, and Brian Harding, who vanished about seven years ago, and we've solved the case!' said Watson.

Slater gave her a wry smile. 'Yeah, I guess that just about sums it up. It'll be a piece of cake!'

CHAPTER SEVENTEEN

Norman walked down Rosie's path and climbed back into his car. It had been a fruitless journey, as Rosie was quite sure William had never mentioned having a brother. He pulled the door closed and started the car, but before he could pull away, his mobile phone began to ring. He looked at the caller ID and took the call.

'Hi Jane, is everything okay?'

'Yes, I'm fine,' she said. 'I've just been down to that storage place on the trading estate and rented a unit.'

Jane had been threatening to pack all her husband's stuff into boxes and put it into storage for weeks, but Norman had thought she had been quite reluctant to actually go through with it. Much as he had wanted to voice his opinion, he had resisted the temptation to get involved on the basis that it had to be her decision — and hers alone. This had come as quite a surprise.

'Oh, right! So you're really going to go through with it?'

'I've been putting it off long enough,' she said. 'And now I know he's going to be coming out soon, I've had to do it. If he came out and found his stuff was still here, he might think everything's okay, and that just wouldn't be fair, so now I've got the unit arranged, all I have to do is move the stuff.'

'You know I'll help you with that, don't you?' he said. 'Just tell me when and I'll take a day out.'

'You know, I was hoping you were going to say that. You really are very kind. I just need to find out when I can hire a van, and then I'll let you know.'

'I always help people I care about,' said Norman. 'And I care about you a lot, so it's a no-brainer.'

There was an awkward, slightly embarrassed silence before Norman spoke again. 'Is that what you called for?'

'Oh, sorry, no. Can you get over here? There's something you need to see. It might be nothing, or it might be a coincidence, but I think you should call in and have a look.'

Ten minutes later, Norman was being ushered inside Jane Jolly's house and through to her kitchen.

'What's this big secret thing you need me to check out?' he asked.

'There.' She pointed to the table.

Norman looked at the brass key that lay on the table. He looked at Jane and looked at the key again. 'It's a key, right?'

'Well, obviously,' she said. 'Perhaps I'm wrong, and I'm wasting your time, but don't you think it looks familiar?'

He looked at it again, then picked it up and turned it over in his hand. 'I suppose it does, now you come to mention it, but there must be millions of plain brass keys knocking around. Where did you get it?'

'That's the key to my room at the storage centre. They have dozens of different units, some are room-sized, and some are just small safes set into walls, but they all have the same sort of key, and they all look just like this.'

Norman looked up at her face. 'You think the key Joe sent Rosie is from the storage centre?'

'I don't know,' she said, uncertainly. 'I thought it was when I first saw it, but now you're asking questions, I'm beginning to doubt my intuition. You're probably right, of course. In fact, the more I think about it, the more I think it's just too obvious, isn't it?'

'Yeah, but isn't the most obvious place often the best place to hide something?' said Norman. 'No one ever thinks to look right under their nose, right?' He took her shoulders, pulled her to him, and gave her a quick kiss on the forehead. 'You're brilliant,' he said, letting her go. 'And don't ever doubt your intuition.'

'But what if I'm wrong?'

'You're still brilliant,' he said. 'And anyway, what if you're right? Jeez, we could be halfway to solving this case if you are! Can I take this key and compare it with the one we have at the office?'

'Of course. But don't forget I need it back.'

'How do you know which room this key fits?' he asked.

'They're all numbered. From one to one hundred and ninety-six, I think the man told me.'

'So, if two little ducks is twenty-two, we could have the key to storage unit number twenty-two. What number's yours?'

'Thirty-eight.'

'Look, I have to go,' said Norman. 'This is brilliant, honestly. It could be the break we've been looking for. I'll call you later, okay?'

* * *

'So, you and Jane think the key Joe sent to Rosie came from the storage centre here on Tinton trading estate?' asked Slater.

'Yeah, why not? Jane says there are nearly two hundred units and they all have the same style of brass key. Now you have to admit when you put those two keys side by side, they look the same, right?'

Slater looked at the two keys. They certainly did look the same, apart from the design cut to fit into the lock, and the piece of tape Norman had stuck onto Jane's key so they didn't get mixed up.

'What do you think, Watson?' he asked.

She briefly looked startled by the question, but quickly regained her composure. 'I have to admit, they *do* look similar,' she said. 'Maybe we could get some sort of forensic examination done.'

'That would take time,' said Slater, 'and the chances are it would only prove they were made of the same material and maybe made in the same workshop. That won't really help much.'

'Couldn't we just take the key down there and ask if it fits?'

'That would be good, but you can't just roll up with a key and ask if you can try all the locks to see if it fits. Anyway, they have security at these places,' he said. 'You'd have to have the correct ID to get in, and we have no idea what that is.'

Norman picked up Jane's key and held it up in front of them. 'You're forgetting — this is Jane's key,' he said, with a wide grin. 'She has the correct ID. She could get us in.'

Slater was grinning too now. 'Now we're cooking! If one of us could get in there, we can take that key and see if it fits storage unit twenty-two.'

'They will almost certainly have CCTV monitoring the inside,' said Watson. 'Didn't you just tell me they'll find it a bit strange if they see someone trying a key in a unit they don't own?'

'That's a good point,' conceded Slater.

'Hang on a minute,' said Norman. 'Jane's just signed up with them. They must have shown her the security setup. Why don't I get her to come down here and tell us about it, and then maybe we can come up with a plan.'

CHAPTER EIGHTEEN

The transit van turned off the road and rolled to a halt at the barrier across the entrance to the storage centre. The driver, a rather rotund figure, rolled down his window and gave a cheery wave to the security guard gazing at him from the window of the small gatehouse.

Inside the gatehouse, Andy Judd, the security guard in question, gazed at the newcomers with the weary indifference of a man bored to tears working mind-numbingly dull twelve-hour shifts. Raising a smile was out of the question, and he failed to manage so much as a grimace. He certainly had no intention of going out into the cold to speak to them, so if one of them wasn't prepared to get out and walk across to him, they could sit out there all day for all he cared.

'Now that's a nice cheery welcome,' muttered Norman to his two passengers.

'Yeah,' agreed Slater, looking past Norman at the guard in the cubicle. He was sitting in the centre seat of the cab with Jane Jolly in the passenger seat. 'That sort of greeting really makes you feel all warm and fuzzy inside, doesn't it?'

She tapped his arm. 'You two stay here and let me handle this,' she said. 'We don't need anyone falling out with the man.'

'I just think it wouldn't hurt him to show some manners, that's all,' said Norman. 'And what does a smile cost?'

'We can worry about his lack of manners another time. Just remember we agreed on a plan, but it will only work if you two stick to it.'

'Yeah, you're right,' said Slater. 'Sorry, Jane.'

She opened the door, slid from her seat, walked confidently across to the gatehouse, opened the door, and marched up to the counter.

'My name's Jane Jolly,' she said, with a sweet smile. 'I'm a new customer. You should be expecting me.'

The man scowled at her, and then looked down at the printed list in front of him.

'What was the name again?'

'Jolly, Mrs.'

'What time did you say?'

'I didn't,' she said, shortly. 'But I called your office this morning to book an appointment. I said I would be here at two fifteen.' Very slowly and deliberately, she turned to look at the large clock on the wall. 'And here I am, right on time.'

The man took his time going down the list in front of him, but eventually he found her name and reluctantly ticked the box next to it. 'What about the geezers in the van?' he asked.

'I have two men to carry the boxes for me, as I said I would.'

The man looked at his list again. 'Oh yeah, you're right. It says so in the notes. You need to drive through the gate and go to the security office at the front of the building. They'll check your ID and everything, and as long as you're who you say you are, they'll let you into the building.' Having delivered his instructions, the guard turned his attention back to the newspaper he had been trying to read before he had been interrupted.

By now, Jane was as irritated by the gateman's surly attitude as Norman and Slater were, but she was disciplined enough to resist the urge to tell him what she thought and made her way back to the van. As she climbed into the passenger seat, the barrier rose slowly into the air, and Norman drove through and headed towards the main building.

As the transit van moved off, a car turned into the space that had just been vacated before the barrier. The security guard looked up and sighed. What was up with all these people today? Why couldn't they leave him in peace to read his newspaper?

He watched as a young woman pushed her car door closed — with some difficulty as she was also trying to manoeuvre around a walking stick — and approached the gatehouse. At least now he could raise a little more enthusiasm. This one was a bit younger, and he had no effort raising a smile for her. He hoped, as she was unaccompanied, she might be a bit more amenable, although he was a little troubled by the clipboard she was carrying under her left arm.

'Yes, love, what can I do for you?' he asked, flashing her his best smile as she walked through the door.

Completely expressionless, she marched up to the counter and flashed her warrant card under his nose, just long enough for him to see what it was, but not long enough for him to read the details.

'DS Brearley, Hampshire Constabulary,' she said, coolly, confident he was no speed-reader. 'I'm here to carry out a check of your security systems.'

'Eh?'

'Well, that's not a very good start, is it?' she said, producing a pen and making a mark on the clipboard. 'That's one black mark already, and I've barely started.'

'Black mark? What d'you mean a black mark?'

'You should have known I was coming.'

The puzzled security guard was scanning his list. He couldn't see any mention of a visit from the police. 'But you're not on my list,' he pleaded.

'That's another black mark, then,' she said, and scored another 'X' on her board. 'What was the point in me phoning to make an appointment this morning if it's not going to be relayed to the man on the gate? I could be anyone pretending to be a police officer.'

'But that's not my fault,' he whined. 'It's that stupid young girl in the office. If she wasn't so busy doing her nails and watching pathetic videos on the internet, these stupid mistakes wouldn't keep happening.'

'Happens a lot, does it?' asked Watson, scrawling yet another 'X' on her clipboard. 'Oh dear me, that's three Xs on the board and not a single tick so far. It's not looking too good, is it? I had an entire security team fired at one of these places the other week, and they only had one bad mark at this stage. I'd polish up my interview skills if I were you, you might be needing them by the time I've finished.'

'Hey, now hang on a minute,' said a horrified Andy Judd. 'You can't get me the sack just because someone else doesn't do their job! That's not fair, is it?'

'What's your name?' asked Watson.

'Andy, Andy Judd.'

Watson made a note on her clipboard. 'Okay, Andy, here's what I'm going to do,' she said. 'As you've been so quick to look out for yourself and point the finger of blame at everyone else, I'm going to make a special recommendation about you to make sure everyone knows just what sort of team member you really are.'

'Really?' said Andy, relaxing. 'You'll do that for me?'

'Oh yes, it'll be a pleasure,' she assured him. 'I'll make sure everyone knows exactly what you're like.'

Andy looked immensely pleased with himself. He was going to get a recommendation. He was special. That'd show those other tossers he worked with.

'Now, could you be a love and open the gate for me?' asked Watson.

'What? Oh yeah, it's my pleasure.'

Watson left the beaming Andy and made her way back to her car. She was hoping the security here was going to be average at best, and if he was anything to go by, she was going to be proved right. Whatever happened, she had decided she would certainly make sure the rest of the team knew what a great team player they had on the front gate.

* * *

Up at the main building, Jane had checked in at the security room and was heading back to the van. They had to drive around to the back of the building and back their van up to entrance B, which gave access to units twenty through forty. This was a real stroke of luck; they hadn't realised both the units they wanted to access would be so close to each other.

She had noted the large bank of screens on one wall, each one displaying the view from the various CCTV cameras dotted in and around the building. It looked as though there were probably two watching over each corridor, but if Watson did her job properly, that shouldn't be a major problem. As she left the security room, she glanced down towards the main gate. The barrier was just reaching the top of its journey, and Watson's car could be seen coming through.

'So far, so good,' she said to Slater and Norman as she pulled the door open and got back into the van. 'Watson's got past the gate, and she's on her way up here right now.'

'Where do we go?' asked Norman, as he fired up the engine.

'Round to the left. Then down to the end of the building and turn right. Entrance B will be the second one we come to.'

'Okay everybody, here we go,' said Norman.

As he pulled away, Watson slipped neatly into the space he had vacated.

* * *

Norman followed Jane's directions and reversed up to a van-sized door marked with a large 'B'. As he pulled up and they climbed from the van, the door rolled upwards to reveal a short passageway to yet another door. Jane walked down to the end of the passageway and pushed the door. Beyond, there was a wider corridor with numbered doors set at regular intervals on either side, starting with twenty-one on the left and ending with thirty-nine on the right. She made a quick note of the two CCTV cameras, and then went back to the van.

'We're in luck,' she said. 'Numbers thirty-eight and twenty-two are right opposite each other.'

'What about CCTV?' asked Norman.

'As we thought, they're in opposite corners, far left and near right.'

'Let's stick to the plan,' said Slater. 'Watson will be expecting us to unload this stuff first, and take it to room thirty-eight. We'll try room twenty-two once we're done.'

'Let's just hope she can distract the guy long enough,' said Norman.

'She'll be fine,' said Slater. 'She can always revert to being a real police officer if she has to. The chances are he won't know she can't just go anywhere she pleases without a search warrant.'

They quickly unloaded the dozen boxes Jane had packed full of her husband's belongings and began carrying them down to room thirty-eight. Jolly slid the key in the lock, and with a nice smooth twist, the door opened.

'Nice and easy,' said Norman. 'If number twenty-two's like that, it'll be a breeze.'

'If that's even what the key's for,' said Slater.

'Have faith,' said Norman. 'It's all cool. We'll be fine.'

* * *

Back in the security room, the guard responsible for watching the screens was trying to keep an eye on the three people heading for room thirty-eight and also deal with the surprise arrival of the seemingly uber-efficient DS Brearley, who had apparently arrived to carry out an inspection. He wondered why that idiot Andy Judd hadn't given him a call from the gate to warn him and made a mental note to have words if he ever managed to get rid of the woman. And, thinking about it, why hadn't the office warned them all, if, as she insisted, she had called this morning to make an appointment?

Looking over the guard's shoulder at the screens, Watson could see Slater and Norman loading boxes into room thirty-eight. Jolly seemed to be watching their every move, but was gradually edging across towards door number twenty-two.

'Right,' she said. 'First I need to go through this checklist, then we'll go into a bit more detail. Before I start, I have to tell you — your friend down on the front gate didn't exactly cover himself in glory, and as a company you have yet to score a single positive point. Is there any particular reason why you think he was quite so unprepared for my visit?'

'Why don't you ask him?' said the guard. 'I don't know what the hell he's doing up here, but he's just about to come through the do—'

There was just the slightest noise of a door opening behind her, but it was the sudden look of alarm on the face of the man stood opposite her that told Watson she was in trouble. Before she had time to react, someone crashed into her back and suddenly she was on the floor in a tangle of arms and legs with Andy Judd, her stick flying across the room. At first, she thought *he* had attacked her, but then she became aware two other figures had come through the doorway. Andy had obviously been shoved into her.

'Right, let's all stay calm,' said a voice. 'There's no need for anyone to get hurt.'

Watson shook herself and looked up at the two figures, and as she did, her blood seemed to run cold and her mind was flooded with memories of pain and the smell of her own blood and being rushed to hospital. Both the men were armed with pistols.

'Get up off the floor, you two,' said the man who appeared to be in charge. 'And no funny stuff. Like I said, I don't want to hurt anyone. If you all do as you're told, you'll be home in time for tea, with no damage done. Understand?'

Andy climbed gingerly to his feet, gave Watson his hand, and helped her up. She caught his eye, but the blank look she got in return showed her he was terrified. She understood. There was no point in arguing with a man holding a gun. At least, not right now. It would be much better to play along and see if an opportunity presented itself.

Once they were all on their feet, Watson noticed the two guards were looking at her. Of course, she was the police officer. They expected her to know what to do.

'Just do as he says,' she said, 'and there's no reason why he should shoot anyone.'

'Clever girl,' said the leader, and then peered at her suspiciously. 'How come you're the only hero in the room? What are you, a copper?'

She said nothing.

'Search her pockets, Denny.'

The second man came over, the gun pointing straight at her, but now just inches from her heart. He slipped a hand into first one pocket, and then the other, pulling her warrant card from her pocket.

'DS Brearley,' he read.

He showed it to his boss, who took a quick glance but quickly dismissed it. 'Never mind about that,' he said. 'It doesn't matter who, or what, she is. She can't do us any harm on her own. Come on. Let's get going.'

He addressed the three captives. 'Right, we're all going for a little walk. You three are going to form a line and put your left hand on the shoulder of the person in front. If you drop that hand, I'll shoot you in the back, and make no mistake, I mean it. Is that clear?' He didn't wait for a response. 'Right, follow Denny here, keep five yards behind him, and behave yourselves.'

Denny led the way out of the room, making it quite clear he was watching them as well as where he was going. The boss kept behind them, constantly moving from side to side and watching the three prisoners like a hawk.

* * *

Down at the other end of the building, Jane had slipped across to the door of room twenty-two and placed the key in the lock. It wasn't quite as smooth as her own, but it turned easily enough.

'I'm in,' she hissed and pulled the door ajar and slipped inside. There was a solitary table in the centre of the small storage room, and on top lay a small attaché case. As she took it all in, Norman and Slater slipped into the room with her.

'Shall we open it?' she asked.

'It'll be quicker to just take it and go,' said Slater.

'Yeah,' agreed Norman. 'There's nothing else in here, so either this is what we're looking for or we've wasted our time. Either way, we need to get out of here before we get spotted on the CCTV.'

Slater grabbed the case and made for the door. He pushed it open slowly and carefully peered around the corner. Then he felt his guts turn to icy water as he experienced something he'd felt once before — and had hoped he'd never have to face again. He was looking down the barrel of a pistol.

'I think this is where I'm supposed to say hands up, isn't it?' said the man holding the gun, with a menacing, icy smile. He waved the gun at Slater. 'Go on, back up, back inside that room.'

Slater stepped carefully and slowly back into the room, the barrel of the pistol never more than a foot from his face.

'Stevie Scanlon!' exclaimed Norman as they came into the room.

In Slater's mind, several pennies seemed to drop into place. Of course — Bradshaw had told them Scanlon had set them up to find the diamonds; he'd just forgotten to mention the man would be following their progress all the time.

'Do you know me?' asked Scanlon, looking suspiciously at Norman.

'We've never met, but I know you by reputation.'

'Yes, I think I'd remember if I met you. Good, is it, my reputation?'

'That would depend on what you call good.'

'In my world, a good reputation means people are scared of me, and if you aren't scared, you should be!'

'Yeah, right. I'll try to remember that,' said Norman, almost casually.

'You've got a big mouth for a guy who's unarmed,' said Scanlon. 'And you really ought to have a little more respect for the gun, don't you think?' He studied Norman's face for a moment. 'You're Norman, aren't you? I was told you were a big fat bugger.' Then he noticed Jane, and his voice was briefly filled with false concern. 'Oh, excuse my language, I didn't notice we had a *lady* present. Are you all right, love?'

Jane was almost too frightened to speak, barely managing to whisper a hoarse, 'Yes'.

Scanlon smiled crookedly at her. 'Don't be frightened, darling,' he said. 'I didn't come here to shoot anyone. If everyone does as they're told, no one's going to get hurt.' Then his face changed and he turned back to Norman, his voice filled with menace once more. 'Unless, of course, this big lump keeps on trying to get under my skin. If he doesn't shut up, someone will get hurt, and it won't necessarily be him.'

'All right, Scanlon, what do you want?' asked Slater, trying to be the voice of reason.

Scanlon flashed a half-smile at him. 'Well, well, well, Mr Slater, isn't it? I was beginning to think you'd lost your voice.'

Slater wondered exactly how much he really knew about them. Did he know about Bradshaw?

'Wondering how I know who you are?' he asked. 'I'm the bloke who suggested Rosie should come and talk to you. Of course I know who you are. You've been working for me all this time.'

Slater resisted the urge to announce this wasn't exactly news, and he was relieved Norman kept quiet about it too.

Now Scanlon beamed a big sunny smile at them, and Slater got the distinct feeling this man was definitely unhinged. Suddenly, he seemed a whole lot scarier.

'I must say, I'm very impressed with your work,' continued Scanlon. 'We've been looking for those diamonds for years, although, of course, we thought we were looking for Kenny Wingate, or whatever he's called now. And then he disappeared, and for a while we didn't know who we were looking for. We thought we'd got close when we finally found old Joe, but then the silly sod dropped dead before we could find out where he'd hidden the bloody things. That's when we thought of hiring two private detectives. Now, that was stroke of genius, I reckon, because no sooner do you two get involved and suddenly it's case closed within two weeks. It makes me wonder how you managed it.'

'I guess we're just not as dim as we look,' said Slater.

'Or you could be working with the police.' The menace was back in Scanlon's voice.

'Don't make me laugh,' said Slater. 'I just walked out a few weeks ago. Wild horses wouldn't get me back into bed with them, and as for Norman, he was forced to quit. Neither of us have any reason to want to help them out.'

'What about the girl?' asked Scanlon.

'What girl?'

'The one outside waving the warrant card around.'

Slater and Norman looked blank.

'Bring them all in here, Denny,' called Scanlon.

The two security guards and Watson were marched through the door, closely followed by Denny, who made Watson gasp and wince with a painful prod in the back with his pistol.

Scanlon took Watson by the arm. 'This girl,' he said. 'DS Samantha Brearley.'

Slater smiled. 'Her real name's Emma Watson,' he said, calmly. 'She's our office clerk. We had the warrant card made up so she could be a diversion while we came in here.'

Scanlon looked at Watson and gave her a crooked smile. 'Emma Watson? Weren't you at Hogwarts?' He laughed in her face then turned back to Slater. 'I don't believe you.'

'You've seen the warrant card,' said Slater, hoping he remembered it correctly. 'There's no constabulary listed. You know as well as I do there's always a constabulary. Mine used to say Hampshire Constabulary.'

'That's right,' said Norman. 'Mine used to say Metropolitan Police Force.'

'So, what went wrong?'

'We hired the wrong forger,' said Norman. 'And we didn't have time to get it changed.'

Scanlon didn't look convinced. He moved close enough for Slater to smell the garlic on his breath and rested the barrel of his pistol against Slater's chin.

'I haven't got time for this now,' he hissed, 'but I promise you, I'm going to check when I get back home, and if I find you're lying, I'm going to come back and find you, and your fat friend, and Emma Watson here, and I'm going to fix all three of you. You really don't want to cross me. Do I make myself clear?'

He studied Slater's face, but with a supreme effort of will, Slater was managing to contain his fear. It wasn't the man, it was the gun — and what it was capable of — that terrified him.

'You know what?' said Scanlon. 'I'm not sure you and your mate are really listening to me, so why don't I make a start now?'

He stepped back, just far enough to raise the pistol at arm's length, looked down the barrel, and placed it against Slater's forehead. Slowly, his knuckle began to whiten as he pressed the trigger. Slater could feel the slight tremor in the hand through the gun, and it seemed as if everyone else around them had ceased to exist. He knew he had stopped breathing but he didn't seem to be able to take a breath of his own accord.

Even Scanlon's crony, Denny, looked worried. Finally, the finger on the trigger reached the point of no return and Slater flinched, but instead of the expected explosion, there was a loud click.

'Bang! You're dead!' yelled Scanlon and roared with laughter. Slater felt his entire body unclench, and he suddenly felt light-headed enough to stick out an arm, which Norman grabbed to stop his friend from falling over.

'Come on, Denny,' said Scanlon, still laughing as he took a tight hold of the attaché case. 'Let's get out of here.'

They retreated from the room and pulled the door closed behind them. Slater rushed to the door, but he could hear the key turning. He banged futilely on the door a couple of times.

'The bastard's locked us in!'

CHAPTER NINETEEN

'Is anyone hurt?' asked Norman. He turned to Jane and slipped an arm around her shoulders. 'Are you okay?'

'Slightly terrified,' she said, 'but I'll survive.'

'Are you okay, Watson?'

'I'm going to have a rather nasty bruise on my back where that pig jabbed me with his pistol,' she said. 'Otherwise, it's just my ego that's a bit bruised.' She turned to Slater, who was still over by the door, holding his head in his hands. 'Are you all right, sir?'

He looked up, slightly dazed. 'Yeah, I think so. I'd forgotten how much fun it is to have some maniac point a gun at me. I doubt it's done much for the state of my underwear, though.'

Watson looked somewhat shocked by Slater's underwear reference, but Norman let out a loud guffaw.

'Well,' he said, 'I, for one, think you definitely qualify for the Joe Cool award of the year. Knowing how terrified you are by guns, I would never have believed what just happened if I hadn't seen it with my own eyes.'

'If we ever get into a situation like that again, can someone remind me to run and hide?' said Slater.

'You're gonna be working with him, Watson,' said Norman. 'That'll be your job, right?'

'Gosh, yes, I suppose it will,' she said. Then to Slater she said, 'Will it? Sir?'

'My whole life has just flashed before my eyes, Watson,' he said. 'So now is probably not quite the right time to ask me that question. You're going to have to improve your timing when we start working together for real.'

'Right. Yessir, sorry, sir,' she said, contritely, then she slowly realised what he'd actually said. 'You mean?' She looked at Norman, who gave her a grin and a wink.

'You got that, right?' he asked her.

But before she could answer, Slater was speaking to the two security guards who were sitting to one side on their own.

'Is there any way out of these rooms?' he asked. 'Like some sort of escape hatch or something?'

Andy Judd shook his head. 'No, sorry, that wouldn't be very secure, would it?'

'Bugger!' said Slater. 'We could be stuck here for hours. Meanwhile that arsehole gets away with the bloody diamonds.'

'I don't think it will be too long before we're released,' said Watson.

'You sound very sure about that,' said Slater. 'Would you like to elaborate?'

'Well, I know it's not really my place to make decisions over your head, but you did say I should be prepared to make them when there's no DI to turn to, and you had gone off with Mr Norman and Mrs Jolly.'

'You also need to learn to stop waffling and get to the point,' said Slater. 'There is a point, is there?'

'I called Chief Superintendent Bradshaw and told him what we were planning to do. He was worried Scanlon might be watching us, so he promised he would have backup standing by just in case.'

'I hope they're well-armed,' said Norman. 'That Scanlon's some sort of psycho.'

* * *

As this conversation was taking place in the locked room twenty-two, Stevie Scanlon and his friend Denny found themselves surrounded by armed police officers and escorted into waiting vehicles. There was only one problem left for Bradshaw to work out: which room were Slater, Norman, Watson, Jolly and the two security officers incarcerated in? But at least there was a clue. Norman's van was still parked outside door 'B', so he guessed that would be the area to start with. All he needed now were the keys . . .

CHAPTER TWENTY

'You used us as bait!' said Slater to Bradshaw later. 'You knew Scanlon was watching us.'

'That's not true. I didn't know for sure,' argued Bradshaw. 'You should think yourself lucky you had Watson watching your back. If she hadn't kept me informed and called for backup, you could have been locked in there for days, and Scanlon would have had a head start. He would have been out of the country before we had even known what he'd done.'

'He nearly blew my bloody head off!'

'His gun wasn't loaded.'

'Oh yeah, you know that *now*,' said Slater. 'But I didn't know that when he had the damned thing pressed against my forehead, did I?'

'And the guy's definitely at least one sandwich short of a picnic,' added Norman. 'He frightened the crap out of all of us, and he wasn't even pointing the gun at anyone else!'

'He's not as mad as you think,' said Bradshaw. 'All that crazy, mental, psycho stuff is an act. It helps to keep everyone under control when they think the boss is a ticking bomb just waiting to explode. Trust me, you were perfectly safe. He's never fired a shot in anger. He might be his father's son, but he's not stupid enough to risk a murder charge.'

'Did Watson know all this?' asked Slater.

Bradshaw shook his head. 'She was as much in the dark as you were. Think about it — if Scanlon had known any of you weren't frightened, don't you think he might have wondered why? He might have realised he was walking into a trap, and we could have lost him. Anyway, there's no harm done in the end, and the case is closed. Congratulations all round I'd say, wouldn't you?'

Slater and Norman exchanged a look.

'And what about the man who called himself Joe Dalgetty?' asked Slater.

'I'm sorry?'

'What about Joe?' said Norman. 'We got into this case because a lady called Rosie asked us to find out what had happened to her friend.'

'What difference does it make? The man died of natural causes.'

'But we don't think he did,' said Slater.

'He had a heart attack, how much more natural does it need to be?'

'Look,' said Norman, 'we know Joe wasn't the protected witness who ran off with the diamonds.'

'But he had the key,' argued Bradshaw.

'Yeah,' agreed Norman, 'but how did he come to have it?'

'And how did he come to be living in that house?' asked Slater. 'The name on the tenancy agreement is William Harding, and the rent and bills are being paid from Harding's bank account.'

'We're sure it's all linked,' said Norman, 'but we're missing something somewhere.'

'Don't all these loose ends worry you?' asked Slater. 'Because they worry both of us!'

Bradshaw considered for a moment.

'Well, I can't stop you if you want to pursue it,' he said, finally, 'but I'm not paying for it.'

'I was rather hoping you might let Watson stay with us for a few more days,' said Slater. 'It'll help us build our working relationship.'

'You haven't confirmed there will be a working relationship yet,' countered Bradshaw. 'I need you to give me a starting date, Slater.'

'Okay, here's a deal. It's Tuesday afternoon now. Let Watson stay until the end of the week and I'll give you a definite start date on Friday afternoon.'

Bradshaw looked doubtful.

'You won't want me to leave cases half-finished when I'm working for you, will you?' asked Slater.

'You will make sure she's on a train on Friday afternoon,' he said finally. 'And you will make sure that train leaves early enough for her to get home for a decent weekend. I don't want to find she was travelling Friday evening.'

'I'll put her on the train myself,' promised Slater.

CHAPTER TWENTY-ONE

'Right,' said Slater next morning, when they gathered at the office, 'we might have solved this case to Bradshaw's satisfaction, but there are far too many unanswered questions for my liking. For a start I'm not convinced Joe died because of Scanlon's diamonds.'

'But he knew where they were,' said Watson.

'Yes, I know that, and your theory that perhaps he came home and found Stevie Scanlon in his house makes perfect sense, but that doesn't tie up with what Scanlon said.'

'I'm not sure I follow,' she said, doubtfully.

'He said it took them years to find Joe and then he dropped dead before they could talk to him about where the diamonds were. On top of that, Bradshaw tells me Scanlon is adamant he didn't kill Joe. He says it was never his intention to confront Joe in his house. Yes, he wanted to get in and have a look around, but if the diamonds weren't there, it was always his intention to let Joe lead him to them, just as he did with us.'

'And you believe him?' asked Norman. 'Just because he says he didn't frighten the crap out of Joe? He's bound to say that, isn't he? If he admits it, he could end up on a murder charge.'

'Scanlon does have a reputation for being a madman,' argued Watson. 'If Joe knew that and he had a weak heart, it's quite possible he would have died of fright at finding his worst nightmare standing there in his house. But whatever Scanlon might be, he's not an idiot. He would have known that was a risk he should avoid.'

'It's not just that,' said Slater. 'Dennis Stockholm said Kenny Wingate was the grass who got a new ID and then made off with the diamonds. But he also said Joe Dalgetty was six inches too short to be Kenny. Stevie Scanlon said they started off looking for Kenny, or whoever Kenny had become, but then he disappeared, and for a while they didn't know who they were looking for. So there's a gap in the middle there. I want to know what happened.'

'You know, you're right,' conceded Norman. 'When you look under the surface, there's a lot of unanswered questions.'

'Exactly!' said Slater. 'What was Kenny Wingate's new ID? We know he didn't have the diamonds any more, but why, and what happened to him? Who was Joe really, and how did he get the diamonds? And did he have anything to do with Kenny's sudden disappearance?'

'There's something else,' said Norman. 'What happened to William Harding? How does he fit into this? Or is he just a red herring?'

'Don't forget the Harding brother, Brian,' said Watson. 'I think it's too much of a coincidence that he was involved at the beginning when he shared a cell with Wingate, and then his brother's house is involved at the end!'

'What do you think?' Slater asked Norman. 'Do we try and work it all out, or do we close the case?'

'Heck, let's do it,' said Norman. 'It's not as if I've got anything else to do!'

'What about you, Watson?' asked Slater. 'You don't have to stay if you'd rather go back.'

'Good heavens no,' she said. 'I'm enjoying myself too much to leave now. This proper detective work is much more fun than keeping Mr Bradshaw's diary straight. Where do you want me to start?'

'Well, I couldn't sleep much last night,' said Slater. 'I think it might have something to do with staring down the barrel of a gun yesterday. Anyway, the thing is, although I didn't sleep, I did spend a lot of time thinking about this case. In particular, I thought about what we learnt before we got distracted by the storage centre. We know Kenny Wingate shared a cell with Brian Harding, and we know when Harding came out he was moving around all over.'

'That's right,' said Norman. 'Didn't you say he was either hiding from someone or looking for someone? Probably Kenny, or whoever Kenny had become.'

'Hold that thought,' said Slater. 'This is probably crazy thinking, but let's suppose Brian actually found Kenny, bumped him off, and got his hands on the diamonds. But then, having got hold of the diamonds, he finds he's not the only one who's been looking for Kenny. Somehow, he finds out Scanlon's looking, and he knows Scanlon's reputation as a homicidal maniac. What's he going to do?'

'Take the diamonds and disappear,' said Watson. 'I'd choose somewhere warm and sunny.'

'Kenny could have done that, but for some reason he didn't,' said Slater. 'Maybe that's what Brian was intending to do, but what if, now he's got the loot, he's found out there's some reason that's not possible.'

'Like what?' asked Watson.

'Now that I don't know,' admitted Slater, 'but just humour me for a minute. Let's say there's no escape and it's not possible to sell them on, or Kenny would have done it. Maybe these diamonds, and the fact Scanlon wants them back, are so well known the only way to move them is one at a time, through a dealer who's crazy enough to take the risk.'

'I get it,' said Norman. 'Brian Harding thought he was going after the Holy Grail that would give him the freedom to do whatever he wanted, but when he actually got his hands on it, he found it was actually the opposite, and the only way to survive was to hide away.'

'But why?' asked Watson.

'Maybe Scanlon was even more powerful than we thought,' said Norman. 'Maybe the price for being caught with those diamonds was so high, no one would even think about touching them.'

'And, of course,' added Slater, 'when Brian put the word out he had some diamonds to sell, the news would have gone back to Scanlon.'

'Making Brian Harding Scanlon's new target,' finished Watson. 'So, to hide, he has to find a new identity. Yes, I see what you mean.'

'Like I said, it's probably just a hare-brained theory,' said Slater, 'but I think Joe Dalgetty was probably Brian Harding.'

'Yeah, it makes sense,' said Norman, 'and it explains why Brian Harding disappeared at about the same time Joe Dalgetty rose from the dead.'

'That still doesn't help us find out who *Kenny* became,' said Watson.

'I have a theory about that too,' said Slater. 'I was thinking about where Brian got the idea to use the name Joe Dalgetty. If you look at the guy's record, and the sort of crimes he's committed, he doesn't strike me as being particularly bright or imaginative. I mean, how would a guy like that come up with the idea of using the ID of a kid who died back in the sixties?'

'He must know people who create fake IDs,' said Norman. 'People like that use those dead kid IDs all the time. Any one of them could have come up with it.'

'True,' said Slater. 'But I have a feeling Brian was pretty much a loner as well as being a bit dim. You would think anyone in the criminal world would have known about those diamonds, and anyone with any sense would steer well clear, but apparently Brian didn't know, or at least not until he was already in so deep there was no way out. Or he was too stupid to understand what he was getting into.'

'Greed is a very powerful motivator,' remarked Norman, 'and it makes a great pair of blinkers.'

'But if Brian's as dim as I think,' said Slater, 'maybe there was something else that helped him choose that particular ID. What did you find when you searched for kids coming back from Germany, Watson?'

'Six families,' she said, and then it was like a light had been switched on inside her brain. 'One of which was the Hardings!'

'Right,' said Slater. 'The Harding family would have known about the two boys who were knocked down by a car, and that means Brian would have known too.'

'So, he chose to use one of those names,' said Norman.

'Yeah,' agreed Slater, 'but why? What was the trigger that reminded him, and why that particular one? Why Joe Dalgetty and not the other one?'

Watson's head jerked. 'You think the other one had already been used?' she asked. 'You think Kenny Wingate had chosen it for himself?'

'But Kenny didn't choose it, did he?' said Slater. 'He was a protected witness. The new identity would have been prepared for him.'

'Of course!' said Watson. She turned back to her desk and began tapping away at her laptop.

'So you think they gave Kenny the name of someone Brian would have known, and he recognised Kenny's new name and decided he would become the other one?' asked Norman. 'That's one hell of a coincidence, don't you think?'

'Yeah, I know, it's a longshot,' said Slater, sorting through their notes. 'But, they have to get these new IDs from somewhere, don't they? Don't forget Harding was ten years older than the kid who died, so would anyone have considered him to be a contemporary? I don't think so. Also, a protected witness is expected to keep his side of the deal and not go around telling people his new name.' He finally found what he was looking for. 'Here it is, Arthur Bradbury. What if Kenny was now called Arthur Bradbury and that triggered a memory? I know it's a stretch, but what else have we got?'

'Well, yeah, I suppose it works,' said Norman, uncertainly.

'Watson, see if you can find Arthur Bradbury,' said Slater.

'I'm already on it, sir. By the time you've made the coffee, I should have an answer.' She kept her head down, but both Slater and Norman could see the edges of her mouth curling upwards in a cheeky grin.

* * *

'Here we are,' said Watson. 'Arthur Bradbury. Killed in an RTA in 1959, suddenly came back to life in 1989, just at the time Kenny Wingate was disappearing into the ether. And then, just as suddenly, he disappeared seven years ago. There's been no sign of him since.'

'And that's roughly when Joe Dalgetty appears,' said Norman. 'This all seems to add up so far, but I can't help but wonder where this Arthur Bradbury is now.'

'It's also not long before William Harding vanished,' said Slater, 'and just three months after that, Joe Dalgetty, a.k.a. Brian Harding, moved into William's house.'

'Sounds to me like Brian Harding didn't just change his name. When he became Joe, he moved up from petty crime to the big league,' said Norman.

'I wonder where the bodies are,' said Slater.

Watson stared at him, looking perplexed. 'Bodies?'

Slater nodded grimly. 'There's usually only one reason people drop completely off the radar like that.'

'Wait a minute,' said Norman. Now it was his turn to sort through their notes.

'What is it?'

'It's here somewhere,' muttered Norman. 'I know it is. Ah! Here we are. When I asked Rosie about William Harding, she said he took off without warning and he was building a patio outside his back door, but he never even finished it. Joe had to finish it when he moved in.'

'Are you thinking what I'm thinking?' asked Slater.

'I remember Rosie saying how unfair it was that Joe had to finish the patio himself, in the cold, with his arthritis.

Now, I think if my arthritis was that bad, I'd get someone else to do the work for me, or at the very least I'd leave it until the weather got a bit warmer.'

'If I moved into a house and there was an unfinished patio, I'd be chasing the landlord,' said Watson. 'That's the landlord's responsibility, I certainly wouldn't be doing it myself.'

'Yeah,' said Slater, 'but what if you had a good reason to make sure no one else went anywhere near that patio.'

'One or two dead bodies would be quite a good reason,' said Norman.

'How good are you with a spade and a pickaxe?'

'Me? Oh no, this is your theory. There's no way I'm doing that. There has to be a better way than that!'

'Can I make a suggestion?' said Watson. 'Mr Bradshaw is very good at getting these things organised. Why don't you call him?'

CHAPTER TWENTY-TWO

Much to Slater's surprise, Bradshaw had been very receptive to his suggestion that they should dig up the patio at the rear of Joe Dalgetty's house. True to his word, by lunchtime it was all organised.

'Apparently, he's getting a local team to do the digging,' Slater told Norman.

'Oh wow! Goodnews is gonna love that,' said Norman. 'She'll go especially ape when she realises all her people have been seconded to an investigation *we're* conducting!'

'Yeah, well, she'll just have to grow up and deal with it,' said Slater. 'I think Bradshaw's going to have a word in her ear about interfering.'

'Oh, great. He gets to light the blue touchpaper and stand well back, while we get caught in the explosion.'

'We'll just have to deal with the fallout when it happens,' said Slater. 'I'm not going to spend the rest of my life tiptoeing around just because she's a bit touchy.'

'Surely she can't be that bad,' said Watson.

'If only that were true,' said Norman. 'Let's just hope you never have to deal with her. Since he dumped her—' he indicated Slater with his thumb — 'Detective Chief Inspector Marion Goodnews is about as predictable as an active volcano. Eruptions can happen at any time, without any warning.'

Watson looked at Slater.

'I made a mistake,' he explained, ruefully. 'It was just a fling, but she doesn't seem to accept it's over.'

'Ah, I see. That can be a bit awkward.'

'That's something of an understatement, if ever I heard one,' said Norman.

There was a knock on the door, and a young man opened it halfway and stuck his head in. 'Are you the detective guys?'

'We are,' said Norman. 'Why don't you come inside? You're letting all the cold air in.'

The young man shuffled in and swung the door closed.

'What can we do for you?' asked Norman.

'I heard something about some diamonds being found and they belonged to some old bloke who died recently. Is that right?'

Slater and Norman exchanged a look.

'What's your name, son?' asked Norman.

'Kerry. Kerry Jones.'

'Have a seat, Kerry,' said Norman, pointing to a couple of chairs, 'and then you can tell us what's on your mind.'

Kerry Jones was a fresh-faced young man with brown hair and brown eyes. Standing an inch or two shorter than Slater and a little taller than Norman, he was dressed in baggy jeans and wore a dark blue fleece over a white T-shirt, which nearly reached his knees. He was obviously very nervous but was doing his best to look relaxed and casual. Unfortunately, his leg started to twitch as soon as he sat down, and it rather spoiled the illusion.

Norman dragged another chair over and did the introductions. Jones offered what Slater would have described as a flabby handshake, his hands clammy.

'What can we do for you, Kerry?' said Norman, once the three of them were settled. Norman had arranged the chairs so they were in a triangle and there were no desks or tables between them to act as barriers.

'You're not official, are you?' asked Kerry.

Norman looked puzzled. 'How do you mean, official?'

'Err, well—'

'We're not the police, if that's what you mean,' said Slater.

Jones swallowed loudly. 'Right. Yeah, that's what I meant.' He looked down and studied his hands, which seemed to have taken on a life of their own, wringing first one way and then the other.

'I can see you're very nervous,' said Norman. 'Are you in some sort of trouble?'

'Well, no, not yet, but I think it's possible I'm going to be. That's why I've come to you, rather than the police. I heard you're like them but not sort of official.'

Norman exchanged another glance with Slater. 'We can't help you if you don't tell us why you're here.'

'Yeah, right, course not. The thing is, I heard you were investigating that old man who died. The one who had the heart attack.'

'You mean Joe Dalgetty?' asked Slater. 'D'you know something about his death?'

Now Jones looked like a frightened little boy. 'I didn't kill him!'

'We know you didn't kill him,' said Norman. 'He had a heart attack.'

'Yeah, I know. I was there.'

'You what?' said Slater, his voice almost a shriek.

'I was there in his house when he came home. He took one look at me, and it was like he'd seen a ghost or something.'

Slater looked at Norman. It sounded as if Watson *had* got the scenario right, but the wrong person as the intruder.

'Before I could say or do anything, he just sort of grabbed at his chest and dropped dead, right there, on the spot. I swear I didn't touch him.'

'But you didn't do anything to help him either, did you?' asked Norman, accusingly.

The boy spread his hands appealingly. 'Well, I couldn't, could I? Not without having to do a lot of explaining.'

Norman looked at him in disgust. 'You could at least have the decency to look embarrassed!'

'But he was dead. It's not as if there was anything I could have done.'

Norman's dismay was obvious. 'How could you know for sure? You look a bit young to be a qualified doctor. Maybe a paramedic might have been able to save his life if you'd taken the trouble to call one.'

'But like I said, I would have had to explain what I was doing there.'

'You could have called one before you ran!'

'What were you doing there?' asked Slater, already guessing what the answer was going to be.

'Looking for cash, of course,' said Jones. 'What do you think?'

'I don't think you're in any position to get cocky, do you?' said Slater. 'If you're saying you're the guy who's been going around robbing pensioners, you're admitting to being one pretty sad specimen.'

'Of course, he could just be some pathetic attention-seeker,' said Norman to Slater.

'Now there's a thing,' said Slater, deliberately ignoring Jones. 'I hadn't thought of that. You mean you think he's just some sad loser trying to impress us?'

Jones was up out of his chair like a shot, pointing his finger at Norman and spitting out his words.

'I don't need to impress wankers like you two,' he shouted. 'I *am* the real robber, and I can prove it!'

'Whoa!' said Slater, jumping from his own chair, ready for action. 'D'you really want a fight, Kerry? I'd back myself against you any time, and you really don't want me holding you down while a big guy like Norm jumps on you.'

'And now I know what you've been doing, I'd be happy to do it too,' said Norman. He hadn't changed his position, still sitting back in his chair, looking completely relaxed. 'It's the least you deserve.'

Now Jones wasn't quite so confident. He looked from Norman to Slater. Slater was pleased to see the young man's face made it clear he didn't fancy a fight any time soon. This was good news, because if he was honest, Slater didn't much fancy it either.

'Sit down, Kerry,' he said.

Jones looked at Slater nervously.

'Come on now, Kerry, don't make me flatten you. Just take it easy and sit down.'

'Trust me, Kerry, you don't wanna be fooled by his appearance. I've seen him in a fight,' said Norman. 'He's beaten the crap out of guys twice your size. I think what he's saying is if you sit down and calm down, we're going to give you another chance. If I were you, I'd accept the offer and sit down.'

Jones edged slowly back to his seat, obviously not sure if he could trust Slater not to beat him up anyway. Eventually, he sat down, and then Slater sat down too.

'Good choice, Kerry,' said Norman, cheerfully. 'We just decorated this place and, frankly, I'd be quite happy if I never see another paintbrush for the rest of my life, so I really don't need your blood splattered everywhere.' He smiled from Jones to Slater and back. 'Now then, where were we? Oh, yeah, you were just telling us how you're a screwed-up, low-life thief.' The smile was gone from his face now, replaced by a much darker expression.

'I'm not that bad,' said Jones. 'I never take anything that might have sentimental value or can't be replaced. I only take cash.'

'Can you hear yourself?' said Norman. 'Do you really think it's easy for a pensioner to replace the cash you steal? You stupid piece of shit! That's often all the money they have in the world, and you think it's fine to just help yourself? Picking on people like that is the action of a coward.'

'I am not a coward!'

'Sure you are,' said Slater. 'That's why you left an old man to die while you ran for it.'

'I panicked!'

'Like a true coward would. It doesn't matter how you try and dress it up, the fact is you left a man to die.'

'He was already dead!'

'We've already established you're not a doctor,' said Norman. 'You had no way of knowing he was dead.'

'I would have had to explain why I was there. It would have been a confession,' said Jones desperately.

'What do you think this is?' asked Norman. 'You're confessing now, aren't you?'

'Well, yeah, I suppose I am,' said Kerry.

'So how come you feel the need to confess now?' asked Norman.

'It was that old geezer. When he snuffed it, I did a runner, but I realised later that I should have helped him. I thought if I came in here and told you—'

'You'd need a conscience to feel bad about that,' said Norman. 'And if you had one of them, you wouldn't have been stealing in the first place.'

'Why did you go back to the old man's house after he was dead and buried?' asked Slater.

'What? I never did!' said Jones. 'I'm prepared to admit what I've done—'

'And what?' asked Norman. 'You think by telling us it makes everything all right? And even if you think it's going to get you a lighter sentence, I can tell you, you have no idea!'

'What do you mean a lighter sentence? You can't charge me with anything. You're not the police! What I've told you is confidential.'

'You're right, we're not the police, but we're not priests either,' said Norman, fishing his phone from his pocket. 'What makes you think we have to keep this quiet? I don't remember making any sort of deal, and I certainly didn't sign any agreement.' He found the number he wanted and pressed call.

'But you can't—'

'Just watch me,' said Norman, raising the phone to his ear.

'I'm afraid we can,' said Slater. 'You don't seriously think we're going to hide your criminal activity, do you? That would make us as bad as you.'

'Yeah, but—'

'Hi, Naomi?' said Norman, into his phone. 'I think we just found a way to repay one of those favours we owe you. Can you get over here? You might want to bring a couple of uniforms. We have a young man here who says he's been robbing pensioners. He says he wants to make a confession.'

Kerry looked as if he was going to make a run for it, but he hadn't noticed Watson make her way quietly over to the door.

'Go on, try it,' said Slater. 'I think I'd actually quite like it if you gave me an excuse.'

Now Kerry had noticed Watson waiting by the door, and the way she held her walking stick suggested she'd be happy to use it as a weapon if she had to.

'You don't seriously think you could get past her, do you?' said Slater. 'You think she'd be the easier fight because she's a woman? That would be a major faux pas. She's tougher than me and Norm put together. She'd batter the crap out of a creep like you with one hand tied behind her back.'

Watson blushed. But Kerry seemed to have realised the hopelessness of his situation and was now slumped in his seat, looking defeated.

CHAPTER TWENTY-THREE

At eight o'clock the next morning, Slater, Norman and Watson stood alongside DC Darling and watched as the first few slabs were lifted from the patio behind Joe Dalgetty's house.

'Are you all right with this, Naomi?' asked Norman. 'It's a big responsibility for a DC.'

'Oh, don't worry,' she said. 'I'm not going to get any glory out of this. DS Dumb-arse Biddeford has only left me in charge until they actually find something. If that happens, I've got to call him so he can come down and take over. It was the same with that Kerry Jones fella yesterday. I bring the guy in, and he does the interview and gets all the credit. Really, it should be you two.'

'We didn't do anything,' said Norman. 'He just walked in off the street. He seemed to think telling us about it absolved him of all blame.'

'And I told you I thought he was clever,' she said, laughing.

'He can't have been completely stupid. He didn't leave any evidence, did he?' argued Norman.

'He's some sort of sociopath or something,' said Darling. 'He seems to have no conscience, and no concept of being responsible for what he's done. I bet he'll probably get a psyche assessment that says exactly that, and he'll get off because of it. You just wait and see. Not that I care. Another few days and I'm done.'

'I think it's a pity they're letting you go,' said Slater.

'They're not letting me go, I'm leaving. Technically, it's not the same thing.'

Slater pulled a face. He felt he wasn't really in a position to argue the pros and cons of anyone's decision to leave the force.

'You realise this has made you even *more* popular with her ladyship, DCI Black Witch Goodnews, don't you?' said Darling.

'Now there's a surprise,' said Slater, dourly. 'And there I was thinking this would make me her favourite.'

'Her favourite target, maybe,' said Darling. 'If you start to get any sharp stabbing pains, that'll be on account of the voodoo doll she's sticking pins in.'

'Where is she anyway?' asked Norman. 'I expected her to be here giving us grief about this.'

'Yeah, me too,' said Darling, then turned back to Slater. 'Anyway, who's this Bradshaw bloke?'

'Why? What about him?' asked Slater.

'He's my boss,' chipped in Watson. 'Why? What's he done?'

'Apparently, he called her up and told her she wasn't to interfere with what's going on here.'

'Oh, my,' said Watson.

'Oh, crap!' said Slater. 'That's all I need.'

'Apoplectic would be the best word to describe her mood yesterday afternoon after she finished speaking to him,' said Darling. 'I found it in the thesaurus when I got home yesterday. It means—'

'Overcome with a furious anger,' finished Slater.

'Oh, you know it, then?' she asked.

'I know *her*,' said Slater, with a grim smile. 'To know one is to know the other!'

Their conversation was interrupted by a shout from one of the diggers.

'I think I've got something over here. It looks like a bone!'

'Right, stop digging,' called Darling. 'Clear the site. We're going to have to get the forensic pathology people down here.'

She turned to Slater and Norman and Watson. 'I'm going to have to call DS Bighead, and I can't see the Black Witch staying away much longer. Do you want to stay? We've got very specific orders regarding calling the forensic pathology people, so there's no need to stay, if you don't want to.'

'Yeah, I can pass on seeing her,' said Norman. 'And you'll be like the red rag to her bull, Dave. C'mon, let's go and have some breakfast. They can let us know what they find.'

CHAPTER TWENTY-FOUR

If there was one thing Jenny Radstock really loved, it was a nice hot shower followed by a long soak in a hot bath. After spending several months living on the street, where getting access to a shower was almost impossible, she was still making the most of the opportunity she now had to shower and bath as often as she wanted to, and this morning she was finding it particularly relaxing.

She still couldn't quite believe how lucky she was to have stumbled across Dave Slater when she had just about reached the end of her tether. Why he hadn't turned his back on her when so many others had she couldn't say, but once he had recognised her and learnt about her fall from grace, he had had no hesitation in offering her his spare room, and thus had begun her journey back to good health and fitness.

That had been almost eight weeks ago, and she thought it was no coincidence that the speed of her recovery had gone hand in hand with the deepening of their relationship. Indeed, the spare room was only used for storage these days. She couldn't remember exactly when she had started sharing Slater's bed, but she was glad it had happened. Being with him felt safe and in fact, since she had been with him, she hadn't seen any sign of the people who had spent so long harassing her, they had almost destroyed her.

She had originally intended to seek revenge, but now she was beginning to enjoy her new life, she wasn't sure she really wanted to stir that all up again. Her life now was stress-free, and feeling loved was a new experience she had quickly become used to. She had no desire to be a kept woman and had every intention of finding a job so she could contribute her fair share, but the longer it went on, the less she felt the need to go back to the stresses of her old life. Maybe it was time for a change.

Her thoughts were interrupted briefly by what she thought was a sound downstairs, but when she listened more closely, she couldn't hear anything. She thought it was amazing how paranoid she had become during her time on the street, but when you were being persecuted that's what happened — it rather went with the territory, and it wasn't an easy thing to shake off.

It was probably time to get out of the bath, but first she took a deep breath and slipped under the water, where she lay for about thirty seconds. Then she resurfaced, took a deep breath, ran her hands through her hair to remove the excess water, stood up, and stepped from the bath. As she reached for a towel, she thought she heard something downstairs again.

It was her imagination playing tricks on her, of course; she knew it was. Dave had gone to work, and the front and back doors were locked, as he insisted they had to be if she was in the house on her own, so there *couldn't* be anyone else in the house. But even so, she felt compelled to tiptoe across to the door and have a peep.

As she eased the door open just an inch or so, she felt a small rush of smoky air, which made her cough and splutter as she breathed it in. She looked towards where the stairs should be, but all she could see was a thick grey haze. Then there was a brief burst of colour behind it. It all happened so fast it was instinct, not rational thought, that made her slam the door and take a step back.

'Oh my God!' she said aloud. 'The house is on fire!'

For maybe ten or fifteen seconds she stood statue-like as panic threatened to engulf her, but Jenny was a survivor, and through sheer force of will, she managed to regain control of her thoughts. It had looked as though there were flames at the foot of the stairs, so there was going to be no escape that way. She looked to the bathroom window, but even her slim figure wasn't going to slip through the small opening at the top.

'Come on, think, Jenny, think!'

Then it came to her. If she could reach the spare room, she could possibly escape through that window. It might be her only chance. She slipped on her dressing gown, then snatched up her mobile phone and stuffed it into the pocket. She could worry about calling for help when she had escaped. She quickly dampened a towel and slipped it over her head, then, taking several deep breaths, she opened the door and fled across the small landing through the thickening smoke. As she ran, she felt the heat from the fire downstairs, and she was sure she could hear crackling sounds as it took hold.

She barged open the spare room door, slammed it behind her, rushed to the window, and looked down. Dave had recently suggested it would be good for both of them if they took up cycling, and although he hadn't actually got round to buying the bikes yet, he *had* bought a shed to store them. As luck would have it, the only place he could put the shed had been at the back of the house under the spare room window. It meant she had to drop onto the apex of the shed roof, but it was better than dropping all the way to the ground. Besides, it was her only option.

She threw the window open and eased herself over the edge, reaching for the roof with her feet, but when she looked down, she could see she was a couple of feet short. Then a loud crash from inside the house made her mind up for her and she let go of the window ledge and braced herself. Her right foot made the first contact with the roof, just to one side of the apex. She lost her balance and toppled spectacularly from the roof, landing on top of a couple of small shrubs, which were just enough to break her fall.

She was winded, and knew she would have a few bruises, but she was otherwise unhurt and, more importantly, she was alive. She scrambled to her feet and sprinted away from the house. Then she dragged the mobile phone from her pocket . . .

CHAPTER TWENTY-FIVE

Slater, Norman and Watson were sitting at a table in the pub where they served an all-day breakfast. They had just decided what they wanted to eat, and Slater had been volunteered to go up to the bar and place the order. He had no doubt he was also going to be manoeuvred into paying. He had hung his jacket on the back of the chair next to Watson's, and just as he got up from the table, his mobile phone began to ring deep in one of his pockets.

'Aren't you going to answer that?' asked Norman.

'I'm just going up to order the breakfasts. If it's important, they'll leave a message.'

As if the caller had heard him, the phone stopped ringing.

'There you go, you see? It can't have been important, can it?'

No sooner had he begun to walk away than it began to ring again. He turned to them as he walked.

'Could you get that for me please, Watson? Tell whoever it is I'll call them back.'

He walked over to the bar, leaving Watson to answer the phone. As he waited for someone to take his order, he amused himself by counting all the different brands of bottled cider he could see on the shelves behind the bar.

'Sir', said Watson, rushing over and offering Slater his phone, 'it's someone called Jenny.'

'Can you tell her I'll call her back?'

'I think you should take it now.'

Slater turned, irritated. 'But we're busy here, and—' Then he caught the expression on her face. He grabbed the phone.

'Jen? What's up?'

He listened.

'Fire service? Whoa, now slow down,' he said, patiently. 'You're not making any sense. Why did you need to call the fire service? It's *what*? Christ! Okay. I'm on my way.'

He handed the phone back to Watson. 'Here, keep her talking, and calm her down, can you? I've got to go.'

He rushed for his jacket, as a bewildered Watson started talking on the phone. 'Hello, Jenny? You don't know me, my name's Watson.'

'My bloody house is on fire!' Slater said to Norman as he headed for the door.

'Wait!' yelled Norman, 'I'll come with you!' He looked up to see a puzzled Watson, who had come back to their table. She looked at him and then at the phone and shrugged her shoulders.

'She seems to have hung up.'

'Let me take that phone,' Norman said. 'I'll see if I can call her back.'

She gave him the phone and he rushed after Slater, who barely gave him time to get inside the car before he screeched away, leaving a trail of rubber to mark his path.

'What the hell's happened?' asked Norman, pressing buttons on the phone.

'Dunno,' said Slater. 'She was near hysterical. All I know is the bloody house is on fire!'

'Christ! Is she okay?'

'I think so. She didn't actually say, but I think so. I certainly bloody hope so.'

Norman knew just how attached Slater and Jenny had become, and knew his friend's concern was for her, not for his house.

'It'll be okay,' he said, hoping he sounded more convincing than he felt. 'She's probably still jumpy, right? Maybe it's just a smoke alarm and she's overreacted.'

'Jeez, Norm, I hope you're right, mate, I really hope you're right.'

By the time they reached Slater's house, the fire was out, but wispy threads of black smoke could be seen curling from the upstairs windows, one of which seemed to have shattered from the heat, and it was obvious from the soot-blackened state of both windows that the damage inside was pretty extensive. Two fire engines were parked in the road outside the house, with an ambulance in attendance just behind them. A paramedic was tending to a young woman in a dressing gown sitting on the back step of the vehicle, a thin fleece blanket around her shoulders. Slater could see it was Jenny and headed straight for her.

'Is she hurt?' he asked the paramedic as he approached.

'She's had a nasty shock,' he said, looking up at Slater. 'But then so would anyone if they got out of the bath and found their house was on fire. Who are you, her husband?'

'Err, partner,' said Slater, not wanting to get into long-winded explanations.

Jenny suddenly seemed to notice him and immediately burst into tears. She jumped up and threw herself into his arms.

'I'm so sorry,' she wailed. 'One minute I was having a soak in the bath, and the next thing I knew, the house was on fire.'

'It's okay,' he said, stroking her hair. 'As long as you're okay. That's all that matters.'

She was sobbing her heart out now, clinging to him so tightly he could hardly breath. He just held her close and continued to stroke her hair.

'You sure she's okay, mate?' he asked the paramedic again.

'Yeah, it's just shock. Physically, she's fine apart from a few bruises,' he said. 'It's lucky she had her wits about her and was prepared to climb out of the window, or it might have been a different story.'

Slater looked back at his house. There was a night, many months ago now, when he'd watched helplessly as flames had engulfed Norman's flat. Now it seemed it was his turn.

'Is she okay?' asked Norman, putting a hand on his shoulder. He had been speaking to one of the fire officers.

'Paramedic says it's just shock.'

'Well, thank the lord for small mercies,' said Norman. 'You might want to have a chat with that fire service guy over there with the white helmet.'

'Who?' asked Slater.

'Eddie Brent, he says he knows you.'

'Isn't he the guy who did the investigation work when your flat burnt down?'

'That's him,' said Norman. 'I think you should have a chat. I can look after Jenny for a few minutes.'

Slater looked down at Jenny. She was still clinging to him, but at least now the sobbing had subsided.

'Jen?' he said. Gently, he placed a finger under her chin and raised her tear-stained face, but she couldn't look at him. 'I've just got to go and speak to the fire service. I'll only be a couple of minutes. Norm will look after you. Okay?'

She sniffed and nodded, but still avoided his gaze. 'I'm so sorry—'

He pulled her to him and tucked her head under his chin. 'Hey, come on, hush now,' he said, gently. 'It's okay. It's just a house.' As he said it, he realised it probably sounded quite absurd, but right at that moment he really meant it. She was all that mattered.

'Hey, come here, good looking,' said Norman, placing his hands on her shoulders, and turning her around. He fished a clean handkerchief from his pocket. 'Here, let me dry some of those tears and clean you up a bit. You go on,' he said to Slater. 'Jenny'll be okay with me for a few minutes, won't you, Jen?' She nodded slowly, and tried a smile, but it was no good and she began sobbing again.

Slater wasn't sure if he should leave her, but Norman enveloped her in his big arms and nodded at him over her shoulder.

'Go on,' he said. 'I'll look after her.'

'Bloody hell,' said Eddie Brent as Slater walked over to him. 'So it really *is* your house. What is it with you guys?'

'We're just lucky, I guess,' said Slater.

'Who have you pissed off this time?'

'D'you think it was deliberate?' asked Slater.

'It's too soon to say. Statistics say it's probably an accident that started in the kitchen, but I can't say for sure until I've had a chance to look around inside.'

'Any ideas?'

'Like I said, we need to do a proper investigation, but I can tell you it definitely started downstairs. The problem is the downstairs windows were wide open, and so was one of the bedroom windows, so once it started there was a good through draught fanning the flames, and it quickly turned into an inferno.' He nodded his head in the general direction of Norman and Jenny. 'Is the young lady your girlfriend?'

'Yeah, something like that,' said Slater.

'Well, she's a lucky girl,' said Brent.

'And you say all the downstairs windows were open?'

'You can see for yourself,' said Brent, nodding towards the house. 'We didn't open them, that's how they were when we arrived.'

'Really?' said Slater, puzzled.

'Sorry if it's not what you want to hear, but perhaps your girlfriend left them open.'

'That's not like her.'

'It happens,' said Brent, then he seemed to realise his opinion, honest as it may be, wasn't helping the situation. 'That's probably not much help, is it? But I can only guess at the moment. If you let me have your phone number, I'll give you a call when I've got something definite to tell you.'

'I'd really appreciate it if you could,' said Slater. He fished in his pocket and found a card. 'Here you go.'

Brent took the card without looking at it and slipped it into his pocket. 'I'll be in touch.'

'Right, thanks,' said Slater. 'I don't suppose there's anything left inside to rescue?'

'I can't let anyone go inside. We're not even sure if it's safe yet.'

'What about the neighbouring houses?' asked Slater.

'We seem to have got here in time to stop it spreading,' said Brent. 'So hopefully they won't have suffered any serious damage. We're trying to contact the owners so they can come home and open up for us. I'll feel happier when I've had a look inside the houses adjoining yours, especially up in the roof spaces.'

'Right,' said Slater, gloomily. 'Is there anything I can do now?'

Brent gave him a rueful smile. 'Call your insurance company? Oh, and you'd better find somewhere to stay for a while.'

'Bloody hell, yeah,' said Slater. 'I hadn't even thought about that!'

'Good luck,' said Brent. 'I'll call you as soon as I have some news.'

Slater walked back to Norman and Jenny.

'Come on,' said Norman, handing Jenny over to Slater. 'There's not much we can do here, is there?'

'No, I guess not.' Slater put his arm around the inconsolable Jenny and they began to walk towards his car.

'I'll drive,' said Norman. 'I think you probably need to sit in the back with Jenny. I think she needs someone to hold her.'

He ushered Slater and Jenny into the back seat of the car, then mumbled something about needing to make a call. When he climbed into the driver's seat a couple of minutes later, he turned to Slater.

'There's an empty room next to mine at the pub,' he said. 'My landlord says you can have it for as long as you want.'

CHAPTER TWENTY-SIX

Norman made sure the drive back was considerably more sedate than the frantic white-knuckle ride he had endured earlier. He totally understood why Slater had been driving that way, but even so, he had closed his eyes and prayed more than once on that journey. As he drove now, he couldn't stop himself from taking an occasional surreptitious glance in the mirror at his passengers on the back seat. He couldn't recall ever seeing Slater show so much concern for another person.

He took them straight back to the pub where he lived, collected the key from the landlord, and led them upstairs to their room. The paramedic had given Jenny a sedative, so Slater put her to bed and then went across the landing to Norman's room.

'So, what happened back there?' Norman asked.

'I'm not sure,' said Slater. 'Eddie says he thinks the fire probably started in the kitchen. The downstairs windows were open so the fire spread quick.'

'And he knows this for sure?'

'No. It's his best guess based on statistics. He wouldn't commit to anything without having a good look inside.'

'You don't think Jenny left those windows open?'

'I dunno,' said Slater. 'I know she likes to have the bedroom window open, but I can't believe she had all the downstairs windows open. We make a point of keeping those closed and the doors locked, just in case anyone is still looking for her.'

'D'you think that's what's happened? Has someone found her and decided to take care of her for good?'

'At the moment, I'm trying to believe it's just an unfortunate accident,' said Slater. 'I don't want to jump to any conclusions about what happened, but I'm finding it hard not to.'

'But if you're right about the windows, this definitely wasn't an accident.'

'But that means they know where she is, right? If that's the case, wouldn't it be easier to get to her when we're out running?'

'Yeah,' agreed Norman, 'but that would involve you too, and maybe they don't want to involve anyone else.'

'They've just burnt my bloody house down!' said Slater, testily. 'I think that sort of involves me, don't you?'

'Well, yeah, when you put it like that, sure it does. But what I mean is, if they had really wanted to hurt you as well, they could have burnt the house down at night with the two of you inside, but they chose not to.'

'She didn't think she was in danger any more. Her argument was that if they knew where she was, they would have got to her by now. I was going to get her a key cut today so she could come and go whenever she wanted. She says she feels like a prisoner.'

'I suppose she has a point,' said Norman.

Slater sighed. 'Yeah, I know, I just don't want her getting hurt.'

'You can't keep her in a cage forever, you know. She's a—'

'I know what you're going to say,' said Slater. 'She's a strong-minded, independent woman who can look after herself. Can you imagine how many times she's told me that over the last couple of weeks?'

'Well, if she keeps telling you, maybe she has a point,' said Norman.

'Yeah, maybe, but don't forget it was being strong-minded and independent that got her into this mess!'

'And you told her so? Jeez, I bet she loved hearing that!'

Slater looked suitably guilty.

'Anyway,' said Norman, 'that's all for you and her to discuss. What bothers me is what happened this morning and why.'

'At the moment, it's just an unfortunate accident.'

'Except you don't think she left those windows open?'

'I'm not going to ask her while she's still upset.'

'I'm not suggesting you do,' said Norman. 'What I'm suggesting is we discount the accident theory and consider the alternatives, such as maybe it's your turn to experience what happens when you upset a Serbian gangster.'

Slater considered this for a moment. 'But the guy who torched your place watched and waited until he knew you were out. He made sure there was no one inside.'

'Maybe he watched you leave and didn't know Jenny was in there?'

'You don't really think they still have a grudge against us, do you? I mean that was well over a year ago. Why come back and start it all up again now?'

'I don't have any answers,' said Norman. 'I'm just exploring theories. Anyway, if you dismiss that possibility and it's not an accident, there are only two other alternatives. Either someone started the fire knowing Jenny was upstairs and she was the target, or someone started the fire to get you for Stevie Scanlon. Out of all those, I think I'd prefer it to be my first suggestion, or, better still, that it really was an accident.'

Slater put his hands to his face and rubbed hard. 'I can't think about this now. It's a bloody nightmare, and it's making my head ache.'

Norman looked at his friend. He certainly looked a little rough around the edges.

'You know, I think you're probably right. We might be wasting all this time on speculation when it was just a silly accident. Let's wait until we get some news. In the meantime, my stomach is telling me I missed breakfast and I really do need to eat. Do you want to come downstairs?'

'I'm going to pass, if you don't mind, Norm. I'm not really hungry, and I need to make some phone calls.'

'I understand,' said Norman. 'Finding your home burnt down does tend to spoil your appetite. I'll be back in a while.'

He made his way quietly from the room, leaving a rather dazed-looking Slater with some space and time alone to sort out his thoughts.

* * *

It was four thirty that afternoon. Slater was sitting on the bed next to Jenny, holding her in his arms again.

She looked up at him, her face pale and anxious. 'Can I ask you something?'

'Sure,' he said, and her head tucked under his chin once again. 'Ask away.'

'Are you going to ask me to leave now?'

'Why would I do that?'

'Because I'm nothing but bad news. I don't contribute anything, and now I've even burnt your house down.'

'Well, yeah, I suppose there is that,' he said, matter-of-factly. 'And, worst of all, you *did* push me into a hedge the other morning.'

This clearly wasn't quite the response she had expected. 'I mean it,' she said, seriously. 'I really think I should go.'

'And where exactly are you going to go?'

It seemed bizarre to be having this conversation while she was holding him like this and he was stroking her hair.

'I don't know. I just don't think this situation is fair on you.'

'I seem to recall it was my choice, wasn't it?'

'Yes, but—'

'I mean, you didn't force me to get involved, did you? And if I chose to get involved, surely it's up to me when my involvement ends, isn't it.'

'Is that a question?'

'No, it's a statement of intent.'

She looked up at him, or at least at the underside of his chin. He leaned back, looked down into her eyes, and held her gaze.

'You don't need to go anywhere,' he said.

'I'll be fine.'

'I don't believe that any more than you do. The time to go is when your confidence is at its peak, not when you're down in a trough.'

He was still holding her gaze, but she didn't look away.

'We both know I'm right,' he said. 'If you really feel you want to go, you can go as soon as you're ready to face the world, and when that time comes I'll give you my blessing if it's what you really want to do, but in the meantime, I think you should stay, and you can stay as long as you like.'

She looked down and rested her head on his chest for a moment.

'In that case,' she said, looking up again, 'can I ask another question? Well, it's two questions actually.'

He sighed a big, exaggerated sigh. 'Jesus,' he said, still gazing into her eyes. 'All these questions. It's like an interrogation. Go on then.'

'If I stay, can I have something to do? And I don't mean cooking and cleaning. I don't mind doing that, but I need to do something constructive and to feel as though I'm putting something in as well as taking out. Besides, if we're going to live here in just one room, even if it's only for a few days, I think I might go mad.'

He pursed his lips as he considered her suggestion. 'Yep. I can understand that,' he said.

'So?'

'We'll find something. I promise we will.'

He waited for the second question. 'What was the other question?' he asked when it seemed she had forgotten.

She had been dozing, and suddenly started when he spoke. 'Sorry?'

'You had another question.'

'Did I? Oh, yes, I don't understand why you're so calm about all this. Your house burnt down this morning, yet you're so calm. How come? I'd be going spare!'

He smiled. 'I've had my eyes opened a lot recently. First, I was in Thailand and met my dad, then I watched him die, then I came back and got involved in the homeless shelter, and then I found you again. It's made me realise what's really important. Like I said before, it's only a house. Once I got there this morning and knew you were safe, the house didn't really seem to matter. It's not the end of the world, is it?'

'You're weird, David Slater, do you know that?'

He shrugged his shoulders. 'It beats being boring, doesn't it?'

'Mmm, it certainly do . . .' She was asleep before she finished the sentence.

Slater carefully took his arm from around her and pulled the duvet up to keep her warm. Then he slipped his shoes back on and made his way out of the room. More sleep wouldn't do her any harm. As he made his way down the stairs and into the bar to join Norman, his mobile phone began to ring.

'Oh, hi Eddie, thanks for calling. Have you found out what caused the fire?'

'You didn't tell me you weren't working for the police any more.'

'It's true I'm no longer with the police, and yes, I didn't tell you,' admitted Slater, 'but does it matter?'

'I shouldn't really be talking to you.'

'But it's my house that burnt down!' argued Slater, quite reasonably. 'Surely I have a right to know what you're going to tell my insurance company?'

There was a long pause, and Slater began to think there was something wrong with his phone. He took it from his ear, looked accusingly at it, realised how stupid that was, and then tried speaking into it.

'Hello? Eddie? Are you still there?'

'Yes, I'm still here. I'm just trying to decide what to do.'

'What's that supposed to mean?'

'Can you get over here?' asked Brent.

'I can meet you at the house if you like.'

Slater became aware of an awkward hesitation before Brent replied. 'Err, no, I can't do that. I think it will be better if you come here,' he said, finally.

'Can't do it, or won't do it?' asked Slater. 'Is there some sort of problem?'

'We can talk about it when you get here—'

'There is, isn't there?' insisted Slater.

'I'm not discussing this over the phone,' said Brent, before adding, 'and I suggest you need to get here sooner rather than later.'

'Yeah, but—' began Slater, but Brent had hung up. He gave the phone another accusing look.

'What's up?' asked Norman, who had been unable to avoid hearing Slater's end of the conversation.

'That was Eddie Brent.'

'What's he saying?'

'I dunno, he says he won't talk to me over the phone, and he won't meet me at the house. I have to go to him.'

Norman's expression reflected Slater's ominous feeling.

'Ah right, I see what you mean. That doesn't sound so good. D'you want me to come with you?'

'Would you stay here in case Jenny wakes up? Whatever this is, it's my problem and I have to deal with it.'

'Okay, but if you need me you only have to shout, right?'

CHAPTER TWENTY-SEVEN

'Before I tell you anything, I need you to know I'm not obliged to do this, and I'm doing it as a favour,' said Brent.

'Jesus, Eddie, this is all a bit cloak and dagger, isn't it?' asked Slater. 'It is *my* house we're talking about.'

'Yes, well, the thing is, I should really go straight to the police.'

'Why do the police need to be involve— Wait a minute! Are you telling me this wasn't an accident?'

Brent's look confirmed Slater's suspicions.

'But you said it was a kitchen fire, right?'

'I'm sorry,' said Brent, 'but I did tell you that was just a guess based on statistics. My job is a bit like yours. When I've gathered all the evidence, I have to take a good look at what I've got and ask myself a few questions.'

'What questions?'

'Well, in this case, I have to ask myself: was it an accident every ring on the hob and the grill were on full blast? Was it an accident cooking oil was poured all over the hob? Was it an accident there are traces of an accelerant around the cooker? Was it an accident newspaper had been stuffed in the grill? Was it an accident all the downstairs windows were left open to provide plenty of airflow to fan the flames?'

Slater couldn't quite make sense of what he was hearing. 'You're kidding me, right?' he asked, foolishly.

'I never joke about arson,' replied Brent, solemnly. 'If someone hadn't called nine nine nine when they did, your house would have been destroyed along with every other house in that row.'

'But Jenny said she was only in the bathroom for half an hour . . . '

'How well do you know Jenny?' asked Brent suddenly.

'What? You're not suggesting she started the fire, are you? Why the hell would she set fire to the only place she can call home?'

'Is she worried about anything?'

'She's not bloody suicidal if that's what you mean,' said Slater. 'That's a ridiculous idea! And anyway, if that was her intention, why did she jump out of the window?'

Brent shrugged. 'Maybe what she's telling you is bullshit. Can she prove any of it?'

'Does she need to?'

'She might have to when I go to the police.'

'Whoa,' said Slater. 'Now hang on a minute. You can't just go accusing her like that. Christ, she used to be a barrister.'

'Harold Shipman was a doctor,' replied Brent.

'What's that supposed to mean?' demanded Slater angrily. 'He was a bloody serial killer!'

Brent held his hands up. 'I'm sorry if that offends you, but I wasn't trying to compare them. All I was trying to suggest is someone's position in society doesn't necessarily make them incapable of committing a crime.'

Slater was struggling with this undeniable truth. Deep inside, he knew he couldn't argue with what Brent had just said. He also knew he needed to calm down, because getting angry wasn't going to solve anything. The poor guy was just doing his job, and the fact was, he didn't have to tell Slater any of this before he went to the police. Maybe he could stall for time.

'I'm sorry,' he said, 'but I just can't believe Jenny would do this. Do you really have to go to the police?'

Brent sighed. 'You know how it works. If I find something suspicious I have to report it.'

'How sure are you?'

'I have absolutely no doubt this was arson. I'm sorry, but I can't ignore that.'

'But why would she want to burn my bloody house down?' asked Slater.

'That's where the police come into it,' said Brent. 'I just hand over my findings. It's up to them to work out who did it — and why they did it.'

For a moment, Slater wasn't sure if Brent was being patronising.

'Yeah, actually, I *do* know how it works,' he said.

'Yes, I know you do,' said Brent. 'So you should know I have no choice about what I have to do next.'

'How about if I ask you to give me forty-eight hours before you report it?'

'Now *you're* kidding *me*, aren't you?'

'Do you always report your findings this quickly? I mean what's the rush? No one died.'

'It depends how busy I am.'

'Aw, c'mon, Eddie,' pleaded Slater. 'Jenny's had enough shit over the past couple of years. I know she didn't do this, but I also know she won't stand a chance if the police think she's involved. This could be the final straw for her. Do you really want that on your conscience?'

'What do you mean the final straw?'

'It's a long story,' said Slater, 'and I don't know it all yet. In fact I've barely scratched the surface.'

'How do I know you won't spirit her away?'

'You don't,' said Slater, 'but trust me, if I think she's set fire to my house, I'll be taking her to the police station myself.'

Brent thought about it, but not for long. 'You've got until Monday morning,' he said, walking across to his desk. He picked up a slim folder and handed it to Slater.

'What's this?'

'It's a copy of my report. I can't imagine how you managed to get hold of it.'

'Wow! Thanks, Eddie.'

'I'll be going to the police on Monday morning. Understand?'

'Perfectly.'

'Just remember the first thing I'm going to have to do is explain why I didn't notify them sooner.'

'What will you tell them?'

'I haven't a clue, but I expect I'll think of something.'

'Thanks, Eddie, you're a mate.'

'I am at the moment,' said Brent, 'so I'd be grateful if you just make sure I don't have reason to stop being one.'

* * *

'Did she ask where I was?' asked Slater as he slipped back into Norman's room.

'As far as I know, she's still asleep,' said Norman. 'I didn't see any point in disturbing her for no good reason.'

'Good,' said Slater, and he wiped a weary hand across his forehead.

'Okay, let's hear it,' said Norman.

Slater gave him an enquiring look.

'He wouldn't have asked you to go all the way over there if he had good news,' said Norman. 'And I've known you long enough to know you're not happy about what he's told you.'

'He says it was arson,' said Slater indignantly, tossing the report down on Norman's bed. 'Some bastard set fire to my house!'

'Holy crap,' said Norman. 'Welcome to the club! So is there anyone, apart from Scanlon, who you've pissed off so much they'd want to torch your house?'

'His prime suspect is Jenny.'

Norman gaped at him. 'No way. That's absurd! What makes him think that?'

'He says every hob ring was switched on, and then oil was poured all over it. The grill was stuffed with newspaper and then turned on, and then all the downstairs windows were left open so there would be plenty of through draught to make sure the fire spread really quickly once it got going. Oh, and he also found traces of accelerant, probably petrol.'

'So how does that prove it was her?'

'His theory is it was an inside job.'

'Why would she burn down what was her home too?' asked Norman.

'Yeah, those are the same questions I came up with,' said Slater. 'It makes no sense, does it? It's not as if she's an attention-seeker, either. Becoming the centre of attention in a police inquiry is the last thing she needs.'

'What are we going to do?'

'This isn't your problem, Norm.'

'Of course, it is. We're best mates, aren't we?'

'Well, yeah, but—'

'Never mind, well, yeah, but,' said Norman. 'Just tell me where you want to start.'

'I'm going to have to ask Jenny some awkward questions.'

'Would you prefer if I did it?' asked Norman.

Slater smiled ruefully. 'Thanks, Norm, I really appreciate the offer, but I think this is something I have to do.'

'Should I sit in?'

'I think that might come across as a bit intimidating. I think it might be better if you stay out of it, then if I make a mess of it, maybe you can try to pick up the pieces.'

Norman smiled. 'You mean you want me to be the good cop?'

Now Slater managed a smile. 'She might storm out if she thinks I'm accusing her,' he said, remembering how hot-headed she could be. 'Then again, she might just start throwing stuff at me.'

Norman smirked. 'Should we clear the room before you start talking? She can't throw what isn't there.'

'But then she might beat the crap out of me instead,' said Slater. 'I think I'll take my chances with missiles. At least I might be able to avoid those.'

'Whatever you say,' said Norman, settling on the bed and picking up the report Slater had left there. 'Just leave my door open so I can hear you scream.'

Slater sighed. He left Norman's door ajar, crossed the corridor, and quietly opened the door to his own room. Jenny peered, bleary-eyed, at him.

'Hi,' he said. 'How are you?'

'Sore,' she said, 'but I'll live.'

'I need to ask you a couple of questions,' he said. 'Can I come and sit down?'

She sat up and shuffled across the bed so he could sit on the edge next to her. She looked enquiringly at him.

'Is this like an interview?'

Slater was beginning to feel uncomfortable. He could almost see a barrier going up around her, and he hadn't even started yet.

'No, of course not,' he said.

'Well, go on then,' she said, the challenge clear in her tone. 'Ask away.'

'I've been out to see the fire service investigator who's been examining what's left of the house,' he said.

She didn't say a word, but her expression told him everything he needed to know as her lips tightened and became so thin they almost disappeared. Then, very slowly, and deliberately, she folded her arms. Slater felt a sinking feeling. Now the castle walls had been completed, and the drawbridge had been raised as well.

'It started in the kitchen,' he explained, 'but because the windows were left open downstairs, and our bedroom window was open, it spread really quickly.'

'What happened? How did it start?'

'The cooker.'

'Look,' she said, finally. 'If it was my fault, I'm sorry, but it was an accident. I would never—' She stopped for a split second as his words sunk in. 'But I didn't use the cooker this morning. I didn't even use the kettle to make a cup of tea.'

'It wasn't an accident. He's absolutely certain of that. Whoever started the fire loaded the grill with paper, poured oil and petrol all over the hob, turned them all on full blast, and then opened all the windows to make sure there was a good draught to get the fire going.'

Her eyes blazed with a fierce intensity, and suddenly she was full of animation, arms waving everywhere. 'Are you suggesting I did this?'

'That's no—' he began, but she was in no mood to listen.

'How bloody stupid would I have to be to set fire to the only home I have? And why would I do that to you after you've been so kind to me? What sort of person do you think I am?'

'If you'd ju—'

But now she was in full flow, and he had no chance of being heard. 'Go on, tell me!' she yelled at the top of her voice. 'Why would I do it? What possible reason could I have?'

Finally silent, she sat back, re-folded her arms, and glared at him with a fierce intensity. At that moment, there was a knock on the door and Norman peered into the room. The fierce glare was immediately aimed in his direction.

'Are you two okay in here? Only it sounds a bit heated,' asked Norman, innocently.

'Oh yes,' she said bitterly. 'Do come in and finish the interview. I suppose you must be the good cop, because it can't be him.' She jerked her head in Slater's direction.

Norman stepped into the room and raised his hands in surrender. 'I may be speaking out of turn here, Jenny,' he said, 'but I can assure you we're both on your side, especially him.' He nodded his head at Slater. 'I think maybe you need to listen to what he has to say before you condemn him.'

Slater wondered if perhaps Norman had some sort of death wish, and he held his breath in anticipation, but to his surprise, Jenny didn't seem to have a response. After a few seconds, satisfied he now might be given a chance to speak without being shouted down, he thought he'd give it a try.

'I didn't say you started the fire,' he began. 'I'm just telling you what the investigator guy told me.'

'So *he* thinks I started the fire!' she snapped.

'He doesn't have an opinion about that. All he does is investigate what caused the fire. It's not his job to work out who did it. He will report his findings to the police, and it's up to them to investigate. You were in the legal system; you know how it works.'

Now her face fell as she realised the possible implications. 'Oh great! They'll be all over me like a bloody rash,' she said. 'This is some sort of setup to get me into even more trouble, isn't it? I knew I should have stayed on the street. I was safe there.'

'Well, pardon me for trying to help you out and putting a roof over your head,' said Slater, huffily.

Norman clapped his hands loudly. 'Now wait, wait, wait!' he cried. 'Listen to the two of you. Can we all just calm down and start behaving like adults? Jenny, listen to me. No one is accusing you of anything, and neither of us think you started the fire, but we need to try and work out what happened, then if anyone does accuse you, we're ready to prove you didn't.'

'Well, you'd better be bloody quick,' she said. 'Because once that fire investigation guy gets to the police, they'll be down here like a shot. I bet they'll be here any minute.'

'We've got until Monday morning,' said Slater. Both Norman and Jenny turned to look at him.

'Pardon?'

'He agreed to hold on to his report until Monday morning.'

Norman grinned. At least they had a little time.

'It's true, isn't it?' said Jenny. 'This is all my fault. Someone's burnt your house down to get at me!'

'We don't know that,' said Slater. 'If it was someone after you, why wait until now? You've been staying with me for weeks.'

'Yes, but I only started to leave the house a couple of weeks ago when we started jogging together in the mornings.'

'If they wanted to hurt you, I don't think they would have worried about me being in the way,' he said.

'But it's not an attempt to hurt me, is it?' she said. 'These people wouldn't risk murdering me so publicly. Someone must have been watching me. They've probably been watching for weeks and somehow figured out I'm in the habit of soaking in the bath every morning. They knew they had time to get in and start the fire. I think it's all designed to frame me. I'm going to be charged with arson, aren't I?'

'But how could they be sure you'd escape?' asked Slater. 'This wasn't an attempt to frame you. Starting a fire downstairs when you know someone is upstairs isn't an attempt to frame someone for arson, Jen, it's attempted murder!'

'Oh my God! You think they're trying to kill me now?' she cried.

'Now let's not get carried away,' said Norman. 'You're not the only one who's been a target, you know. It could be the same people who set fire to my flat. Maybe they thought it was time to come back and have a go at Dave. There's also the possibility it could be something to do with the case we're on. Have you thought of that?' He gave her a moment to consider this before he continued. 'No,' he said, 'of course not. You haven't considered any other possibility except it must be all about you, have you?'

Jenny looked suitably chastened. 'You'd think it, too, if you'd had the last two years I've had,' she said, sulkily.

'Yeah, well, we understand that,' said Slater, 'but until you actually tell us what's been going on, we can't help you out with that. We've had this discussion before.'

'Yes, all right, all right!' she snapped. 'I'm just not ready to—'

'Let's not get off the subject here,' said Norman. 'I realise you're both stressed after what happened, but can we try and remember we're all on the same side here. The clock's ticking and we need to establish exactly what happened.'

'Yeah, right,' said Slater, sheepishly. 'I'm sorry, Norm, you're right.' He turned to Jenny. 'Look, I'm sorry, okay? I didn't handle this very well, but it's not every day some arsehole burns my bloody house down and tries to kill my girlfriend!'

His face had turned a neat shade of beetroot red. Jenny was looking at him with a curious expression verging on a smile.

Norman grinned at both of them. 'I think that's what you call a Freudian slip,' he said. 'I think you two need to sort out exactly what your relationship is, but you can do it later. Right now, we need to get on with the matter in hand. Please.'

'Yeah, right,' said Slater. 'Jenny, talk us through what happened after I left for work.'

'Nothing,' she said. 'I did what I usually do once you've gone. I have a shower and then I ran a hot bath, climbed in, and soaked.'

'You didn't turn the cooker on and forget?' asked Norman.

'I promise you, I didn't even turn the kettle on this morning,' she said. 'Dave will tell you, I only drink cold water first thing.'

'Yeah, that's right,' said Slater.

'And I'm sure I checked the front door was locked before I went upstairs, and I certainly didn't open any windows downstairs.'

'What about the upstairs windows?' asked Norman.

'The spare room was closed,' said Slater, 'and the window in our room was open, but only the small one at the top.'

'According to the report, all the downstairs windows had been opened,' said Norman.

'Not by me,' said Jenny. 'They were all closed. It's too cold to have even one downstairs window open, never mind all of them.'

'That's what I figured.' Norman rubbed his chin thoughtfully.

'Anyway,' said Jenny, 'if I wanted the place to burn down, why would I have called nine nine nine?'

'You did?' asked Slater.

'Well, of course, I did, you silly arse! That's what you're supposed to do when your house is on fire, isn't it?'

'When did you do that?' asked Norman, trying to avert a full-blown argument. 'As soon as you saw the fire?'

'I got out first,' she said. 'Survival instinct, you know?'

'How long was it before they got there?' asked Norman.

She looked at him as if he was mad.

'Roughly,' pleaded Norman.

'God, I don't know, five minutes, maybe.'

'But it would have taken at least fifteen minutes from the time you called,' said Slater, puzzled. 'The call has to be transferred to the fire service, then the station has to be notified, and the crew has to assemble, and they have to make the journey . . . It's got to be about fifteen minutes in total. How did they get there so quick?'

'I don't know,' she said, angrily. 'They didn't tell me! I assume one of the neighbours had already called it in.'

'But they were all out. Remember? Eddie said they were trying to track everyone down so they could get into their houses.'

'Well, I don't know,' she said, exasperated. 'What difference does it make?'

'It might make a whole lot of difference,' said Norman.

Slater reached for his phone and started dialling.

'Is it important?' she asked Norman.

'Maybe,' he said.

'Eddie?' Slater was saying into the phone. 'It's Dave Slater. I'm sorry to call you, but it's important. According to your report, you say you estimate the fire had been burning for about fifteen minutes when you got there.'

'That's right,' said Brent. 'Another five or ten minutes and we would have been too late.'

'My guess is it would take you about fifteen minutes from the call being placed to you arriving at the house, is that right?'

'That would be about right,' agreed Brent.

'But Jenny says she didn't call nine nine nine until she had escaped from the house. The flames were already spreading up the stairs by then, so it must have been burning for a good few minutes.'

There was a short, pregnant pause before Brent replied, 'I see what you mean. She would have had to call almost as soon as the fire started.'

'Exactly,' said Slater. 'It doesn't add up, does it?'

'People often get these things wrong when they're in these situations,' said Brent. 'Panic can make time seem to fly by, or sometimes stop altogether.'

Slater couldn't understand Brent's reluctance to accept Jenny was telling the truth, but he resisted the urge to argue with him and asked a question instead. 'Can you do us a favour, Eddie? Can you find out who called nine nine nine to report my house fire, and at what time?'

'If you think it'll help,' said Brent, reluctantly.

'Jenny says she didn't call it in until she had escaped from the house,' said Slater patiently, 'and you arrived about five minutes after that. You've just confirmed that's not physically possible, haven't you? But it would be possible if someone else had already called it in about ten minutes before Jenny. That stuff's all logged, so it should be easy for you to check, right?'

'Ah! Now I see where you're going with this,' said Brent. 'Leave it with me. I'll get back to you later or tomorrow morning.'

'That's great. Thanks, Eddie,' said Slater.

'Have you finished interrogating me now?' Jenny asked Norman. 'Only I would like a shower, and then I need to get some clothes from somewhere.'

'Aw, come on,' said Norman. 'It wasn't that bad, and we had to find out the facts, right?'

'Hmmph!' was her response as she turned to see what Slater had to say.

'Eddie agrees with me about the timings,' said Slater as he put the phone down. 'And he agrees someone could have reported the fire before Jenny's call. He's going to get back to us as soon as he can.'

'Someone must have made an earlier call or it doesn't add up, does it?' asked Norman. 'Let's not count our chickens, but we just might have had a breakthrough.'

'I don't understand,' said Jenny.

'If someone had already called nine nine nine,' explained Slater, 'and it wasn't one of the neighbours, and it wasn't you, there's a good chance it could have been the person who started the fire.'

'Why would they do that if they wanted to kill me?'

'Maybe that wasn't the intention,' said Norman. 'Don't forget — we're only guessing at the moment. It could even be the case that whoever it was didn't even know you were in there. When they did my flat, they actually waited until I had left to make sure I didn't get hurt, and they called the fire service and set off the fire alarm so no one else got hurt either. It was all about doing just enough damage to send out a warning.'

'When you say it like that,' said Slater, thoughtfully, 'it sounds like a familiar scenario, doesn't it?'

'It's somewhere to start, I guess,' said Norman, 'but only if you assume they didn't know Jenny was there, and frankly that would surprise me because they certainly knew everything about us both the last time we met.'

'And why would they come after us now we're both out of the force?' added Slater.

'What if Goodnews has been poking her nose in and stirring things up again,' said Norman. 'She did it once before.'

Slater grimaced. Contacting Marion Goodnews was not something he wanted to do. When their brief affair had ended, she had refused to accept it, and he didn't know what sort of can of worms he might open if he contacted her now.

'We'll have some fun trying to prove *that*,' he said.

'Look, I know she's the last person you want to speak to,' said Norman, 'but we need to know. I'd ask her myself, but she wouldn't tell me if her life depended on it and you know it.'

Slater sighed. 'Yeah, I know. I'll give her a call tomorrow morning. But before we start worrying about a ghost from the past, I think we should confirm it wasn't a neighbour. I'll go and ask them all tonight.' He turned to Jenny. 'In the meantime, I'd better go and buy us both some new clothes while you take your shower.'

* * *

Half an hour later, Slater's phone began to ring.

'It's Eddie Brent,' said the voice in his ear. 'You were right about the nine nine nine calls. Jenny made her call at 10.17, but someone else had already called at 10.06. Our arrival was actually timed at 10.21.'

'Who was the first caller?' asked Slater, excited now.

'That would be too easy, wouldn't it?' said Brent.

'What, no name?'

'No name, and the voice is muffled, like they were talking through a scarf or something. They can't even tell me for sure if it's a man or a woman. I'm going down there tomorrow morning to have a listen myself to see what I can make of it.'

'Okay, Eddie, thanks for calling me back so soon.'

'It's fine,' said Brent. 'I'm as keen as you to find out what's going on now.'

CHAPTER TWENTY-EIGHT

It was nine thirty and pitch black. Slater had spoken to every neighbour but one. He had felt guilty talking to those either side of his house, but they were both very gracious about what had happened, assuring him that their houses were fine and there was nothing for him to feel guilty about. *These things happen*, they both assured him, and as long as he and Jenny were okay, that was all that mattered.

Now, as he walked away from them, he felt guilty he hadn't got to know them better. He made his way back to the one who had been out and was pleased to see there was a light on indoors. He rang the bell and waited. After a minute or so, the door opened to reveal a man of about thirty, clad in a dressing gown. He had a towel in his hands and his hair was wet.

He smiled at Slater. 'Sorry, I was in the shower.'

'No, don't apologise,' said Slater. 'I should be apologising for dragging you out of the shower at this time of night.'

'I just got home from work,' said the man. 'I had a crappy day and needed to wash it away.'

'The reason I'm calling,' explained Slater, 'is my house caught fire.' He waved an arm in the general direction of his own house. 'Lucky for me, someone called nine nine nine otherwise the whole row might have gone up. I'm trying to find out who it was so I can thank them.'

'Well, I would have if I'd been here,' said the man. 'What time did it start?'

'The fire service estimate it was a little after ten o'clock this morning,' said Slater.

'I'd just left for work. I'm on this weird ten thirty until eight thirty shift.'

'Oh well,' said Slater. 'I guess whoever it was wants to remain anonymous.'

'Is your girlfriend all right?' asked the man.

'Yeah, she had a lucky escape, but she's fine. Shaken but not stirred, as they say.'

'That's a relief, because she must have got home just before the fire started.'

'Got home?' asked Slater, nonplussed.

'Yeah, I don't think she noticed me,' said the man, 'but it was definitely her. I'd just got into my car when she jogged down the road to your house and let herself in. She runs a lot, right?'

'Err, yeah, that's right,' said Slater.

'Well, she'd been out for a run, I think. She was wearing her running gear anyway.'

'And this was about ten o'clock?' asked Slater.

'Must have been because the news had just started on the car radio as I drove off. Anyway, whatever, I'm glad she's okay.'

'Err, yeah, right,' said Slater.

'No problem,' said the man. 'And I'm sorry about your house.'

'Thank you, but these things happen, right?' said Slater, philosophically. 'I'd better not keep you from your shower any longer. Thanks for your time.'

As he walked back to his car, Slater was thinking about what he'd just heard. He wasn't best pleased to find Jenny had been going out running when he wasn't around. He had specifically asked her not to go out on her own, but then again, he knew she was beginning to feel like a prisoner. Could he really be angry with her for wanting to get out? She was an independent woman, what did he expect?

He was a bit miffed about her story though. If she *had* got home at ten, she could hardly claim to have had a shower and then soaked in the bath for twenty minutes before she became aware of the fire. Was she lying just so he wouldn't find out she had been out running on her own? Did she really think he was going to make that big a deal out of it? Or was she lying for another reason? But surely she wouldn't have started the fire, would she? And did this have any bearing on the 999 caller? Did Jenny start the fire and then have second thoughts? He couldn't believe she would do such a thing, but the seeds of doubt had been planted now.

* * *

When Slater got back to the pub, Norman was perched on a stool at the bar. 'Can I get you a pint?' he asked Slater.

'No thanks, mate, I'll go up and see if Jenny's all right.'

'Are you okay? Only you look like you've seen a ghost.'

'What? No, no, I'm fine, just a bit tired, you know?'

'How did it go with the neighbours?'

'No one was home when the fire started, and no one called nine nine nine.'

'Someone must have made that call.'

'Well, it wasn't one of my neighbours.'

'It looks like we have a mystery caller,' said Norman. 'That often means it's the person who started the fire, right?'

'It's a strong possibility,' admitted Slater, wondering if he should tell Norman what he'd heard about Jenny.

'Possibility?' echoed Norman. 'Who else would call, and not give a name?'

Slater shrugged. *Yes, who indeed?* he wondered.

'I'm sorry,' he said. 'I can't seem to think straight right now. I guess all the excitement must be catching up with me. I think I'm gonna have an early night.'

'You sure look knackered,' said Norman, 'but you've had a lot to deal with today. Try and get a good night's sleep. I'll see you in the morning.'

Slater made his way wearily up the stairs and into the room he was sharing with Jenny. She was sitting up in bed.

'How are you feeling?' he asked, sitting on the foot of the bed.

'I've been better,' she said, 'but I'm sure I'll survive. What about you? It can't be easy dealing with all this crap and finding you suddenly have nowhere to live.'

He showed her a mask of a smile. 'Yeah,' he said. 'Like you, I've had better days.'

'Norm said you'd gone to speak to some of your neighbours. Did you learn anything?'

'In a manner of speaking,' he said.

'What does that mean?'

'Well, I now know that none of my neighbours made the nine nine nine call,' he said.

'Yes, and?'

'Is there something you want to tell me?'

'About what?'

'About this morning.'

'I've told you what happened,' she said. 'You don't want me to go through it all again, do you?'

'And you didn't miss anything out?' he asked.

She studied his face for a few seconds and slowly folded her arms. 'Are you accusing me of something?'

He let out a long, heavy, sigh. 'You're not going to make this easy for me, are you?' he asked. 'I do understand why you do it, but I don't understand why you're denying it.'

'I'm not making it easy for you? Really?' she asked, her voice became more strident as she went on. 'Has it occurred to you that maybe I'm not making it easy for you because I don't know what the bloody hell you're talking about? What exactly do you understand?'

'I know you've been going out running while I'm out, without telling me,' he said.

'No, I bloody well have not!'

This wasn't quite the response Slater was expecting. *Why wouldn't she just admit it?* Then he had another thought. *Jesus, what else was she hiding?*

'Oh, come on, Jenny. Don't lie to me.'

'How dare you accuse me of lying to you! On my life, I have never lied to you, and I never would. After all you've done for me, do you really think I would repay you by telling you lies? Is that what you think of me?'

He looked at her sadly. 'But one of the neighbours saw you coming back home this morning at ten o'clock.'

'They did not!'

'He was sitting in his car just getting ready to leave for work. He knows it was you — he recognised your running gear.'

'I don't care if he was in your house,' she said, through gritted teeth. 'I swear to you he did not see me outside, in my running gear, at ten o'clock this morning. I was as naked as the day I was born, and I was in the bath.'

'So why does he think he saw you?' asked Slater, exasperated.

'I don't know,' she hissed. 'Why don't you go and ask him?'

'What?'

'You heard!' She threw the covers back, jumped out of bed, and started to put on the clothes he had bought her just a couple of hours ago.

'Yeah, but—'

'Look,' she snarled, 'I don't know what it is you think I've done, but what I do know is you seem to be trusting the word of someone you hardly know and using it against me. I can't believe you would do that, but here you are, bold as brass, accusing me of being a liar.'

'Yes, but—'

'I don't want to hear any lame excuses,' she snapped, so fiercely he took an involuntary step back. 'What I want you to do is go and see this guy and prove I'm telling the truth. I think that is the very least I deserve.'

'But it's ten o'clock!'

'I don't care if it's after midnight,' she said, adamantly. 'I'm not backing down. If this was a police investigation, you'd want more proof than the word of one witness. You'd make a real effort to make sure what he said was right. I'm asking you to make that effort for me. And then, when you've proved I'm telling the truth, you can come back and apologise.'

'Are you telling me you haven't been out running behind my back?' he asked.

'I think it's a bit too late to ask me that now, don't you? You've already made it perfectly clear you think I'm incapable of telling the truth, so you're not going to believe me if I deny it. No, the only way I can clear my name is by proving your *witness* is mistaken. If you won't go and speak to him again, I'll go myself. Is that what you want?'

'But he says he saw you run up to my front door and let yourself in.'

'How could I?' she asked, triumphantly. 'I don't have a bloody key, do I? That's why I keep asking for one!'

Slater went to open his mouth, but then realised the truth in what she had said. Now he was genuinely confused. Could she be telling the truth? He really didn't know what to think.

'Lost your tongue, now, have you?' she asked. 'Well, I suggest you find it pretty quickly because you're going to need it when you get to your neighbour's. The sooner you get there and learn the truth, the sooner you can stop treating me like a suspect.'

'I am not—'

'Oh yes you bloody well are,' she snapped, now fully dressed.

'Christ,' said Slater, snapping back at her. 'Can I get a word in?'

She glared at him so fiercely he took another step back, half expecting her to launch herself at him, but her expression changed to one of sadness.

'Quite honestly, David Slater, I think you might have already said far too much,' she said, grimly. 'If I were you, I'd stop right now.'

'Now wait a minute,' he said, but she was already half-way through the door.

'Jenny, wait,' he said, desperately. 'Where are you going?'

'I need some fresh air,' she said. 'I'm going for a walk.'

'Yes, but . . .'

* * *

Downstairs, Norman was still at the bar, but now he was sharing a pint with Naomi Darling. In the mirror behind the bar, he caught a glimpse of Jenny marching purposefully through the bar, heading for the exit. He spun around on his stool as Slater appeared, following in her wake, desperately trying to catch up. Norman gave Slater an enquiring look as he caught his eye, but Slater just shook his head and rushed on.

'What was all that about?' asked Darling, as they watched Slater disappear through the exit.

'Beats me,' said Norman, turning back to the bar, 'but she looks pretty angry, and she's not the sort of person you want to be on the wrong side of.'

'She's a bit like the Black Witch, is she?' asked Darling.

'Nothing like as poisonous,' said Norman, 'but almost as fierce.' He took a sip of his beer. 'So, anyway, now you've brought her name up, how is she?' he asked.

'She gets crazier by the day,' said Darling.

'Do you know if she's been poking her nose into any old investigations?'

'Like what in particular?'

'How about the guys who set fire to my flat?'

'D'you think they started the fire?'

'We don't know for sure what started it,' said Norman. 'I'm just testing theories, like worst-case scenarios.'

'I'd put my money on it being an accident,' said Darling. 'I'm sure they would have notified us by now if they thought there was anything suspicious.'

Norman quickly looked away. He felt a slight unease at not being totally honest with Darling, but at least now he knew Eddie Brent had kept his word.

'So, anyway,' he said, turning back, 'has she been poking into the past?'

'Not that I'm aware of,' said Darling. 'But if you think you know who's responsible for what happened this morning, you really ought to make it official.'

'Yeah, of course we should,' agreed Norman, 'but you know we're not going to rush to do that, right?'

Darling shrugged her shoulders. It was no secret how Norman and Slater felt about Goodnews, so she wasn't surprised.

'She's become so erratic, I'm surprised she keeps her job,' she said.

'Yeah?' said Norman. 'What's she done now?'

'You remember how she always used to be at work by seven every morning? Well, you were there this morning and where was she? Apparently she didn't appear until midday.'

'Maybe she's decided they're going to get rid of her when Tinton closes and she doesn't care any more,' said Norman.

'That would certainly explain some of her more obscure operational decisions,' said Darling. 'The other day she had us CID officers out on the streets doing the sort of stuff liaison officers should be doing.'

'So why doesn't someone say something?' asked Norman.

Darling laughed. 'They're all frightened of being turned into frogs, I think.'

'What about you? You're not frightened, are you?'

'I need a good reference,' she said, 'so no, I'm not frightened, but until I get away, I'm treading pretty carefully. Trust me, though, once I'm out, I'm going to get my own back on the evil cow.'

'How long is it now?' asked Norman.

She smiled and let out a contented sigh. 'Just one more week. Promise me you'll come to my leaving party.'

'I'll be there,' said Norman. 'Count on it.'

* * *

Out in the car park, Slater had just caught up with Jenny.

'Jen, wait,' he said, but she ignored him and continued walking.

He placed a hand on her arm, and now she stopped dead in her tracks. She looked down at his hand as if she was deeply offended by it, then she looked up at his face.

'Take your hands off me,' she said, her voice icy.

He took his hand away as if her arm had suddenly become red hot.

'Now you listen to me,' she said. 'I know I owe you far more than I can ever repay, and I'm more grateful than you'll ever realise. Through you, I've learnt to trust again, and up until a couple of hours ago, I would have trusted you with my life, but that just makes it all the more disappointing to find you don't trust me.'

'What do you mean up until a couple of hours ago?'

'I'm afraid everything changed the moment you made it clear you don't believe what I told you. How can I have complete trust in you when you don't trust me?'

'But what about us?'

'I'm not sure I believe there is an us.'

'But don't be silly—'

'Silly? I'll tell you what's silly. Silly is me thinking I can trust any man. In the end, you're all the same.'

'What's that supposed to mean?'

'I can't do this now,' she said. 'I just need to be on my own for a while.'

'But it's not safe.'

'Right now, I don't care,' she said. 'And if you follow me, I'm going to scream my head off and cause such a scene the police will be here in minutes.'

'You know you wouldn't do that.'

'Do you want to try it and see? I mean it. Just back off and leave me alone. I need to think, and I'm going to do it on my own.'

She turned on her heel and stalked off, leaving Slater watching helplessly. He wondered if he should follow her, but then his mobile phone began to ring. Out of habit, he raised the phone to his ear without looking to see who was calling.

'Oh, hi,' said the familiar voice of DCI Marion Goodnews.

Slater looked skywards and swore softly to himself. Why hadn't he checked caller ID before he'd answered the call? He knew he needed to speak to her, but he hadn't planned on it being tonight. He wondered how quickly he could get rid of her, or was this going to be a rant about what happened this morning, and then yet another of her attempts to convince him he should never have stopped going out with her?

'Hi,' he said casually.

'I heard about your house fire,' she said, her voice filled with warm concern. 'I was worried about you. Are you all right?'

'Yes, Marion,' he said, wearily. 'I'm fine, thank you.'

'I heard your house was gutted. If you need somewhere to stay, I've got plenty of room.'

'Marion, don't,' he warned.

'But I have!'

'I'm fine. There's a spare room at the pub where Norm lives.'

'That's going to be a bit cramped, isn't it?'

'I haven't exactly got a lot of stuff left to fit in there, so it'll do fine for now.'

'What about what's-her-name, your friend? Is she all right?'

'Her name's Jenny, as you well know,' said Slater. 'And yes, she's fine too, thank you.'

'Oh!' She sounded confused. 'She didn't get caught in the fire, then?'

'She was actually in the bath, but luckily she kept her wits about her and managed to escape through the back window,' said Slater.

'Oh, I see, that was lucky. Good for her,' she said, unconvincingly.

'You almost sound as if you would have liked her to have been hurt.'

'Don't be ridiculous. Of course I wouldn't.'

In his head, Slater could see those words being forced, one at a time, through fiercely gritted teeth.

'Has she found somewhere to stay? Although, I suppose it doesn't matter. When you're used to living on the street, you can just go back whenever you want!' She almost spat the last sentence.

'No, she's not back on the street,' he said, sounding far more patient than he was feeling. 'She's with me.'

He was sure he heard a muffled curse, but he ignored it. However, the warmth had completely disappeared from her voice, which was now icy cold.

'I don't understand what you see in her,' she snapped.

'I've told you before, she's just a friend in need of some help,' he said, reasonably.

'She ruined us,' she spat.

Slater sighed. *Here we go again.*

'Listen, Marion, *us* was over before Jenny appeared on the scene, and you know it,' he said, interrupting what he knew would be a long monologue about how wonderful their relationship had been until 'that awful, dirty, street bitch' had come along and turned his head. 'I'm going to end this call now, and I'd prefer it if you didn't call me again. If there ever was anything between us, it's long over, and I can promise you there's no chance it will ever happen again. Goodbye.'

He ended the call and glared at the phone, almost as if it were the phone itself that had upset him. Then, remembering why he was out in the car park, he took off along the alleyway and out into the High Street, where he stopped and looked frantically in both directions. There was no sign of Jenny anywhere. He guessed she would have turned left, so he headed off in that direction, jogging along to try to make up for lost time.

In the end, he walked the streets for two hours, but it proved to be a futile exercise and eventually he conceded defeat and headed back to the pub. All the way back, he hoped she would be there, curled up in bed fast asleep, but when he got back, the room was cold and uninviting in its emptiness. Exhausted and worried sick, he slipped into bed, and after an hour's tossing and turning, he finally slipped into a deep sleep.

CHAPTER TWENTY-NINE

Slater woke very slowly, at first unsure where he was, and then a sudden, urgent need made him reach out for Jenny's familiar, warm body, but her side of the bed was refrigerator cold. He sat up in panic, then it all came flooding back to him and he recalled the argument and how she had walked off and left him. He reached for the bedside lamp and jumped out of bed. He had to start looking; she couldn't have got far with no money.

And then he noticed the folded note tucked under the lamp, where he couldn't miss it. He sat down on the bed and reluctantly unfolded the sheet of paper to reveal a note written in her beautiful, flamboyant handwriting.

Dear Dave,

By the time you find this letter, I'll be gone. I know you think I set fire to your house, but I promise you I didn't do it. I think it's the people who have been chasing me. I always thought I would have to go if they came for me and endangered you, but the longer I have been with you, the more I've been hoping I would never have to make that decision. Yes, it's funny isn't it? In just a few short weeks, the feisty career girl of old fell in love with you and become so settled she even began to hope there might be a different future ahead.

But none of that matters any more because now they're here, I know what I must do. It's heart-breaking, but last night has actually made the decision a little easier, if no less upsetting. I think we both know we would have had no long-term future if you really don't trust me. It doesn't matter how much you love someone, you can't share a life without trust, can you?

I think this is best for both of us, so please don't try to find me.

Love you always,

Jen

P.S. Sorry, but I've borrowed twenty pounds from your wallet. I will pay you back for everything one day, I promise.

Slater read the note twice, then set it carefully on the bedside table before flopping onto his side and curling into a ball.

* * *

Slater slowly became aware someone was knocking on his bedroom door. He sat up and looked around, feeling slightly dazed and disoriented. The bedside clock told him it was eight o'clock in the morning.

'Dave? Are you okay?' called Norman through the door.

'It's not locked. Come on in.'

'I didn't want to come bursting in on you two lovebirds,' said Norman as he slowly opened the door and poked his head around it. He stopped talking when he saw Slater's face.

'Jesus,' he said, coming into the room. 'What happened? Where's Jenny?'

Slater handed Norman the note. 'Read that.'

Norman unfolded the note, his eyes widening as he read. 'Jeez, I'm sorry, Dave,' he said, sitting down on the bed next to Slater. He placed a consoling hand on his friend's shoulder. 'When did this all happen?'

'We had a row last night,' said Slater.

Norman recalled seeing Jenny storm out of the pub with Slater chasing after her.

'Yeah, I kinda guessed that,' he said. 'Is that what all this not trusting her stuff is about?'

'I went and spoke to the neighbours,' said Slater. 'One of them told me he saw Jenny going into my house just before the fire started, but according to her, she never left the house after we got back from our run, and she said she had been in the bath before the fire started.'

'And what did she say when you told her what the neighbour had said?'

'She denied it,' said Slater.

'And you said you didn't believe her?'

'Well . . .'

'Please tell me you didn't accuse her of starting the fire,' said Norman.

'I wouldn't have minded if she had admitted it,' pleaded Slater. 'I mean, I wouldn't be pleased to find she had started the fire, but she's been through a lot. We could have got her some help . . .'

'Didn't it occur to you that maybe accusing her wasn't the best idea you've ever had? You said yourself she'd been through a lot, and then just as she's starting to think she's actually found her forever hero, he turns on her as well!'

'But what else am I supposed to think?' wailed Slater.

'Are you sure this guy was right?'

'He knows her. He's seen her out running. He described her running stuff.'

'I thought she only went out running with you.'

'Well, yeah,' said Slater, 'so did I, but he says he recognised her because he's seen her out running on her own, and he recognised her gear. He said he saw her running up to the house and letting herself in.'

'I thought she didn't have a key. I thought you lost the spare one.'

'Well, maybe it wasn't so lost after all,' said Slater.

'You mean she had it all the time?'

Slater sighed. 'Yeah, it seems that's another lie.'

'But that can't be right, can it? That key was missing before she moved in, wasn't it?' asked Norman.

'What?'

'Don't you remember? You told me there was a spare key in that kitchen drawer when you went to Thailand, but it wasn't there, was it? We searched the house for it when you came back but we couldn't find it anywhere, so how come Jenny managed to find it?'

Slater raised a hand to his mouth. 'I'd forgotten about that. But the guy said he saw her with a front door key, and she let herself in!'

'Did it occur to you to that maybe he was wrong?'

'Why would I think that? What's he got to gain?'

'I don't know,' said Norman, 'but maybe you should have asked yourself that question when you were accusing Jenny. Reading this letter, it looks to me like she was hoping you might ask her to become Mrs Slater. How would burning your house down help her achieve that?'

'We need to look for her,' said Slater, determinedly.

'And where do you propose to start?'

Slater was puzzled, and then he realised what Norman meant. They didn't have the resources they used to have at their disposal.

'What about Naomi? Would she look for me?'

'Yeah, I'm sure she would keep her eyes open for you,' said Norman, 'but I wouldn't be in such a hurry to start a major search. If Jenny's right and these people *are* responsible, they might well have someone on the inside who's looking out for just such a search to appear on the database.'

'Shit, yeah, you're right,' said Slater.

'You're also forgetting Jenny's done all this before. She knows how to disappear, and how to stay disappeared.'

'But she can't go back on the streets!'

'Oh, but she can,' said Norman. 'And my guess is she already has.'

'And it's all my fault. What have I done?'

Norman patted Slater on the shoulder.

'I think you should have a shower and clean yourself up,' he said. 'We've got work to do, and I suggest we start with this witness and find out what he's up to.'

CHAPTER THIRTY

Slater steered his car slowly past his house, the front door and windows now boarded-up.

'Let me handle this,' Norman said as they pulled up outside the house Slater had pointed out. 'I think it would be fair to say you're a little stressed right now.'

Slater climbed wearily from the car, followed Norman up to the front door, and stood to one side as his friend rang the doorbell. It was probably no more than ten or fifteen seconds before they heard someone moving to the door, but for Slater, it seemed more like ten or fifteen minutes. Finally, the door opened just enough for the man to show his face. He looked uncertainly at Norman, but then recognised Slater standing to one side.

'Oh, it's you again,' he said, relaxing and opening the door wider.

'Err, yeah, I'm sorry to disturb you again,' said Slater. 'This is a bit awkward.'

'It's Tom, isn't it?' asked Norman.

The man nodded. 'Yeah, that's right.'

'Last night you told Dave here you saw his girlfriend going into his house at ten o'clock yesterday morning, just before the fire started.'

'That's right,' said Tom. 'I was just leaving for work. She'd been out for a run.'

'Are you absolutely *sure* it was her?' asked Norman.

'Yeah, I'm sure. I've seen her running in the area before. Slim girl, always wears black running gear.'

'And you're sure it was her?' asked Slater. 'Only she says you were mistaken and it wasn't her.'

'Of course I'm sure. She ran up to your front door and let herself in. Who else would it be?'

'Well, that's the thing,' said Norman. 'In our line of business, we make plenty of enemies.'

'What? With a front door key? You're kidding, right?' asked Tom, staring at Norman in disbelief.

'It's not that long ago my own flat was turned into an oven,' said Norman, matter-of-factly. 'The arsonist let himself in with a duplicate key. They had to evacuate an entire block of flats because some idiot wanted to warn me away from an investigation we were involved in.'

Now Tom turned to Slater. 'You think someone set fire to your house?'

Slater shrugged.

'Bloody hell! I thought that sort of thing only happened in movies. Is that really what happened here?'

'We don't know exactly what happened yet,' said Norman. 'That's why we need you to be absolutely certain you saw who you think you saw. Have another think. Can you describe the face you saw?'

'Well, I didn't actually see her face,' said Tom, awkwardly, beginning to blush. 'I wasn't exactly looking at her face. I mean that running gear is a tight fit, and she has a really ni—' He stopped, embarrassed.

'Nice arse?' suggested Norman. 'Is that what you're trying to say? You were staring at her backside?'

'Well, yeah,' he admitted, guiltily, but then rallied. 'There's no law against it, is there?'

'Actually, I'm not interested in your guilty little secrets,' said Norman. 'I'm only interested in who you saw going into the house yesterday morning.'

'It was her. I told you, I recognised the gear she wears, and the blue hat. She always wears that blue hat.'

This was just the spark Slater needed.

'She doesn't have a blue hat!' he snapped, taking a step towards Tom. 'She doesn't like hats, whether they're blue, red, or any colour!'

'Yes, she does,' argued Tom. 'Every time I see her she's wearing it.'

'Listen, mate,' snarled Slater. 'I live with her, and I run with her at six o'clock every morning. Don't you think I might have noticed if she had a bloody hat?'

'Whoa, steady on, Dave,' said Norman, placing himself between Slater and Tom. 'Just keep it calm now. Tom's just telling us what he saw.' Then, turning back to Tom, he said, 'It's just he might not have seen quite what he thought he saw.'

Tom was looking confused and had taken a step back to keep away from the advancing Slater.

'Please excuse my friend,' said Norman. 'He's under a lot of stress, as you can imagine.'

'Well, I suppose that's understandable,' said Tom, sulkily. 'I'd probably be the same.'

'The thing is,' continued Norman, 'without you recognising her face, I'm not convinced you saw who you think you saw. You're obviously some sort of connoisseur of ladies' backsides, but I don't think you'll find too many people have been found guilty on account of their arse being recognised.'

'I know what I saw,' argued Tom.

'I'm not disputing you saw a young woman letting herself into the house,' said Norman, firmly. 'But I am disputing your conviction that this young woman was definitely Dave's girlfriend. You say you're certain. I say it's a possibility. That's not the same thing, is it?'

'Well, I suppose, when you put it like that,' said Tom, sheepishly. 'But if it wasn't her, who was it?'

'If we knew that, we wouldn't be standing here asking you these questions,' said Slater.

'I would guess it was someone trying to look like her,' said Norman.

Tom looked puzzled. 'But why?'

'Just in case someone saw her,' replied Norman. 'Anyone seeing her would assume it was his girlfriend, just like you did.'

'You really think so?' asked Tom. 'It all sounds a bit far-fetched to me.'

'The idea that my girlfriend would set fire to my house is what's far-fetched,' said Slater, bitterly. 'It's just a pity I didn't realise it yesterday when I spoke to you.'

* * *

'I'm an idiot,' said Slater, once they were back in the car and on their way.

'You were stressed,' said Norman. 'We all make mistakes when we're stressed.'

'But I should have asked the questions you just asked him.'

'Like I said, you were stressed.'

'And I should have trusted her!'

'Jeez, will you stop all that!' said Norman, sharply. 'If you really want me to say it, then yes, you messed up. Do I think it's the end of the world? No, I don't. Listen, Jenny's a bright girl. Okay, she's mad at you for not believing her, but I'm sure, when she calms down, she'll understand you had to ask after the guy was so adamant it was her.'

'You really think so?' asked Slater, hopefully.

'Sure,' said Norman, confidently. 'It'll all work out, trust me. You two are made for each other.'

They headed back towards town, but they'd barely gone two hundred yards before Norman's mobile phone began to ring.

'Yo,' he said into the phone as he raised it to his ear. 'Oh, hi, Naomi.'

Slater listened impatiently as he drove, just catching Norman's end of the call.

'You have? Jeez, that was quick . . . Yeah, well, we all need a bit of luck now and then . . .'

Norman glanced in Slater's direction once or twice as he was talking, which convinced him he must somehow be the topic of conversation, but all he could think was, *Come on, Norm, get off the phone. We need to get on.*

'You're sure about that?' continued Norman, into his phone. 'Only I don't wanna see any blood spilled . . . Yeah, we can do that. Where exactly? . . . Right, we'll be there in a few minutes.'

He ended the call, shoved the phone back into his pocket and turned to Slater. 'Go to the bypass, and head north.'

'Why? Where are we going?' asked Slater, irritably.

'We're meeting up with Naomi.'

'Why? Is it important?'

'Just do it, and don't keep arguing,' said Norman, his patience wearing thin. 'Trust me, you'll be glad you did this.'

Slater sighed, but didn't argue, and set off for the bypass.

'You seem to be seeing rather a lot of Naomi,' he said, accusingly.

'You think so? Well, maybe it's because I like her. She's a nice kid when you get to know her. Her real father left when she was little and she's never seen him since, so I think she's sort of adopted me as a father figure.'

Slater didn't quite know how to respond to that.

'Yeah, I know what you're thinking,' said Norman. 'I'm not exactly a shining example for anyone, am I? But there's no accounting for taste, right? Besides, I always wanted a daughter and never had one, and she always wanted a dad and never had one, so, it sort of works for both of us.'

'Actually, I think you're a great example to a lot of people,' said Slater.

'You do?'

'Yes, I do, as it happens. Anyway, that's another matter, why are we meeting her this morning?'

'She has something for us,' said Norman. 'By the way, I sent Watson home yesterday afternoon. I didn't see any point in her hanging around on her own. I gave her my number and told her to call me over the weekend and I'd let her know what's going on.'

'Yeah, right, good thinking,' said Slater. 'It's a good job you're still thinking clearly. My head seems to have turned to mush over this bloody house fire.'

'I don't think it's the fire,' said Norman, slowly. 'I think you'll find it's the girl, and the sooner you realise it, the better.'

Slater looked across at Norman in open-mouthed surprise, but Norman just stared straight ahead. Two minutes later, he directed Slater to pull off the bypass into a lay-by. A small car was parked up ahead.

'That's Naomi's car,' said Norman. 'Just pull in behind it.'

Slater did as he was directed, pulled up behind the car, and switched off the engine.

'Now what?'

'Just stay there a minute,' warned Norman, climbing from the car.

He walked up to the other car, opened the passenger door, and leaned down to speak. For the first time, Slater realised there was a passenger in the car, and then his heart seemed to miss a beat as Norman stepped back to allow the passenger to climb slowly from the car. Norman took her arm and guided her carefully back to Slater's car. When they got alongside, he opened the door and leaned in.

'Right. Naomi's gonna run me back home so you two can have some space. I think you have things to talk about. I'll catch you later.' Then he stepped away and headed back towards the small car.

'Can I get in?'

'Oh, Jenny, of course you can get in,' said Slater.

She climbed into the car, pulled the door closed, and turned to look at him.

'I'm really sorry about what happened,' he said, thinking it sounded trite and inadequate and certainly didn't express what he really felt.

She looked down at her hands and for a moment, he thought she was going to tell him what he could do with his inadequate apology, but instead she turned and looked straight into his eyes.

'It doesn't matter,' she said.

'But I should have trusted you,' he said.

She gave him a brief, sad half-smile.

'Maybe,' she said, 'but Naomi told me what that man said he saw. What else would you think?'

'Yeah, but—'

'I missed you, you know,' she said. 'I know it was only a few hours, but I missed you so much.'

'Yeah, me too,' he said. 'I'll never doubt you again.'

'You'd better bloody not, Dave Slater,' she said. Then suddenly she was in floods of tears, and he was reaching for her.

CHAPTER THIRTY-ONE

After what could best be described as a rather heavy weekend, Slater and Jenny had decided they really didn't want to fall out, whatever might have happened. In fact, they had decided they were sticking together now, come what may. Even leaving Jenny on her own in the bedroom above the pub didn't seem to be an option that Monday morning, so Slater had brought her with him to the office.

'What are you doing here, Watson?' he asked. 'I thought you were supposed to be going back to Bradshaw.'

'But the case isn't finished yet, is it?' she said. 'And when I left a message about your house fire and suggested I should come back for a few more days he didn't call back to say no, so here I am.'

'So you don't actually have his permission, then?' asked Slater. 'You're here by default.'

He was feeling so weary he felt as if his very bones ached, and he was wondering what he should do about Watson when his mobile phone began to ring.

'Good morning, and how are you today?' It was Marion Goodnews again.

Slater sighed and cursed himself for failing to check the caller ID, yet again.

'I thought I asked you not to call me again,' he said, rather testily.

'Yes, sorry about that,' she purred, 'but this is police business, so don't think you can hang up on me like you did last time.'

'What do you mean police business?'

'I've just had a report from the fire service investigations officer. He's convinced the fire at your house wasn't an accident, and having seen his report, so am I. This is a courtesy call to let you know I shall be investigating this case myself.'

'I didn't think house fires came within the remit of a DCI,' said Slater. 'I would have thought you had more important things to worry about.'

'Oh, I do have plenty of important things to worry about,' she agreed, 'like the discovery of two bodies under a patio, but if we've got an arsonist on the loose, I want to make sure she gets caught as soon as possible. But first of all, I need you to come in and make a statement.'

Slater silently cursed Eddie Brent and wondered if he had told Goodnews he thought Jenny was responsible for the fire? He would be having words with him later.

'I can't help much, I wasn't there,' he said, trying to think how he could stall her.

'I still need you to come in and make a statement,' she said. 'And I'd like to speak to Ms Radstock, whom I know was there. I would *especially* like to speak to her.'

'I'll come in later,' Slater said. 'I'm a bit tied up right now.'

'Make sure you do,' she hissed down the phone, 'I'm doing you a favour here. Don't make me have to come and find you. And make sure you bring your *friend* with you.'

Slater realised she had cut the connection. He had expected some sort of investigation, but he had felt quite sure it would probably be handed down to someone like Naomi Darling. Why was Goodnews getting involved? This could only mean trouble.

Norman was just ending his own call. 'We have a problem,' he announced. 'Goodnews is on the warpath.'

'How do you know?' asked Slater. 'She's only just called me.'

'That was Naomi calling to warn us.'

'She wants me to go in and make a statement,' said Slater. He looked at Jenny. 'And she wants me to take my friend with me.'

'Who, me?' asked Jenny.

'I wouldn't do that,' said Norman. 'It appears our favourite Black Witch has already decided who started the fire, and her one and only suspect is Jenny.'

'Why would she think that?' asked Jenny. 'They haven't even spoken to anyone yet, have they?'

'I need to speak to Eddie Brent,' said Slater. 'He must have told her—'

'Naomi says he told them nothing of the sort,' interrupted Norman. 'So you can forget about blaming him. She says there's nothing in the report that points the finger at anyone, and he didn't offer any opinion about possible suspects.'

'So how come she thinks I'm responsible?' asked Jenny.

'Maybe I'm being paranoid, Jen,' said Slater, 'but it sounds to me like she's going to try to make the evidence fit the suspect. She's going to fit you up.'

'But why?'

'Because she blames you for ending her relationship with me.'

'But that was nothing to do with me, was it?'

'No, it was over before you came along,' Slater said. 'And she knows it was, but she wants someone to blame, and you're the obvious choice!'

'Oh my God. What do I do? Perhaps I should go in and make a statement?'

'No! You don't go anywhere near there,' said Norman. 'You stay out of the way while me and Dave get to the bottom of this.'

'And how am I going to do that?'

'Lemme make a call,' said Norman. 'I think I know somewhere you can hide out for a few days.'

'But I don't want to be a bloody fugitive,' she wailed.

'Would you rather get locked up? Just trust me. We can sort this out.'

Watson had been an interested bystander while all this had been going on, but now she got to her feet and picked up her bag. They all looked around at her.

'Sorry, I just need a cigarette,' she said. 'I'll go outside.'

'And I need to make this call,' said Norman. 'I'm just gonna step outside for a minute too.'

'I didn't even know she smoked,' said Slater to Jenny, when Watson and Norman had left the office.

'Perhaps it's just when she's stressed,' said Jenny. Then she let out a big sigh. 'D'you know, sometimes I wish I was someone else. Trouble just seems to follow me everywhere.'

'We'll get through this,' said Slater. 'But Norm's right, you need to keep your head down for a few days while we get to the bottom of all this.'

'You're supposed to be wrapping up a case and deciding on your future, not worrying about me.'

Slater smiled and pulled her into his arms. 'Yeah, I know, but like I told you, it's also about what's important in my life. Right now, you're the most important part of my future, so it's a no-brainer.'

'Where's this hiding place of Norm's?' she asked, settling against him.

'I think I can guess,' said Slater, 'but I'll let him tell you.'

'How long do you think it will take? Will I be there until Christmas?'

'You're spending Christmas with me,' he said. 'And the New Year.'

'Let's hope it'll be a new year and a new start.'

'About that,' he said. 'If I take this new job, will you come with me?'

'Where is it going to be?'

'I haven't a clue. Does it matter?'

She leaned back far enough to allow her to study his face for a few, silent moments, and then she settled her head back against his chest before she spoke.

'Yes, I will come with you, and no, I don't think it matters one little bit where it's going to be. Getting away from here and starting over might be the best thing that could happen.'

Their quiet moment was suddenly shattered as Norman burst through the door, rubbing his hands together.

'Jeez, it's damned cold out there,' he said as he came in. 'Oh, sorry! I didn't mean to interrupt anything.'

'You're not interrupting anything. I was just promising Jen we can sort this out.'

'Sure we can,' said Norman, looking at Jenny. 'But in the meantime I've found somewhere you can stay. You'll have to stay indoors and resist the urge to go jogging for a few days, but you'll be safe, warm and welcome. Oh, and I hope you like kids.'

'Are you sure Jane's okay about this?' asked Slater.

Norman smiled. 'You guessed?'

'Just a hunch.'

'She's fine about it. She said she would have been annoyed if I hadn't suggested it.'

'What about her husband?' asked Jenny. 'Isn't he coming out on parole soon? I don't want to make things difficult for everyone.'

'That's a month away at least,' said Norman. 'Trust me, you're not even going to be there for a week. All we have to do is get you over there and hope no one sees you in the process, and just in case anyone's watching our cars, Jane's coming over to get you herself. She'll be here in about fifteen minutes. And you have to understand that you won't see either of us until this is over, right?'

'Is that really necessary?'

'It will be once we tell Goodnews we don't know where you are,' explained Norman. 'She won't believe us and might even have us watched.'

'This is like a nightmare! Have I got time to get my things from the pub?'

'Sure,' said Norman. Then he turned to Slater as Jenny rushed off to collect her things. 'Do you still have that note

Jenny left for you? You can use that as your excuse for not knowing where she is.'

'Yeah, I have it right here in my pocket.'

'Right then,' said Norman. 'We're all set. The story is Jenny ran away when you accused her of starting the fire.'

Slater winced as Norman said the words.

'I'm sorry to remind you, but you have to admit it's a good cover story.'

'It makes it look like she's guilty,' argued Slater.

'Yeah, but from what I hear, Goodnews has already decided that anyway,' countered Norman. 'So what's to lose? When are you going to make your statement to the police?'

'As far as they know, I'm really busy,' said Slater. 'They'll have to wait, but I can't put them off forever. And I was told to take Jenny with me.'

'That's not what you said earlier,' said Norman.

'What?'

'Didn't she say you had to bring your friend?'

'Well, yeah—'

'So, why not take me?'

'She's not going to wear that one for long.'

'I know,' said Norman, 'but we need to stall 'em for as long as we can. And don't worry about getting picked up, Naomi will warn me if they decide to come for you.'

The outside door opened and Watson crept back into the office.

'Okay, let's hear it,' said Slater.

She looked at him, startled. 'I'm sorry?'

'You don't smoke, do you?'

'Ah, so you noticed,' she said, nervously.

'I think even the dimmest detective would have noticed you haven't needed one before, and besides, I can usually smell a smoker from a hundred yards, and there's not a trace on you. So my guess is you've been making a phone call.'

'Right,' she said. 'Yes, I suppose it wasn't very discreet, was it?'

'Well, I'm guessing you're not calling the bad guys,' continued Slater, 'so my guess is Bradshaw. You're going to have to get out of the habit of running to him every time things get a bit sticky. He'll think you've got no faith in me.'

She had reached her desk now and she fidgeted nervously; her cheeks were reddening, but it didn't seem to be embarrassment that was causing her face to flush.

'It's all right,' said Norman. 'You can sit down, we don't bite — or at least we don't bite those on our side. You are on our side, right?'

'Of course,' she said, angrily, 'but this isn't about running to him because I don't have faith in anyone here. As I said before, he's still my boss, and we still have a case to close. You two seem to have forgotten the fire is almost certainly related to the case. I think the prime suspect has to be the Scanlons or one of their employees. I just thought Mr Bradshaw should know the local DCI has just thrown a huge spanner in the works.' She looked challengingly at them. 'Well, her investigation doesn't look as if it's designed to help us, does it?'

The boys were slightly stunned by her outburst. This was the first time she had been anything other than cool and calm.

'I'll admit it doesn't look very helpful,' said Slater. 'But if we can persuade Goodnews it wasn't Jenny who set the fire and they do a proper investigation, it could be a big help.'

'And you think you can do that, do you?' she asked, raising an eyebrow. 'Have you never heard the expression "hell hath no fury like a woman scorned"? Because that's exactly how DCI Goodnews sees herself. There's only one thing on her mind right now, and it's called revenge. She doesn't give a damn about who started that fire, she's just trying to hurt you. I'm trying to make sure she doesn't succeed!'

Watson slammed her bag down on her desk for emphasis, dragged out her chair, and dropped into it. She folded her arms and crossed her legs, her right foot twitching angrily. It was clear she was fuming.

A tense, deathly hush had descended on the room. Slater felt himself blushing. He shouldn't be getting at Watson; this situation certainly wasn't her fault.

'Well, yeah, I suppose that's probably true,' he admitted, sheepishly. 'I'm sorry. I didn't think about it like that.'

'I'm a woman,' she said. 'I know how other women think. I've seen it before.'

'What I mean,' he said, quietly, 'is right now, all I care about is making sure Jenny doesn't get accused of starting that fire.'

'I know it wasn't her,' she said.

'What do you mean, you know it wasn't her? Are you telling me you know who started it?'

Watson looked horrified. 'If I knew who had attempted to murder Jenny, do you really think I'd keep quiet about it?'

'Hey!' said Norman. 'Listen to you two! Come on, let's lighten up a bit. Aren't we all supposed to be on the same side here?'

Slater sighed. 'I'm sorry,' he said. 'I guess I'm a bit personally involved here . . .'

'No, *I'm* sorry,' said Watson. 'Of course you care about Jenny first. I do understand that, but I care about closing this case too. If we mess this up now I could end up back on the shelf.'

'I thought you said they'd just find someone else if Dave didn't fit in,' said Norman.

'Yes, but that could take months,' said Watson. 'And I'm not sure I can take much more of being a PA. It's driving me mad. I want to be doing the job I was trained to do.'

'You sound just like Jenny talking about being trapped in my house,' said Slater. 'She said exactly the same about it doing her head in. Because of her, I think I understand where you're coming from.'

'Sounds to me like you two have got good reason to work together and stop arguing,' said Norman. 'So let's get back to it, shall we?'

They both murmured their assent.

'Okay then, Watson,' continued Norman. 'You were saying you know it wasn't Jenny. How come you're so sure?'

'Because the boss told me so, and I'm not in the habit of questioning what he tells me.'

'But how can he be so sure?' asked Slater.

She looked at her watch before she answered him. 'He didn't tell me that, but you can ask him yourself in about an hour and a half. He's on his way here, and I can promise you he's not a happy bunny.'

'He's not happy?' said Slater. 'Well, I hope he realises I didn't ask someone to set fire to my bloody house, because, to be perfectly honest, I'm not very happy either.'

'I'm pretty sure he's not coming down here because he's angry with any of us,' she said. 'All he said was to tell you he's on his way and to stay put until he gets here.'

There was a sudden, brief tension in the room, but Norman was determined nothing was going to spoil the harmony of their little team.

'Can I ask a question?' he asked, looking at Watson.

'Sir?'

'Where's the walking stick?'

'Ah. I see. I felt I was in danger of relying on it, when I really don't need it, so I've left the damned thing at home. I know I'm fit and ready for real work, even if I've yet to be given the all-clear.'

CHAPTER THIRTY-TWO

It was almost midday. Jenny had been whisked away by Jane Jolly a couple of hours previously, and Norman had spent the intervening time coaching Slater about what he was going to tell the police. Watson, meanwhile, had been carrying out one more check on William Harding's background to add to their case notes.

'Well,' she announced, 'as far as I can see, William Harding was squeaky clean. We know from earlier that he went to Windsor Grammar School, and from there he went to university. He wasn't exactly a star graduate, but in 1975 he left with a good enough degree to get him a job with a High Street bank. He spent the next twenty years at Richmond, and then in 1995 he moved to Tinton, where he spent the next thirteen years as assistant manager. He was made redundant in 2008 with a generous payoff and good enough pension to be able to retire aged fifty-five.'

'Didn't Harding move into that house in 2008?' asked Slater.

'That's right. He bought it with cash, which came from his parents' estate when they died.'

'So where was he living before that?'

'Apparently he never married, and he lived with his parents in Windsor,' she said.

'What, all his life?'

'Perhaps he was a devoted son. It does happen, you know. I think it's quite sad to think he spent his entire working life commuting, and then when his parents died, he finally moved to the town where he worked, and no sooner had he done that than he was made redundant.'

'Now that's real irony,' observed Norman. 'Is there any mention of his brother getting a share of the estate?'

'No, he was estranged from the family. It looks as though he'd been cut out of the will. Maybe his parents didn't approve of his criminal lifestyle.'

'So William inherited everything when his parents died?'

'Can't say for sure,' she said, 'but it looks that way, and if he looked after his parents and his brother was the black sheep, it would explain why he had so much money. Unless, of course, he robbed a bank.'

'Well, that *would* explain his hurried disappearance,' said Slater.

'There's nothing to suggest he's ever so much as been given a parking ticket,' said Watson.

'An older brother looking for his share of the inheritance could be a better explanation for his disappearance,' said Norman.

'No one ever suggested there was any foul play,' countered Slater.

'Yeah, but did anyone ever look?' asked Norman. 'It all seems to tie in with your theory. And it would certainly explain one of the bodies under the patio. And if Kenny Wingate is the other, that just about wraps it all up.'

Slater nodded his head in acknowledgement.

'It was a lucky guess,' he said. 'When you think about it, it's surprising how much we rely on luck. We think we solve these things with detective work, but half the time it's a bit of luck that leads to the breakthrough.'

'Yes,' agreed Watson, 'that's true, but I think you make your own luck, don't you? If you don't keep looking, you never actually have that lucky break, do you?'

Not for the first time, Slater noted Watson's positive attitude, and he thought he would probably enjoy working with her — and if her bionic knee didn't make the grade, he thought he'd be happy to have her as his backroom staff; that was if he hadn't already put her off.

His thoughts were interrupted by a sharp rap on the door, and Chief Superintendent Robin Bradshaw pulled open the door and strode into the room.

'Good afternoon, everyone,' he said, taking in the three faces turned towards him. Then he focused on Slater. 'Are you okay?'

Slater nodded. 'A bit stressed at having my house incinerated,' he said, 'and now I've got the local police hassling me for a statement.'

'What about Miss Radstock?'

'She's okay. She's made of tough stuff.'

'So, have you worked out who you've upset yet?'

'We think there are three possibilities,' said Slater.

'Go on,' said Bradshaw.

'Well, not so long ago we crossed paths with this Serbian gangster. He sent some Russian thug to set fire to Norman's flat to warn us off. Now we know we haven't been anywhere near them, but if someone else has been stirring them up, they might think it was us.'

'You're definitely barking up the wrong tree, there,' said Bradshaw. 'I can tell you for a fact the Russian hasn't been over here since, and there's no reason to think anyone else from that organisation has been here either.'

Slater was surprised Bradshaw knew all this apparently off the top of his head. Bradshaw smiled at Slater's confusion, and winked at Norman, who had kept quiet so far.

'I told you we're not your normal, everyday police squad,' said Bradshaw. 'I have access to such information, and I make it my business to keep up to date with certain people.'

'Okay,' said Slater. 'In that case, it's probably someone working on behalf of the Scanlons.'

'That's a better idea, but it's not that either,' said Bradshaw, quite definitely.

'How can you be so sure?' asked Slater, irritably. 'I'm beginning to think we've only got half the story.'

'Why do you think that?'

'Well, for a start, I thought you were the guy who had suggested Rosie came to see us.'

'That was your own assumption,' said Bradshaw. 'I didn't mislead you about that. If you recall, you never raised the subject when we first spoke.'

Slater felt a retort on the tip of his tongue, but swallowed it back as he realised Bradshaw was right. He had just assumed.

'All right,' said Slater. 'I admit I did make an assumption there, but if you're so sure the fire has nothing to do with the Joe Dalgetty case and the Scanlons, that means you know a lot more than you've told us so far. So what haven't you told us?'

Bradshaw studied Slater for a few seconds, then his face broke into a broad smile. 'Are we all on the same page here? Everyone trusts everyone?'

'Yes,' said Slater, 'we're all on the same side, but it would have been a lot easier to solve this case if we'd had all the information to start with. I get the impression you knew what had happened before we started.'

'I didn't have all the answers,' said Bradshaw. 'If I had, I wouldn't have needed you to solve this case for me — I would have already done it myself.'

'And how can you be so sure the Scanlons have nothing to do with the fire?' asked Slater.

'Because I know none of their associates have been near your house.'

'Wait a minute,' said Slater. 'Are you telling me you've been watching my house?'

'Please don't be such a drama queen,' said Bradshaw. 'I told you I'd been keeping an eye on Miss Radstock. It's one thing to know who caused her all that grief, but it's quite another thing to prove it. I was rather hoping someone might come to your house and lead us back to the ringleaders.'

'You mean you've been using her as bait?' asked Slater.

'I wouldn't put it like that,' said Bradshaw. 'It was unlikely it would happen, so the risk was minimal.'

'You can't have someone sitting there watching, so you must have a camera set up somewhere.'

'It was just a precaution, I never expected anyone to do anything. If I'd thought there was a serious threat I would have told you, and I would have had someone there.'

Somewhere in Slater's head a penny dropped. 'You know who started that fire, don't you?'

'Yes, I do,' said Bradshaw.

'Well, tell me who it is!' demanded Slater. 'And tell the bloody police. They think Jenny did it. They'll arrest her if they find her.'

'I can promise you that won't happen,' said Bradshaw.

'How can you be so sure?'

Bradshaw looked at his watch. 'You'll just have to trust me on that one. You do trust me, don't you?'

'Quite frankly I'm beginning to wonder if I should,' said Slater. 'You don't make it easy when you're spying on me and keeping us in the dark.'

'What about you, Watson? Do you think you can trust me?'

'Absolutely,' said Watson. 'But, to be fair, I have known you longer.'

'What about you, Norman?'

'Yeah,' said Norman. 'But I gotta say — this new way you have of building trust doesn't do you any favours. If I didn't know you already, I'd be finding it pretty hard. And

I'd be pissed off if you'd been spying on me. Why didn't you just tell him?'

'I had to make sure I could trust him,' said Bradshaw.

Norman shook his head. 'Jeez, you have some weird ways of doing things, that's all I can say.'

'I'll take your comments on board. Maybe you're right, and I can understand why you think I haven't exactly covered myself in glory, but hopefully, in a little while, you'll see things differently and you'll understand why I've done what I've done. You might even think, like me, that it was the best thing to do.'

He looked at his watch again. 'I'm afraid I'm going to have to leave now,' he said. 'Watson? Would you walk me out to my car?'

'Yes, sir, of course,' she said, and followed him out of the office.

'What the hell was that all about?' asked Slater. 'Was he taking the piss or what? "Hopefully you'll see things differently." Cheeky bugger. He knows who set fire to my bloody house and he won't tell me who it is. Why does he think I'll agree it was the best thing to do?'

'I know you're pissed off at him,' said Norman, 'but he really is a good guy. Trust me, whatever he's up to, he'll have his reasons.'

Watson came back into the room. She was carrying an envelope. 'He says I have to give this to you at one o' clock,' she said mysteriously.

Slater looked at his watch. 'It's ten to,' he said. 'You might as well give it to me now. Ten minutes won't make any difference.'

'Sorry,' she said. 'I can't do that. Trust me, it's for your own good.'

'Jesus!' said Slater. 'Why does everyone think they know what's best for me? If we're going to work together, you're going to have to sort out where your loyalty lies.'

'That won't be a problem if we're working together,' she assured him. 'But at the moment, Mr Bradshaw is my boss, and you're just two ordinary blokes, I think that's what you told me when we first met, wasn't it?'

'Well, yeah,' admitted Slater, reluctantly.

'So, there you are then. My loyalty has to be to my boss,' she said, firmly.

Norman grinned at Slater. 'Ha! Checkmate,' he said. 'I tell you what, this here is one smart cookie. I wish I was being offered a chance to work with her.'

'All right,' said Slater, sounding far more patient than he was feeling. 'I'll wait, but I'm telling you it won't make any difference.'

'We'll see,' said Watson, triumphantly.

'I have to say, I am seriously impressed with this new Dave Slater,' said Norman.

'What's that supposed to mean?'

'Well, if the events of the past few days had happened a year ago, you would have been climbing the walls by now. I'm sure I would have been holding you back from doing something really stupid, and yet here you are, keeping remarkably calm in the circumstances.'

'I've always been calm,' protested Slater.

'Yeah, right. Of course you have.'

'I don't know what you mean.'

'You know exactly what I mean,' said Norman. 'Before, you would have been throwing all your toys out of the pram and storming off in a huff. But look at you now!'

Slater felt his face redden. 'Yeah, well, I told you I see things from a different perspective these days.'

Norman winked at Watson. 'This thing with Jenny is obviously having beneficial side effects on you.'

'You seem to be forgetting all the other things that have happened recently.'

'No,' said Norman. 'I'm not forgetting any of that. Your values have changed, I get that, but the way I see it, if your new values are the cake, Jenny provides the icing.'

Slater looked at Norman and nodded towards Watson.

'What? You think we shouldn't talk about this now?' asked Norman. 'I disagree. Watson needs to know who she's going to be working for, right? Well, she's read up on all the old stuff, I'm just making sure she's got the latest update. I figure she'll appreciate the fact you're a bit more considered and not quite so headstrong, these days. Am I right, Watson?'

Watson looked mortified to be drawn into this conversation, which Slater was beginning to find excruciatingly embarrassing.

'Err, well, I, err, I suppose it's always good to get a well-rounded view of your colleagues,' she stuttered. Now she, too, looked deeply embarrassed.

'Hey, look,' said Norman. 'I don't want to embarrass you guys, but I have to tell you, I think you'll make a great team. You have empathy. I always thought that was one of the things that made us a good team, Dave, don't you?'

'You seem to have made your mind up about where I'm going to be working,' said Slater. 'But you seem to have forgotten I've just discovered my would-be boss has been spying on me.'

'He was looking out for Jenny,' said Norman. 'You should be happy about that.'

'What about not telling me who started the fire?' asked Slater.

Watson looked at her watch. 'That was for your own protection,' she said, as she slid the envelope across the desk to him.

'So you know who it is too?' asked Slater.

'No,' she said. 'I just know it was for your own good.'

'So, what's in here?' he asked, grabbing the envelope and tearing it open.

Norman moved to look over his shoulder as he pulled out a photograph and stared at it.

'You're kidding me!' said Norman, staring open-mouthed at the image.

'What is it?' asked Watson.

Slater dropped the photograph onto the desk and pulled a second from the envelope.

'Holy shit!' said Norman. 'Isn't that your house? And look at the date and time stamp!'

'Bitch!' said Slater, tossing the second photo down with the first. 'I'm going to kill her!' He made to rush for the door, but Norman wrapped his arms around him before he could move.

'Get off me, Norm!' Slater cried.

'Watson, lock the door!' yelled Norman, struggling to hold Slater back. 'Don't let him out!'

Watson rushed over to the door, turned the key in the lock and pulled it from the door. When she turned back, Norman and Slater were embroiled in an unseemly wrestling match that seemed to involve lots of cursing, swearing and heavy breathing. The curses were Slater's; the heavy breaths were Norman's.

She rushed back to her desk and snatched up the photos. The first one showed a good-looking woman in black running gear and wearing a blue hat. She was obviously at some event — possibly a fun run, or something similar. The second photo showed the same young woman at someone's front door. She was slipping a key into the lock and looking furtively over her shoulder.

The two men had collapsed in a heap on the floor, and she rushed over to try to stop the fight.

'Stop it!' she yelled at them. 'Stop!'

There was a new noise in amongst the chaos, which she recognised as Norman's mobile phone. They weren't listening to her attempts to break up the fight so, for want of something better to do, she picked up the phone.

'Hello?' she said, showing remarkable poise in the circumstances, 'Norman's phone. Who's calling, please?'

'Who's that?'

'This is Watson. Who are you?'

'This is DC Naomi Darling. Is Norm there?'

'Err, he's a bit busy at the moment. Can I take a message?'

'What on earth is that noise?'

'It's Norman and Mr Slater. They're fighting.'

'They're *what*?'

'Mr Slater made a rush for the door, and Norman stopped him. I don't really understand, and I don't know what to do. It's something to do with a woman in a photograph. My boss gave it to him.'

'Ah! A woman in a photo? And Norm tried to stop him? Is she a strawberry blonde?'

Watson scrabbled for the photos. 'It's difficult to tell, but yes, she could be.'

'Right. Now I get it! Suddenly things are beginning to add up.'

'Not at this end,' said Watson.

'I'll explain when I get there,' said Darling. 'Just get it through to them that DCI Goodnews has just been arrested. That should stop them fighting, and tell them if they haven't calmed down by the time I get there, they'll have me to deal with. I'll sort the silly buggers out!'

Watson put the phone down and turned her attention back to the floor, where things seemed to have quietened down quite considerably. There was a metal tea tray on the end of the desk. She grabbed it and began to slam it against the desk. The din was appalling, but it got their attention.

'Now, stop it!' she shouted. 'I've never seen anything like it! How dare you start behaving like animals in my office!'

They had stopped writhing around now, and both looked decidedly sheepish.

'That was DC Darling on the phone,' continued Watson. 'She said to tell you DCI Goodnews has just been arrested and driven off to Winchester.'

'What?' said Slater, sitting up and then climbing gingerly to his feet. 'But how did they kn—'

'That's why Mr Bradshaw wanted me to keep hold of the photos,' said Watson. 'He guessed you'd be out of here like a shot once you knew, that's why he had her whisked away. He didn't want you doing anything we would all regret.'

'But she could have killed Jenny!' said Slater.

'Exactly,' said Watson. 'That's why she's been arrested. I hear attempted murder has been mentioned.'

'Which is probably what you would have been arrested for,' puffed Norman, to Slater, 'if we'd let you get there.'

'It would have been more than just attempted,' remarked Slater.

Concern shadowed his face as he looked down at Norman, who was lying flat on his back, his hands to his chest. He was still puffing hard, and his face had turned a rather unhealthy shade of grey. There was a blueish hue to his lips. Slater suddenly felt worried.

'You knew about this?' he asked, trying to behave as normally as possible.

'I knew as much as you,' gasped Norman, 'until I saw those photos. And if I'd known she was going to be arrested at one, I wouldn't have been wrestling with you, would I?'

'So Bradshaw—'

'Guessed you'd be mad enough to go after her, yeah,' said Norman. 'I just wish he'd told me. Jeez, I feel like I'm going to have a heart attack.'

'Oh, good lord,' said Watson, bending down over Norman.

Now the words had been spoken aloud, Slater was seriously concerned by the way his friend was struggling to breathe.

'Bloody hell, Norm, don't say things like that.' He knelt down next to him, took hold of his wrist, and felt for a pulse. It was there, but like a wounded butterfly; it seemed to be fluttering wildly just to keep going.

'Well, that's a relief,' he said, gently releasing Norman's wrist. 'There is a pulse, so you must still be alive.'

'Just don't tell me if it stops,' said Norman. 'I'd rather not know, but if it does, you can have my night-vision goggles.'

'Christ, Norm, it's not going to bloody stop. Don't say things like that. I've just lost my dad, I'm not ready to lose you, too. I'm really sorry, I didn't mean to hurt you.'

'Hurt me?' said Norman weakly. 'What makes you think you hurt me? I had you completely subdued.'

'Yeah, right,' said Slater. 'Of course you did. Here, let's try to make you comfortable.'

'Should I call an ambulance?' asked Watson, quietly.

'No, I'll be fine,' said Norman, struggling to breathe.

'Yes, please, Watson,' said Slater, making himself comfortable next to Norman. 'Let's get one here and get him checked out.'

'I'm okay,' insisted Norman, his face sallow. 'I'll be as right as rain in a few minutes.'

'If you go any greyer, Norm, you'll look like you were made of concrete,' said Slater. 'We're calling an ambulance and that's that.'

'Well, at least help me up,' said Norman.

'No, you're staying right where you are. I admit you're making the place look seriously untidy, but then you always do, so we can live with that.'

'You're not gonna rush off, are you?' asked Norman, clutching anxiously at Slater's hand. 'Only I don't wanna go on my own.'

'Go?' said Slater. 'The only place you're going is to the hospital in the ambulance when it gets here.'

'If it gets here in time.' Norman closed his eyes.

'Where did Mr Bloody Negative come from all of a sudden?' asked Slater. 'What have you always told me about that?'

'Jesus, don't you go on about it now you've got it?' said Norman, opening his eyes again. 'Sometimes I wish I'd let you carry on being Mr Doom-and-Gloom.'

'The ambulance is on its way,' said Watson, 'and I've unlocked the door. I'll go and keep an eye out for it.' She headed off for the door, worry etched all over her face.

'Can you do me a favour?' asked Norman.

'Sure.'

'Can you call Jane? She was going to come over for a drink later, but that's probably not going to happen now, right?'

'Yeah, I'll call her just as soon as we get you sorted out.'

'You can probably tell Jenny she's safe to come back too.'

'I'll make sure she's not still on the wanted list first,' said Slater.

'No, she's not,' said a female voice behind him.

'Naomi? You got here quick.'

'Not quick enough by the look of it,' she said, kneeling down next to Norman and taking his free hand. She looked worried sick, but she kept it out of her voice.

'Is this because you don't want to come to my party, you silly sod?' she asked him. 'You could have just said no. You don't have to make such a drama out of it.'

He managed a half-smile. Darling looked around at Slater.

'What on earth were the two of you doing fighting? I thought you were supposed to be mates.'

'Watson was exaggerating,' said Norman, raising his head a couple of inches from the floor. 'We weren't fighting. I was just trying to make sure this idiot didn't do anything he would regret. And don't blame him, it's that Black Witch. It's all her fault. If she hadn't started the fire, none of this would have happened.'

As he finished speaking he lay back and closed his eyes, and for a moment Slater thought the worst, but then he could see Norman's chest was still rising and falling.

'The ambulance is here,' called Watson from the doorway.

There was the sound of running feet, and then two paramedics came rushing through the door and across to Norman.

'What have we got then?' asked the first as he came through the door.

'Possible heart attack,' said Slater, moving aside.

'Right then, mate,' said the paramedic as he sank to his knees next to Norman and began to examine him. 'You just lie there and we'll soon have you sorted out.' He looked at Slater. 'He's a big lad.'

Slater gave him a sad little smile. 'Yes, I'm afraid you'll need the extra-wide stretcher.'

‘Hey!’ said Norman, without opening his eyes. ‘I might look it, but I ain’t dead yet, so watch what you’re saying.’

The paramedic grinned, and winked at Slater. ‘I think he’ll be all right,’ he said. ‘He’s got spirit.’

CHAPTER THIRTY-THREE

'The hospital rang. Norm's okay. He's had a close escape, but he's going to get through it,' Slater said, beaming.

'But there must be some sort of underlying problem,' said Watson.

'Well, yeah, I think we can all see what the problem is. Maybe now he'll do something about it.'

'Do you think he will? I rather got the impression he's not the sort to be worrying about his weight.'

'You're right there,' said Slater, 'but I was talking to Jane at the hospital last night, and she told me she's not prepared to sit back and watch him kill himself, so I don't think he's going to have much choice.'

'Are they actually an item? Isn't her husband coming back?'

'He's coming out of prison, but she won't have him back. She's divorcing him. In fact, it was his stuff in the boxes we put into storage.'

'Have the doctors said anything about how they're going to treat Norman?' she asked.

'He's got at least one blocked artery, but they think they can sort him out with a stent rather than having to open him up.'

'Gosh! That will put him out of action for ages, won't it?' Watson said. 'Do you think he'll come back to work afterwards?'

'I suppose it will all depend on how he feels when he's recovered, but I'll be very surprised if it stops him for long. I mean, he could be retired now, but he isn't.'

'So what happens in the meantime?'

'I had a long chat with Norm about that yesterday, and I was talking to Jenny about it last night,' he said. 'How d'you feel about you and me working together?'

Her eyes widened as he spoke. 'You mean you're going to take the job? Oh, how wonderful! Mr Bradshaw will be so pleased, and I think I'd rather like it too.' She was so excited she didn't seem to be able to stop talking. 'What does Jenny say? Where is she, anyway?'

'She's going to stay at Jane's to help her out with the kids for a couple of days. She says we should go for it.'

'Well, there you are then!'

'I want to know about your bionic knee,' he said.

She looked a little pensive. 'What about it?'

'Like how long is it before you get the all-clear to use it? If I'm going to be a DI, I need a DS I can trust and rely on, and if I have my way, I'd like you to be that person.'

'Oh, goodness! Really?'

'Yes, really, but you need to be able to get around, and not by stuffing yourself full of painkillers.'

'I stopped using those over a month ago,' she assured him, 'and you know I've ditched the walking stick.'

'Well, for what it's worth, I thought you managed fine at the storage centre, and you were quick enough and agile enough when you needed to be, so what's the situation, honestly? Are you really ready?'

'Yes, I am. It's just a question of passing the medical. It's a formality, honestly.'

'So you'd be up for giving it a go, then, as my DS? I don't know how long it's going to take to sort things out with Bradshaw, and I haven't a clue where we're going to be based, so you might be hanging around for a few weeks.'

She seemed to have swelled with pride and was beaming from ear to ear.

'I'll be ready whenever you are, sir,' she said.

'One more thing,' he said. 'I can't keep on calling you Watson. Didn't you say your real name is Samantha?'

She was actually blushing. 'Gosh, sir, isn't that rather informal?'

He smiled at her. 'Is Sam okay?'

'Oh! I don't think anyone's ever called me by my first name at work.'

'Well, someone does now!'

EPILOGUE

'I don't understand, Mr Slater,' said Rosie. 'How on earth did Joe come to have all those diamonds? And if they were worth so much money, why was he living here, like a pauper?'

Slater put down his cup and saucer.

'To really understand, you need to go right back to the 1980s when a gangster called Ronnie Scanlon and his gang pulled off a big diamond robbery. The police caught the gang, but they never found out what happened to the diamonds. They managed to convict them all because one of the gang, a man called Kenny Wingate, gave evidence against the others in exchange for a short sentence and a new identity.'

'So where does Joe come into it?' asked Rosie.

'I'm coming to that,' said Slater. 'Now, Kenny Wingate shared a cell with a man called Brian Harding. The thing is Kenny was a bit of a bighead, and he couldn't resist bragging to Brian about how clever he was, and how he knew where all these diamonds were stashed away. We think he even told Brian his new name was going to be Arthur Bradbury.'

'That was a bit daft,' suggested Rosie.

'It certainly was,' said Slater, 'because Brian figured if he could find Kenny, or Arthur as he was now known, when he got out of prison, he would also find the diamonds. It took him over ten years travelling up and down the country, but eventually Brian found Arthur, bumped him off, and took the diamonds. He thought he was going to live the high life, but he soon found out Ronnie Scanlon's son was also looking for the diamonds, and they were hot on the trail.'

'Sounds to me like these diamonds were more trouble than they were worth,' said Rosie.

'That's exactly right,' said Slater. 'Now Brian had a big problem. He had a body to hide, and loads of diamonds he couldn't sell, and a big London mobster looking for him. We believe that was when he decided to come and pay his brother, William, a visit. We think he murdered William, buried both bodies under William's half-finished patio, let things lie for a couple of months, and then moved into William's house, using the name Joe Dalgetty.'

'Oh my God,' said Rosie, horrified. 'You mean to say I was friends with a murderer?'

'I'm afraid so,' said Slater.

'But why would he kill his own brother?'

'William had looked after his parents all his life, whereas Brian was very much the black sheep of the family. When the parents died, William inherited everything and Brian got nothing, so there was a long-standing grudge which probably made it a lot easier.'

'So Kenny became Arthur,' said Rosie, 'and then Brian became Joe, and they were both the names of two schoolboys who died in the sixties? I don't know what the world's coming to.'

'It makes you wonder, doesn't it?' agreed Slater.

'So what about this money Joe left me?' asked Rosie. 'I don't think I want it now I know what's been going on.'

'We're still not really sure where that came from,' said Slater. 'It looks as though he may have sold a couple of the diamonds to raise that cash, but in the process he alerted the Scanlons, and that's why they were looking in this area. It just happens he came across that young burglar before the Scanlons got to him.'

'And that man who sent me to you, who I thought was a detective, was that Ronnie Scanlon's son?' asked Rosie. 'It just doesn't bear thinking about. He made a complete fool out of me, but I suppose it could have been worse, he could have murdered me!'

'He made fools out of all of us,' agreed Slater, 'but he got his come-uppance in the end.'

Rosie seemed to take a few seconds to consider this, before she spoke again.

'So how is Mr Norman? He's not going to die is he?'

Slater smiled. 'The doctors say he's going to make a full recovery. It'll take a few months, but as long as he does what they tell him, he'll be fine.'

'He needs to lose some weight,' she said. 'He's a lovely man, but he really needs to look after himself a bit better. Perhaps that young fancy woman of his can keep him under control. What was her name?'

'Jane,' said Slater.

'That's right,' said Rosie, with a smile. 'I saw the way he looked at her. I reckon he'd do whatever she tells him.'

'Yeah, that's what we're all hoping,' agreed Slater.

THE END

THE JOFFE BOOKS STORY

We began in 2014 when Jasper agreed to publish his mum's much-rejected romance novel and it became a bestseller.

Since then we've grown into the largest independent publisher in the UK. We're extremely proud to publish some of the very best writers in the world, including Joy Ellis, Faith Martin, Caro Ramsay, Helen Forrester, Simon Brett and Robert Goddard. Everyone at Joffe Books loves reading and we never forget that it all begins with the magic of an author telling a story.

We are proud to publish talented first-time authors, as well as established writers whose books we love introducing to a new generation of readers.

We won Trade Publisher of the Year at the Independent Publishing Awards in 2023. We have been shortlisted for Independent Publisher of the Year at the British Book Awards for the last four years, and were shortlisted for the Diversity and Inclusivity Award at the 2022 Independent Publishing Awards. In 2023 we were shortlisted for Publisher of the Year at the RNA Industry Awards.

We built this company with your help, and we love to hear from you, so please email us about absolutely anything bookish at feedback@joffebooks.com

If you want to receive free books every Friday and hear about all our new releases, join our mailing list: www.joffebooks.com/contact

And when you tell your friends about us, just remember: it's pronounced Joffe as in coffee or toffee!

ALSO BY P.F. FORD

SLATER AND NORMAN MYSTERIES

Book 1: DEATH BY CARPET
Book 2: DEATH BY PLANE
Book 3: DEATH BY NIGHT
Book 4: DEATH BY KITCHEN SINK
Book 5: DEATH BY TELEPHONE BOX
Book 6: DEATH IN WILD BOAR WOODS
Book 7: DEATH IN THE RIVER
Book 8: DEATH IN A SKIP
Book 9: DEATH OF A PENSIONER

THE WEST WALES MURDER MYSTERIES

Prequel: A DATE WITH DEATH
Book 1: A BODY ON THE BEACH
Book 2: A BODY OUT AT SEA
Book 3: A BODY DOWN THE LANE
Book 4: A BODY AT THE FARMHOUSE
Book 5: A BODY IN THE COTTAGE

Printed in Dunstable, United Kingdom

69234036R00143